CLUB BALAFON

CLUB BALAFON

a novel

Stuart Gelzer

BERTIE STANHOPE PRESS
Santa Fe

Cover design by Stuart Gelzer
Cover art © 2023 by Lisbeth Cort

Published by Bertie Stanhope Press

ISBN 979-8-987-80810-8
Library of Congress Control Number: 2023902622

For Milena Jelinek

THE GERMAN'S HILL

THE GERMAN LEFT Marcel in charge. He said, "I have to fly home for an operation. I'll be back in three weeks. The place will be closed, but I want you to keep an eye on everything. I'm depending on you." Then he left. He didn't say what the operation was for, but it could have been almost anything, because he was in bad shape—in truth, he looked awful, even for a white man.

When the German wasn't back at the end of three weeks Marcel didn't think anything of it. After all, delays were normal in medical treatment. So he just did his job. After another week a white man he didn't know drove to the top of the hill and told him the old man had died almost as soon as he got to Germany. He had three children in Europe, and now they were fighting over who owned their father's place, which none of them had ever seen, even though the old man had spent twenty years building and running it. None of them wanted it, but they were fighting over who'd get the money when they sold it.

The man in the suit didn't tell Marcel all that exactly—he didn't think an African needed to hear about disputes between white people—but Marcel could put the pieces together. Anyway, the man, who said his name was Koeffler, finished up by telling Marcel that, while the children fought, the estate was going to continue paying him to watch over the place. It was, after all, in everybody's interest that the property be maintained in good condition for sale. He gave Marcel money for the extra week he'd already worked and said someone would come back up here every week to pay him. Then he got into his car.

Marcel hadn't said anything at all till then: Monsieur Koeffler didn't seem like the kind of white man who liked to chitchat with Africans. The chauffeur had begun backing up the Mercedes when Marcel bent down and gestured, and Koeffler lowered the window.

"Please pass on my condolences to the children."

The window was already going up again as Koeffler nodded without replying, and then the chauffeur drove off, backing down the narrow road to find a place to turn around. That was five years ago, and the estate was still paying him, though after that first time Monsieur Koeffler just sent his chauffeur to deliver the money.

So what exactly was Marcel in charge of? The city was surrounded by a ring of hills, and where the slopes got steep enough the shanty towns gave up and the forest remained. The President's palace occupied the highest hill, on the eastern side of the city, but the German had owned the top of the second-highest hill, west of the city, since before independence. Starting in the Fifties he'd slowly cut and then improved a dirt track that switchbacked its way to the summit, till almost any car could make it up—though at a couple of spots a Citroën Deux Chevaux full of people might still need to unload its passengers and have them push.

At the absolute top of his hill the German built a nightclub, with an outdoor dance floor from which you could look down at the lights of the city five hundred feet below. When they were taking a break from dancing, people liked to lean on the railing and point out streets and buildings they recognized, and those with sharp eyes claimed they could make out the city's single traffic light, between the Catholic cathedral and the railroad station. Sometimes in the sudden silence when the band was resting, you could hear people calling out, "Red!...

Green!... Yellow!... Red!"

Around the back of the club the view from the verandah was at its best by day, especially toward dusk, when you could look out at range after range of forest-covered hills stretching away to the horizon, with each layer a slightly different shade, so when the nearest slope still looked green the furthest was already the color of the sunset. Not a single house or road marred that view—people lived in the valley bottoms, not on the ridges—and at night, if you danced around that far, away from the crowd on the city side, you'd see nothing but the uninterrupted darkness of the African night, a matte black wall close enough to touch.

Because of the shape of the hill, the slope behind the Club Balafon was much steeper than in front, almost sheer, and many patrons who came there only at night would have been shocked to learn how far down the posts supporting the rear verandah had to go before they met the ground. In all its zigzagging, the road up to the club stayed on the front side of the hill, and in fact was never really out of sight of the city. But on the side of the hill facing the forest the German had built himself a long cunning staircase, sometimes cutting into the slope and some-times adding wooden steps. When it was finished his staircase started directly from the business office at the back of the club, passing under the high rear verandah and invisible from it, and then ran down into the forest to a boardwalk.

Built far enough down the thickly forested slope that the nightclub was invisible and almost unimaginable from there— but still many hundreds of feet above the truly unimaginable bottom of what should more accurately be called a ravine than a valley—the boardwalk itself was a triumph of construction and willpower. From its start at the foot of the staircase it ran horizontally along the contour of the hillside, always suspended over the void and always supported on posts made from the tallest forest trees the German could procure. Even in the admittedly dim forest light of midday, if you got down and peered between the gaps in the floorboards, you couldn't quite make out the bottoms of those posts or see how and where they met the ground.

Following the hillside around several turns so its full length could never be seen all at once, the boardwalk squeezed around one last bend and ended at the door of the German's house. After all the dramatic buildup of the way there, and considering the work involved in making the journey possible, the house itself was modest—and maybe on some level the German knew he'd be the only person who ever lived in it. From the boardwalk the front door opened directly into a fashionably open-plan living and dining room, with a tiny kitchenette to one side marked off by a counter at bar height. (The German ate almost all his meals up at the nightclub.) A door off the living room to the right led to a small bedroom, a door off the living room to the left led to a bathroom, and that was it—the house had no other level.

From all three rooms, floor-to-ceiling windows looked out on the forest at tree-top height—it could almost be said the entire outward-facing wall of the house was glass. Even in the bathroom, when the German sat soaking in the long tub, he could look straight out past his toes at the solid green wall of forest. And late at night, once the last drunks had left and he'd closed up the club and found his way down his private staircase and along his secret boardwalk by flashlight, the German went to sleep in inky blackness, surrounded by the thousand sounds of the African forest night—and truly surrounded, even from below, because every square foot of his house was suspended over the ravine.

Marcel had now spent five years watching over both the nightclub and the house. It wasn't hard work, since a gate and a sign put up by Koeffler blocked the road and discouraged casual visitors a hundred yards down the hill, at the last reasonable place to turn a car around. Marcel slept at the nightclub, in one of the private party rooms. He toured the grounds periodically, looking for intruders—mostly lovers seeking a memorable place to make out, but occasionally a looter hoping the club band had left their drum set or saxophones behind.

But Marcel almost never went down the long back stairs to the German's house, because as far as he could tell no one even knew it existed, and in any case the only way to get there was by going through the small business office at the rear of the club. Besides, though he wouldn't have admitted it, the little house suspended in the forest at the end of an apparently floating boardwalk gave Marcel the creeps—even before it became the house of a dead man.

Once, during his second year on the job, Marcel had to go to his village for a funeral. He asked a cousin of his, a man named Danton who lived in the city, to watch the place for him while he was gone. When Marcel got back he found that the liquor storeroom had been broken into, and worse, someone had pried up and taken away one of the teakwood planks from the facing of the bar. They would have needed a truck to get more, because each piece was almost ten feet long.

Danton claimed the looters had been well organized, and had created a loud distraction that drew him down the hill while they did their work quietly up here. But Marcel thought that was a load of shit—how could you quietly tear apart a teakwood bar? —and anyway Danton seemed hung over. Marcel didn't say anything, because the man was a relative, but he was glad he hadn't told Danton anything about the German's house, and that he'd locked the little door that led to the back stairs and taken the key with him to his village.

After that Marcel asked a nephew of his father's junior wife, a teenager named Théophile who'd just moved to the city and had no job, to come stay at the nightclub with him. The idea was that when one of them had to go away—even just down to the bottom of the hill, where the German's road met the main road, to hitchhike to the outdoor neighborhood market at the edge of the shanty town—there'd still be someone to watch the place. It was only a temporary arrangement at first, but Théophile, though of course he couldn't help being a bit of a simple village boy, proved to be better company than solitude, as well as unexpectedly serious and conscientious about the work.

The fifteen-year age difference between them allowed Marcel to feel sometimes like Théophile's older brother and sometimes like his father—though no one would have mistaken them for relatives of any kind. Théophile was tall for an Mtom, and skinny to the point of looking fragile, with a face that seemed too narrow to contain his broad smile. Maybe to look less like a village yokel, or maybe just under the influence of an American movie he'd seen at the Palais de Versailles theater downtown, he'd begun to grow his hair out in what Americans were calling an Afro, though in Africa it looked nothing but American. Marcel, on the other hand, was a small man with a heavy chest and shoulders and strong hands. Even in his early thirties his hair had begun to thin and recede, and his high forehead joined with his habitually thoughtful expression and deliberate movements to give him the gravitas of a man to be trusted with serious responsibilities.

After a couple of months, when he thought Théophile had earned it, Marcel revealed to him the secret of the German's house. One day, without telling him anything, he took him into the owner's office and opened the little door that looked like a closet but that led to the stairs, and then to the boardwalk, and then to the house. They didn't go inside, but stood just outside the front door on the boardwalk, shaking their heads and snapping their fingers at something they would have had trouble putting into words but that could be summed up as the genius and folly of the German.

Several years passed peacefully. They shooed away the occasional lovers, but there were no more looting outrages. They were both pretty good mankala players, and they played a lot of games out on the verandah, not for money but for chores. Marcel was saving his money for when he got married someday, but he spent some on a guitar and replaced the missing string, and after he'd taught himself to play a little he began to teach Théophile what he knew.

Now and then they invited a couple of girls up the hill to the nightclub. They turned up the volume on the little transistor radio Théophile had bought with the money Marcel gave him out of his own salary, propped the radio on the verandah railing, and shuffled slowly and happily around the dance floor, the girls exclaiming in the most gratifying tones at the beauty of the city lights far below every time the dance brought them around to face that way.

When he thought about it, Marcel knew he wanted the things any serious man wanted from life: a wife, a business of his own—because how long could he remain the servant of unknown people far away in Europe?—and a house in his village, next to his father's house. But some evenings, at the end of the best days, as they sat on the verandah and Marcel let his fingers practice a new guitar progression his mind no longer had to concentrate on, and across from him Théophile studied the mankala board, his eyes flickering back and forth along the pits as he chose his next move, Marcel imagined he could live this way forever.

After a while he noticed that time and the forest were accomplishing what looters couldn't. Vines and even tree roots began to break apart the boards. Animals got into the ceiling of the club and made a hole big enough that, when the rainy season came, water soaked the café tables in the restaurant area next to the bar. He and Théophile had to move their beds to a different room when the floor of theirs began to sag noticeably if they were both standing in it at the same time.

Marcel gave a detailed account of each new development to Koeffler's chauffeur when he drove up with the pay, describing the damage and asking Monsieur Koeffler to please arrange for repairs to save the property. The chauffeur always nodded, and nothing ever happened. The black Mercedes backed down, turned around, and drove away, and Marcel and Théophile resumed their quiet enjoyment of what remained of the Club Balafon as it gradually returned to the forest.

MORNING

1.

WHEN MARCEL WOKE he thought it was because he'd heard a dog bark. He lay on his cot in the second-best private party room, looking up at the ceiling and listening to the forest birds greet the dawn. He'd decided it must have been a dream, and was trying to reconstruct the dream, which it seemed to him involved a beautiful dog running on a beach—he'd never owned a dog like that, and sitting on the sand with his feet in the surf while the sun sank into the Atlantic was something he'd imagined for as long as he'd wanted a dog, so he regretted waking too soon from the dream—when he heard another bark.

He sat up and reached over to shake Théophile in the other cot. They'd been up late the night before, dancing on the verandah with a couple of girls who, in defiance of all reasonable expectation, at some point just picked up their purses and tottered off, laughing and waving, down the road to where they'd left their car. Maybe Marcel didn't know the going rate for girls with their own car. Anyway now, as Marcel shook him, Théophile rolled over and went back to sleep.

Marcel left him and went out past the small musicians' stage and the round café tables to the outdoor dance floor. The sun was just rising over the city, which lay hidden under a haze of smoke from morning cooking fires. He needed to figure out what direction the barking had come from. Looters, lovers, even just inquisitive tourists had never shown up so early in the morning, and he'd heard no engine straining to climb the hairpin turns of the road, so maybe a freak gust of wind had carried the sound of the dog up from the shanty town that lapped at the foot of the hill far below. He waited at the railing, enjoying the sun while it was still mild enough to enjoy. Then he followed the verandah slowly around to the back side of the nightclub.

There it was again, a single bark, this time followed by a high voice, a woman's voice maybe, scolding the dog. The sheer hillside and the dense vegetation made it hard to be sure, but the sounds seemed to be coming from the direction of the German's house. Marcel walked back into the club, intending to drag Théophile to his feet to go with him, but then he remembered what his cousin Danton had told him about a diversion pulling him away from the club while the looters went to work—not that he believed Danton, then or now, but he favored caution.

He looked into their room, where Théophile was now sitting up—he too had heard the bark and the voice—and told him to stay here and be alert. Then he went into the owner's office and got the German's pistol out of the bottom drawer of the desk. He checked that it was loaded and ready to go—in the bush, if you had a weapon you should be prepared to use it—and opened the little door to the stairs.

Marcel had imagined that the greatest challenge in approaching the intruders would be to get down the decaying stairs and along the old weathered boardwalk without making a sound that would give him away. But the staircase turned out to be so bad —loose boards, missing steps, previously anchored sections yawning away from the hillside—that he thought he'd be lucky just to get to the bottom of the stairs alive. He tried to remember how long it had been since he'd come down here, and decided it was before the last rainy season. He was impressed by the power of three months of rain—not that the stairs had been in excellent condition before that, but still.

When he reached the bottom of the staircase he gave up a silent prayer of gratitude—a prayer which he almost retracted, if it were possible to retract a prayer, when he saw the condition of the boardwalk stretching away ahead of him: boards split or rotted hollow, boards missing entirely, the whole structure sloping away from the hillside and seeming to rock gently just from the impact of his arrival at the bottom of the stairs.

As he paused to gather his courage to cross the boardwalk, music—enormous, glorious music—filled the morning. Marcel felt as if he and the entire forested slope had been transported to the nave of the cathedral downtown. He didn't know he was listening to the young Albert Schweitzer playing a Bach toccata on the pipe organ, but he did know he had goose bumps all over his body, and he knew they came from a mixture of ecstasy and terror. He wanted to fall to his knees (a bad idea on that iffy boardwalk) and he wanted to run—because why was music like that coming from the dead man's house?

The Bach toccata cut off in the middle of a chord, and in the silence Marcel could hear his heart pounding. But he reminded himself that earlier he'd heard a dog and someone scolding it, and that didn't seem to suggest any kind of ghostly visitation he knew about. He took a deep breath and set out along the boardwalk, moving slowly, testing the health of each board ahead of him before committing his weight to it, keeping to the uphill side so he could at least grab at a nearby branch if the whole thing gave way.

Enormous music filled the air again—this time Bruno Walter conducting a Brahms symphony—but now Marcel was prepared and didn't lose his careful footing. His fear was gone, and he thought of the music merely as a helpful noise to cover the sound of his approach. As he crept around the last turn in the boardwalk and finally caught sight of the house ahead, on top of the flowing strings and brass he heard the sharp percussive sound of shattering glass. He couldn't see the back side of the house from here, but, as he watched, something fell crashing through the forest canopy behind and below the house, like an animal jumping from branch to branch and missing repeatedly. Something else followed it, this time flying horizontally away from the house before hitting a tree and beginning the long, much-interrupted drop whose end was hidden in the forest.

The front of the house looked intact, though the door was ajar. With his pistol up—not only ready but clearly visible—Marcel carefully pushed open the front door, the volume of the Brahms rising as he did so. The living room was a shambles: furniture overturned, the few dishes broken and scattered, and, most importantly, the record collection—the German's prize possession—strewn across the floor, half of the shiny black discs already out of their sleeves. The old man had told Marcel he owned more than a thousand records, counting 78s, and his correspondingly good stereophonic system was now pumping out Brahms to an empty room: Marcel could see no one.

He waited in the doorway. When a quieter musical passage arrived, he heard voices coming from the left, the bathroom. Pistol raised and leading the way, Marcel crossed the living room, trying without much success not to step on record albums. Music covered his approach as he eased through the bathroom doorway, but he needn't have been so cautious, because all the occupants of the bathroom were facing the other direction.

Four white boys—truly boys, barely teenagers, as far as Marcel could judge—were gathered around the window, much larger than any normal bathroom window, that looked out onto the forest. The glass was shattered and mostly missing. Each of the boys held a handful of record albums, and more albums lay around them on the floor. They were taking turns pulling discs out of sleeves and whipping them out the window. (Marcel thought of it as the discus throw, though the boys would have called it a frisbee toss.) They seemed to be competing to see who could throw a disc the furthest, but the loudest cheers came when the record hit a tree hard enough to shatter before it dropped into the forest.

They were all talking at once, and over the music Marcel couldn't understand a word, but he thought they might be speaking English. Next to the boys, in the long bathtub aligned to face the forest, stood a large German shepherd, straining to watch the flight of each record and each time barely holding himself back from lunging out the window after it.

Marcel said "Hey!" but his speaking voice was drowned out by the triumphant Brahms. Another record went wobbling out the window, and the boys howled with laughter at the weakness of the throw. Marcel screamed at the top of his lungs in French, "Stop that right now!"

In a movie his words would have been followed by shocked silence, but in reality of course the Brahms kept going as loud as ever. The boys spun around to face him, screaming, ducking, and either dropping the records they were holding or trying to hide behind them. The dog, taken aback that a threatening stranger had managed to get within three feet of him without his noticing, tried to make up for his lapse by barking and lunging for the man's throat. But he was facing the wrong way in the tub, and the high sides hampered his turn, and his toenails found no traction on the smooth enamel, so his lunge came out as a helpless comical scramble, and Marcel had plenty of time to aim his pistol at the dog and yell in French over the music, "I'll kill him!"

One of the boys grabbed the dog's collar and held him back. Marcel pointed his pistol at each of the boys in turn to give them all a taste of his seriousness. He couldn't believe it: four white boys, some of them not even as tall as his shoulder, and he wasn't a tall man. But before he could find out what was going on he had to shut off that music. He backed out through the bathroom door, motioning with his free hand for the boys to follow him.

He kept on backing up till they were all in the living room—he wished they weren't all standing on the unprotected records, but he didn't have any choice. It was even louder in here, so he didn't try to speak. He gestured to one of the boys to switch off the stereo. The needle lifted off the groove, and in the sudden silence they could all hear the series of clicks as the tone arm automatically arced over to its cradle.

Before Marcel could figure out where to start, one of the boys, a skinny little kid with red hair, began to cry. Next to him, the solid blond boy still holding the dog said in decent French, "Please don't hurt us. We're just children and we didn't mean any harm."

That set Marcel off. "What are you talking about? You didn't mean to throw those records out the window? They just fell?" The boys said nothing, but the tallest one, a dark boy who looked to Marcel like he might be Spanish or maybe even Arab, smiled to himself as if he appreciated Marcel's sarcasm.

"Is this your house? Are these your records?" Marcel could hear himself sputtering with fury, and he realized he sounded like his father, so he stopped. If these had been boys from his village, he would have beaten the shit out them with his open hand and then turned them over to their mothers for a further beating, but he admitted to himself that he didn't dare beat these white boys in their American-looking clothes and haircuts. "Where are your parents?"

The fourth boy had straight brown hair hanging to his shoulders like a girl. His face was flushed bright red, but it was hard to tell whether from fear or from anger. Now he said, "In bed, asleep. It's Saturday morning." He spoke French like an African, and Marcel couldn't tell if that was the boy's real accent —if so, it was note-perfect—or if he was talking like that to mock Marcel.

"Do they know where you are?" None of the boys answered, but Marcel thought he saw the skinny little red-haired one, who was still crying, shake his head slightly. The boys' ability to reach the German's house without passing through the nightclub owner's office at the head of the stairs bothered Marcel maybe even more than the vandalism. "How did you get here?"

Three of the boys said nothing. The little red-haired one pointed through the door at the hillside—but in the direction away from the boardwalk, the side that was just forest and almost sheer slope. "We were exploring the forest. We didn't know this house was here." His French was ungrammatical and his accent was terrible.

Finally the Spanish-looking one with the amused eyes spoke up. In perfect Parisian French—at least to Marcel's ear—he said, "This is the house of that old German guy who built the Club Balafon, isn't it? I heard he's dead, so what does it matter what we do with his stupid records? No one's ever going to listen to them anyway."

Furious, unwilling to lay a hand on these punks but equally unable to let them go, Marcel forced himself to reason beyond his immediate visceral response and think through a plan while the boys watched him. He should send Théophile down into the city to find the German Embassy and get that man Koeffler to deal with these boys in whatever way white people thought was normal for the treatment of bad children at that age. Monsieur Koeffler might even be able to make the boys' parents pay for the damage. But before Marcel could dispatch Théophile on his mission he had to get all four boys and their dog across the boardwalk and up the staircase to the nightclub.

❖

The mysterious loud music rising out of the forest had made a big impression on Théophile, and when Marcel and the boys finally emerged from the staircase into the small office they found Théophile waiting for them with a spear in one hand and a machete in the other. Since the German had left them only one pistol, Théophile had made the spear himself when he first came to live here—choosing the wood, whittling it patiently on the verandah while Marcel worked on his guitar, and hardening the tip over a slow fire till it was as black and shiny as steel. The machete he also kept very sharp, to cut the grass in the little strip next to the road.

Marcel led the boys out to the café tables by the bar and made them sit down. He thought about tying up the dog, but it would take him a while to find a strong enough rope, and he decided to wait till Théophile was on his way down to the city. He explained the job to Théophile in Mtom: find the German Embassy, bring Monsieur Koeffler back here. But Théophile was barely listening. He kept staring, sometimes at the four white boys—it was unbelievable that these rich men's children could have had such lack of respect for a dead man's house and property—sometimes at the big mean-looking dog still in the blond boy's grip. The dog stared back at him with yellow eyes.

Marcel wondered if he ought to go get Koeffler himself, but that would mean leaving Théophile here with the boys and the dog and the pistol... So he started again: "Théophile, pay attention and repeat after me. Walk or hitch a ride to the market. At the market get a taxi. Tell the driver to go to the German Embassy. Don't pay more than fifty francs for the ride, no matter what—for fifty francs you could get all the way to the airport. What did I just say?"

"Fifty francs, go to the embassy."

"If he wants more than fifty, get a different taxi. Any driver will know where it is. At the embassy—"

Marcel stopped. He could hear a car laboring up the road. It was still early morning: who would be coming up here? He looked at the boys to see if their expressions gave anything away, but they were talking quietly amongst themselves around the table. Either they hadn't heard the car or it meant nothing special to them. Marcel signaled to the Spanish-looking boy, because he had the best French. "You over there. Before you walked around the back side of the hill, who drove you up here from the city?"

The boy waited a while to reply, a long enough pause that Marcel both doubted the truth of the answer and realized the boy meant him to doubt it. "Nobody drove us. We walked all the way."

"From the city?" That would have taken them hours, since they obviously didn't live in the nearby shanty town neighborhoods. From the good part of town where white people mostly lived, on the slopes of the hill near the President's palace, it would have taken Marcel a couple of hours just to walk through the city, much less reach the foot of the hill, much less climb it, much less find a way through the forest around the back side to the house. And these were children, and white children. "You're lying. When did you leave home?"

The dark boy pointed at the skinny red-haired boy. "The others left his house at midnight and picked me up about twelve-thirty." Marcel still looked skeptical, and the boy repeated defiantly, "We walked the whole way."

The car coming up the hill made the downshift Marcel recognized as the mark of the final switchback before the turnaround point. He felt a rising sense of panic that complications were arriving faster than he was ready for. He looked at the blond boy and held up the pistol. "If you let go of the dog because you think I'm not paying attention, I'll shoot him first and then I'll shoot you." He looked around at all of them.

"Nobody knows you're up here, so if I kill you all and bury you in the bush nobody will ever know."

Théophile's expression suggested he thought Marcel had lost his mind, but Marcel didn't have time to explain that he just needed to frighten the boys to keep them under control. Instead he told Théophile in Mtom, "Go out on the verandah and see who's coming."

The one with long hair like a girl said, "Who says nobody knows we're here?" He still spoke French with an African accent, and Marcel decided it wasn't mockery.

"You're what, thirteen years old? Boys who are thirteen don't tell their parents before they leave their houses at midnight."

"How do you know we didn't leave a note?"

"Because that car coming up the hill now would be one of your parents, and I can tell none of you are expecting someone you know."

Marcel made the boys go around behind the bar and sit down on the floor out of sight. Then he perched on the barstool at the end of the row, so he could see the boys—from far enough away that he would have a moment to react if the dog got loose—as well as the door out to the verandah, where Théophile had gone to wait. He rested the hand holding the pistol in his lap, where the boys could see it and see that the barrel was still aimed at them, but where it would be hidden from the rest of the room.

They all listened as the car stopped at the turnaround and doors opened and closed. The people walking up the last stretch of road sounded like Africans from their voices, and maybe even Mtom, but Marcel couldn't tell for sure. There was a silence, then an explosion of laughter. Théophile came in from the verandah accompanied by Marcel's smooth-talking cousin Danton, and a soft, round-faced Mtom man named Auguste who was also a cousin of some kind—as well as a friend and hanger-on of Danton's—and a third man whom Marcel didn't recognize, with sharp closed features and fancy sunglasses. All three were dressed in motley military camouflage castoffs, all three were carrying rifles, and all three were laughing in the pushy way people use for laughing when they just want to show you they're laughing at you.

Danton was yelling at Théophile in Mtom, "Did you steal that from the ethnographic museum? Because I think I saw a spear just like it there."

"You almost made us shit our pants, son!" shouted his sidekick Auguste. "And you still might—from laughing!"

Then they all laughed some more, circling around Théophile and snapping their fingers. Théophile just pursed his lips and said nothing, because both Danton and Auguste were elder relatives.

Danton finally noticed Marcel in the deep shadows by the bar. "Wise man, Marcel! You got this kid to scare people away with his homemade spear, so now you're free to hang out at the bar."

Marcel just nodded and said, "You know me."

Danton perched on a stool at the other end of the bar. If he had just stood up on the cross rung of the stool and leaned over a little he would have seen the white boys behind the counter, but he didn't. Instead he fingered the broken teakwood facing. "Hey, what happened here? Oh, yeah." Danton's shaved head, shiny with sweat even in the cool of the morning, accentuated the squareness of his face and chin and nose.

Auguste and the third man sat at one the café tables and looked around at the ruined but still grand nightclub, impressed but trying not to show it. Théophile, happy to be out of the spotlight, moved past Marcel to a place from where he too could keep a distant eye on the boys still sitting in a row on the floor behind the bar, their knees under their chins. The blond boy had one hand on the dog's collar and one hand around his snout.

Marcel said, "I'm a little surprised to see you up here so early in the morning, Danton."

Danton rapped his knuckles on the bar as if to get the bartender's attention, but of course there was no bartender, nor any liquor. "I brought my friends up here for some hunting. You know our cousin Auguste. And that's Prosper."

Marcel nodded the necessary greeting at Prosper, who was not an Mtom and therefore not following the conversation, but who'd heard his name. Auguste waved cheerfully, and Marcel nodded but didn't return the wave. He turned back to Danton. "You can't hunt up here. It's private property."

Danton laughed. "I hunt on private property all the time."

"But this private property has a watchman, and the watchman says you can't hunt here." Even as he was saying the words, and recognizing how ugly they sounded, Marcel wondered what had made him choose impulsively to refuse Danton. He decided it was partly the crack about the missing teakwood facing and partly the memory of all those record albums strewn across the floor or flying out the broken window. The old German's property had been abused enough already today.

Danton stared at him down the length of the bar. Finally he said, "What village are you from?"—an open insult, because all four Mtom men knew Danton and Marcel had grown up together in the same village.

Marcel drew a slow breath, reminding himself that only a rude man echoed rudeness. "You were laughing at Théophile's spear, but this kind of thinking belongs in the same museum. The rules don't change just because we're from the same village. You can't hunt up here."

Both Théophile and Auguste looked uncomfortable at this quarrel between their relatives. The third hunter, Prosper, still not following the words but understanding there was not only a problem but a serious breach of manners, said nothing and smoked a cigarette.

Danton continued to stare at Marcel. "Why can't I? I'll leave plenty for you."

"I already told you. It's private property, and the owner never allowed hunting up here, and I'm responsible."

Danton laughed. "Fuck that shit, Marcel! It's 1973, and the big white man doesn't tell us what to do anymore. And by the way, your particular big white man is dead." He slapped the bar as if he himself were delivering the death blow to the old German.

"That doesn't make any difference," said Marcel calmly, "because—" But at that moment the dog barked. Danton's hand slapping the bar just inches from his head had been the final provocation, and he'd squirmed free of his master's grip. While Danton was still turning his head in puzzlement and disbelief that he'd really heard a dog bark behind the bar of the Club Balafon, the German shepherd lunged over the bar to attack him, and Marcel stood up on his bar stool with his pistol extended, and Danton jumped back out of reach of the dog, but also out of reach of the rifle he'd put down on the next stool, and the blond boy lunged after the dog and threw his arms around its neck to hold it back, and Auguste and Prosper leaped to their feet with their rifles aimed, and Marcel realized he didn't have a clean shot at the dog without hitting the boy too, and the other three boys jumped up from behind the bar to help the first boy hold the dog, and Auguste and Prosper realized they didn't have a clean shot at the dog without hitting Danton too, and all four boys ended up sprawled across the bar with the dog still squirming, but with the blond boy's weight holding it down and his grip on the dog's collar firmly restored.

Still standing foolishly empty-handed, his heart pounding, while around him three men with guns aimed more or less at him had come within a finger twitch of firing, Danton took a moment to recover his cool. Then he laughed and said in Mtom, "What's the matter, Marcel? You don't like our girls anymore? You prefer little white boys now?"

Auguste laughed, but Marcel said nothing. Danton pressed on. "Come on out of there, boys," he said in French, "and if you let go of that dog I'll shoot him and then I'll shoot you."

The Spanish-looking one muttered, "Yeah, we know."

"Smart guy, huh?"

The four boys climbed off the bar and came around the front, pulling the dog with them. Danton, still irked by Marcel's pigheadedness about the hunting, saw he had the advantage now and shouldn't let go. He smiled at the boys. "That's a fine-looking dog. What's his name, son?"

The blond boy with his hands on the dog's collar said, "Clint."

"Clint Eastwood?" The boy nodded. "The Man with No Name—that's cool." Out of the corner of his eye Danton could see that Marcel was still standing over by the bar, his pistol hanging by his side, looking passive and unsure how to regain the initiative. Danton made clicking noises at the dog. "Good boy, Clint." Clint growled and strained to get free, and Danton changed his mind about going closer. He turned to the other hunters and said, still in French so Prosper could understand, "My friends, I think our hunt is over, and we're going to bring home some prize game."

"The white boys have nothing to do with you, Danton." Marcel took a step toward him. "They're not your business."

Danton said, "The dog tried to attack me. That makes them my business. What are they doing here, anyway?"

The conversation continued in Mtom. Auguste translated in

a whisper for Prosper, who kept his eyes and his gun on the boys.

The boy with long brown hair, whose name was Jesse, said quietly to the others in English, "The guy with the shaved head is talking about holding us for ransom." Since his nanny when he was an infant had been an Mtom girl, the first words he ever spoke were in Mtom. When Marcel had caught them in the German's house this morning Jesse had assumed the watchman was a local Yoa-speaking man and had addressed him only in his African-accented French. He was grateful for that in hindsight, and now he meant to hang on as long as possible to the obvious advantage of overhearing conversations in Mtom that the men assumed were unintelligible to the boys.

The tall dark one, Nabil, said, "That means they think our parents are rich. So we have to say they're poor."

The stocky blond one, still holding Clint by the collar, was named Ben. "Come on—what white people out here are poor?"

Nabil said, "How about Peace Corps volunteers? They're poor as shit."

The skinny red-haired boy, whose name was Roddy, said, "But Peace Corps workers are Americans, and we're not all Americans." He himself was Scots, and in fact of the four of them only Ben was American.

The whole expedition had been Nabil's idea at first. In the punchy hour near dawn during a sleepover at Roddy's house a few weeks ago they'd somehow begun to talk about going on a long crazy walk somewhere, an epic trek that would impress the girls in their class, and Nabil, who'd heard about the place from his father, mentioned the old abandoned nightclub on top of the hill overlooking the western end of the city—visible from everywhere, yet almost unimaginably far to go on foot. Ben wanted to start out right then, but the rest of them agreed it was too late to set off that night, and they needed time to do it right.

So it was especially painful to Nabil that, when they set up the next sleepover as cover for the expedition, his father decided he couldn't go: Nabil's grades had slipped this year. The other three snuck out of Roddy's house at midnight, leaving a note saying, *We've gone to Ben's house for breakfast and we'll probably be there all day if we don't go swimming at the club.* That way everybody's parents would think they were somewhere else and no one would wonder where they were all day, probably not till after the Saturday night movie at the American Embassy Club ended, by which time they'd be home, hopefully, or maybe even at the movie for real. When they reached Nabil's house they looked for gravel to throw at his window, but he was already waiting for them outside his gate.

They'd agreed to bring no money at all, to avoid the temptation of flagging down a taxi if they got tired—they had no idea how long it would take to walk all the way across town and up to the top of the hill or even if they really had the strength to do it. As for food, they'd meant to bring the snacks Roddy's mom had set out for the sleepover, but they were so excited they ate everything long before midnight, so they made some Nutella sandwiches just before they left. And when those were gone they stole fresh hot rolls from the shelf outside a hole-in-the-wall bakery on the main road through the shanty town at the edge of the city, and when the baker chased them they sicced Clint on him and he retreated, cursing at them.

Now Jesse said to Roddy, "Africans can't tell who's an American and who isn't, stupid. We all look and sound exactly the same to them."

Roddy said, "I think it's safer to tell the truth. We're in enough trouble already."

Ben said, "Don't be a fucking retard. You want to be held for ransom? And it's not going to be like that Red Chief story either."

Meanwhile the equally heated conversation in Mtom on the other side of the room ended with Danton brushing Marcel aside and calling out heartily in French, "Attention please, my young friends. It's time to get acquainted." He pointed to Nabil, the tallest one. "You, who is your father?" While the question sounded bald and to the point in the context of a ransom plan, it was a normal and perfectly polite way for two Mtom, say, to figure out their ties of kinship.

Nabil said, "My parents are both volunteers with the American Peace Corps. That's how the four of us know each other. All of our parents are in the Peace Corps."

In fact, Nabil's father was one of the biggest businessmen in the country, and certainly the biggest Lebanese businessman. He'd started with the hardware store downtown, the Quincaillerie Chaloub that now filled the whole block across from the central post office, but then he'd invested in a fleet of refrigerated trucks to haul fish from the coast to the capital. Anyone who drove in this country had had the experience of being forced into the ditch on the narrow bush roads by an oncoming truck with the name *CHALOUB* painted across the windshield visor. As for Nabil's mother, she'd left a year ago, taking Nabil's little sister with her, to pursue her dream of a career as a pop singer in France, and had never come back.

Danton pointed next to Jesse, who'd been born at a Canadian mission hospital in the heart of the Mtom region, several hours' drive into the bush south of here, where his father was the doctor and his mother was the chief nurse (a local nurse took over her duties that day). They'd met twenty years ago during medical training in Winnipeg, and come out to Africa the year they were married. Jesse nodded, agreeing that he too was the son of Peace Corp volunteers.

Ben nodded too, though his father was an agricultural adviser to the government and spent most of his time at coffee or cocoa or rubber plantations or at the experimental farm up north. As for Ben's mother, she all but lived at the American Club, working on her tennis and her tan and refreshing her vodka tonic.

That left Roddy. The other boys looked at him. He stood up straight and said to Danton, in his awful French, "My name is Roderick Montgomery. My father is David Montgomery. He is the head of the British Council. He is the most important British citizen in this country after the ambassador. If you do not release us immediately there will be a diplomatic incident. We are very sorry for the damage we caused. We will repay you."

The first person to react was Théophile, almost forgotten off to one side, who began to laugh and snap his fingers, in much the same way he'd laughed and snapped his fingers at the genius and folly of the German's house. The second person was Nabil, who said in English, "You're a fucking asshole, Roddy." Of all of them, Nabil was the one with the most to lose, in fact the only one worth kidnapping at all. Monsieur Chaloub's reaction on getting a ransom note for Nabil would probably have been, "Well, it had to happen sometime."

Danton said to Marcel in Mtom, "We only have room for one of them in the car." He pointed to Roddy. "We'll take that one."

The other boys glanced at Jesse to see from his expression what was being said about Roddy, but Jesse just gazed blandly off into space, pretending not to understanding.

Marcel said, "You can't just take the boy, Danton. He's not yours to take."

"Oh, yeah? Watch me." Keeping an eye on the dog, Danton stepped forward, grabbed Roddy by the arm, and pulled him away from the group.

Roddy shouted, "Let go of me! My father will complain to the President!"

Laughing, Auguste said, "Stay cool, son. We're just going for a drive."

Roddy struggled and shouted even louder, "I don't want to go for a drive! Let go of me!"

Danton swung around and slapped Roddy once, hard. Tears filled the boy's eyes as his face reddened.

Marcel said, "Danton, don't do that."

Danton laughed. "What's the matter? Are you shocked I would dare lay a hand on a white boy?"

Marcel shook his head. "You can't take him or any of them —they're not yours. Let go of him."

"Don't be greedy, Marcel. They didn't grow on one of your precious German's trees, so they're not yours either. I'm letting you keep three out of four—I think that's fair, don't you?"

Marcel didn't quite lift his pistol, but it moved idly at the end of his arm in a way that reminded Danton it was there. "Danton, let him go and get out of here, all of you."

Prosper stubbed out his cigarette and got up from the table where he'd been sitting watching. "Shit," he said in French, "I know people say the Mtom are famous for arguing, but this is ridiculous." He pulled Roddy away from Danton and jammed the tip of his hunting knife under Roddy's chin. "We're taking this one now, and we're coming back for the rest later." He looked at Marcel and Théophile. "And if they're not all here when we get back, I'm personally going to kill both of you. I've had it up to here with all your Mtom village bullshit."

He dragged Roddy out the door. The four Mtom men looked at each other without saying anything. Then Danton and Auguste followed Prosper. Théophile, still carrying his wooden spear, went out onto the verandah and watched as the three hunters dragged Roddy down the road and out of sight. A couple of minutes later he heard the car start and then drive away down the hill.

❖

"So you're telling me these two guys are the good guys?" The three remaining boys sat at one of the café tables, and Ben, still holding his dog by the collar, rubbed Clint's head while he tried to follow what had just happened.

Jesse shrugged. "Well, compared to the other guys, at least."

Ben said, "Because it sure didn't look like that right up till the other guys showed up."

"Yeah, but remember," said Jesse, "we broke into the house. The watchman was just doing his job."

"Listen, it doesn't matter anymore," Nabil said. "Once the quiet guy said he was going to kill these guys if they didn't hold onto us, from then on there aren't good guys and bad guys, there's only one kind of guy. This guy here isn't the boss anymore."

Ben said, "If you say the word 'guy' a lot it sounds really weird."

They all laughed and muttered, "Guy, guy, guy, guy, guy—" then stopped when they remembered Roddy.

Watching them from a stool at the bar, Marcel was struck again by how young they were. Even in the hour or so that had passed since he caught them in the German's house, he'd picked up a sense of them as individuals, not just as a bunch of white boys. He knew Danton had chosen the wrong one—had known it at the time, but he was certainly not going to help Danton. He knew they weren't all children of Peace Corp workers—in fact, judging by the volunteer who'd been posted in Marcel's village for a while, the one most likely to be a Peace Corp child was the red-haired one with bad French the hunters had taken.

No, if he had to pick one of these boys to hold for ransom, it would be the Spanish or Arab one. He tried to figure out why, and decided it was because of the boy's shoes: only a rich man would buy really expensive Adidas for a boy whose feet were still growing.

But Marcel wasn't planning to hold Nabil or any of the boys for ransom. In spite of Prosper's threats, Marcel's first impulse now was to do exactly what he'd planned to do before the hunters arrived: send Théophile down to the city to get Monsieur Koeffler and let him deal with the white boys and their vandalism—and now of course with the kidnapping of one of the vandals.

But Marcel found he was still brooding over what Danton had said about not depending on the big white man anymore, and he recognized that running to Koeffler to solve everything was exactly that. So he ought to find a way to solve this without Koeffler. But he couldn't imagine either sitting here meekly till the hunters came back for the other boys or facing Prosper after letting the boys go, so what was he going to do?

He could take the boys with him to the city and just hand them over to Koeffler. He tried to picture getting into a taxi at the outdoor market with these three white boys and their huge dog. And would he have his pistol out the whole time? If he didn't, how could he keep the boys from just stopping the taxi at some corner—they all spoke French, and any driver would obey them automatically—and getting out and walking away?

And anyway, that would mean leaving Théophile here to face Prosper empty-handed. Unless Théophile came to the embassy too, in which case they'd have to split up into two taxis, with only one pistol between them. And the nightclub would be deserted when the hunters returned, and they'd be angry at being tricked...

Marcel noticed with an inward smile that in spite of all his talk about tribal loyalty not trumping the rules, he wasn't even considering going to the police. First, the idea of letting the local gendarmes step into his family quarrel with Danton was unthinkable. And then he was pretty sure Prosper was a Yoa, just like the gendarmes would be, so that wouldn't lead anywhere, at least not without a bribe to overcome their inertia.

That whole train of thought went through Marcel's mind while Théophile was out on the verandah, watching the hunters leave with Roddy and listening till the sound of their car was lost in the distant murmur of city traffic. Théophile came back inside, still carrying his stupid spear, and it was the sight of the spear and the memory of the hunters laughing at Théophile that made up Marcel's mind.

It didn't matter that Danton would mock him for kowtowing to the big white man like a good little colonial black boy. He needed to get all of them—the children, Théophile, himself—out of here before Prosper and the others came back. Maybe he'd take them to Koeffler somehow, maybe he'd find somewhere else to hide them for now, though all the people he knew in the city were his relatives, who were also Danton's and Auguste's relatives.

He didn't know yet exactly what he was going to do, but he had the long walk down the hill and along the road to the shanty town market to decide. He stood up and set the pistol on the bar. "We're leaving too," he said to Théophile in Mtom. "Watch them for a moment." He went into the makeshift bedroom to get money enough for two taxis.

While Marcel had been holding his internal debate about what to do, a parallel conversation had been going on at the café table, except in English and among seventh-graders.

Nabil said, "I don't know about you guys, but I'm not planning to just sit here till they come back for us. Even if we survive being kidnapped, my father would beat the shit out of me and send me to military school in France and probably deduct the ransom from my allowance."

"See, I'm just not sure what this guy's plan is," said Jesse.

"Like, is he actually going to obey the other guys."

"I told you," said Nabil, "there's no difference now. There's just one group of guys, and they're kidnapping us."

"Either way," said Ben, "they took Roddy. So that means the police will get involved, and that means our parents will find out about the house and the record albums. So we're all fucked even if Roddy comes back safe."

Nabil said, "Not if we solve it ourselves."

Jesse said, "Solve what?"

"If we get free, and we get Roddy back, then it's over."

"We're in seventh grade, moron."

Ben said, "And now they know who Roddy is, because he was a retard and told them, so they can always get us for the vandalism."

Jesse laughed. "What are they going to say: 'Excuse me, we learned your son's name and address while we were kidnapping him, and we're very upset about some records albums he broke'?"

Nabil said, "Be serious. This is serious shit. We have to concentrate." They all stared at the floor, concentrating. Then Nabil said, "I think the thing we need to ask ourselves is, what would Sean Connery do?"

In reverent silence they all pondered the subtleties of *Diamonds Are Forever*, which they'd seen together a few weeks earlier, breaking into the dusty old Palais de Versailles theater downtown through a fire door so they could save their ticket money to buy Gentleman brand menthol cigarettes, and then ice cream afterward to cover the smell. Two of them didn't have permission to see the movie at all: Since Jesse's parents lived hours away in Mtom country, he stayed at the little Canadian mission dormitory in town, and the house parents had told him James Bond movies were sinful depravity, while Roddy's parents had explained to him that James Bond was a chauvinist who demeaned women. Once Jesse and Roddy reported back to the others what each of them had just learned about James Bond, all four of the boys would have paid in blood to see *Diamonds Are Forever*, so it was just a bonus that they got in for free.

Doing his best to focus on practicalities and not get distracted by the crazy plot twists in the movie, Ben said, "What we need is a car that shoots stuff, like missiles and shit."

Jesse said, "Yeah, that'd be cool." But they all knew they had little chance of finding a car like that.

"Well, okay, we're not Sean Connery," said Nabil, "but there's three of us."

"Don't forget Clint," said Ben. "The Africans are terrified of him."

Jesse said, "He's like a secret gadget weapon we got from Q."

Nabil nodded. "So we need to do something all at the same time, and release Clint."

That was as far as they got before Théophile came back inside. But the moment Marcel went into the other room, and before Théophile could pick up the pistol from the bar, all three boys stood up together, and Ben released his grip on Clint's collar. Without making a sound the dog leaped straight at Théophile, and if he'd been holding the pistol he wouldn't have raised it in time to fire.

But he was a village boy, and while it pleased Danton and his friends to make fun of him for being a yokel, he had the skills and reactions of a village boy. His spear hung loosely from his hands with the point resting on the floor, and as the dog lunged —even before it occurred to him to step back—Théophile's arm came up and the dog plunged straight onto the fire-hardened wooden tip of the homemade spear.

Clint had been waiting so long to attack, and every muscle in his body was so thirsty for vengeance on these men, that the force of his leap when his master finally released him carried him onto the spear far enough for the point to puncture his heart. The big German shepherd dropped to the floor of the bar, dead without a whimper, the spear still buried in his chest.

The four boys—for in truth Théophile was still a boy himself, barely five years older than the white boys—all stared at what had happened, their mouths wide open. Then Nabil and Ben and Théophile reached for the pistol at the same time. Nabil was closest and got to it first, but, with a long roaring scream that was the first sound in the room since Marcel left, Ben wrestled it out of his hand. Théophile, who by that time had his own hand on the barrel but was unable to turn the pistol away, yelled in Mtom, "No!" And then Ben fired. Hit in the face from two feet away, Théophile flipped back along the bar, knocking down all the bar stools as he fell.

Hearing the gunshot, Marcel's first thought was that Théophile had stupidly shot one of the boys. As he ran out to see, Ben turned the pistol on him, and Marcel froze in the doorway, taxi money in hand.

Nabil now yelled, "No!" in English, and this time Ben listened, taking his finger off the trigger but keeping the pistol aimed at Marcel. Ben was hyperventilating. "He killed Clint! Why shouldn't I fucking kill them both?"

Nabil said, "No! We need him!"

Crouching down, his hands to his face, Jesse stared at Théophile, whispering, "Holy shit, holy shit, holy shit, holy shit, holy shit!" He'd spent enough time around a bush hospital to know a dead man when he saw one. "We're going to prison."

Ben was still screaming. "Why do we need him? Why don't we just kill him and get the fuck out of here?"

Nabil said, "Because we can trade this one for Roddy, don't you see?" He put his hand on Ben's arm. "You need to calm down, Ben. Give me the gun and calm down."

2.

"It was an accident."
"It was an accident."
"It was an accident."
"It was an accident."
"It was an accident."
"It was an accident."
Once they'd all said it twice, it became true, and now they could move on to figure out what to do next.

In fact, if these modestly delinquent seventh-graders, promising future solid citizens all, had just witnessed a white eighteen-year-old getting shot dead—never mind having done it themselves—they would have been immobilized, nauseous, prostrate with shock, and nothing in the long day to come would have turned out the way it did. But Théophile was an African; and though not one of these boys would have admitted it or could even have made himself conscious of it, that alone rendered him not quite real to them, whether dead or alive. Théophile's unreality made it possible—not always easy, but at least possible—for them to go on playing starring roles in a movie in their heads (while not considering even for a moment that Théophile too had been the star of the movie in his own head), and consequently for the rest of that day to unfold as it would.

Marcel, his wrists bound, lay on his stomach across one of the café tables. The boys had tied him up with the rope they'd found on the shelf behind the bar, the rope Marcel himself should have looked for when he first thought about tying up the dog. In their clumsiness or their unconcern, they'd positioned him so he was forced to look straight at the bloody corpse of Théophile, still sprawled at the foot of the bar. Marcel could have closed his eyes, but he made himself keep them open, and as he stared at Théophile's body he decided revenge against the parents of these monstrous children would be even sweeter than revenge against the boys themselves, who after all knew only what they'd been taught.

The boys sat at another table, far enough away from the bodies but close enough to keep an eye on Marcel. They were drinking Cokes they'd found on Marcel's shelf in the refrigerator in the nightclub kitchen. It wasn't a callous celebration—they were shaking with adrenaline and their mouths were dry from panting. But to go on playing their parts seemed as giddily and dangerously effortless as sliding down a steep gully while red earth filed their shoes, a favorite after-school pastime they called "dirt-surfing."

Jesse said, "It's easy enough to say we're going to trade him for Roddy, but those hunters all had rifles. We have one pistol, and one machete, and one spear."

"I don't think we should count the spear," Nabil said. "Who's going to pull it out, you?"

They all looked over at Clint, still lying a few feet from Théophile. "Okay, so a pistol and a machete."

Nabil said, "If we leave this guy, what's his name, Marcel, just lying here on the table while we negotiate, then the other guys will just shoot us and free him. We need to hide him, so they have to give us Roddy before they find out where Marcel is."

Ben said, "Yeah," and wished he'd thought of it.

Looking around the nightclub, all of whose smaller rooms opened directly onto this one, Jesse said to Ben, "Where are you going to hide him, at your house?"

"Why not?" Ben's father was at the experimental farm up north for another week, and his mother would be on the tennis courts by now and would stay at the American Club till after the Saturday night movie. "It could work."

"Maybe." At Jesse's dorm the house parents were always around, and a dozen noisy elementary school kids were always underfoot. He envied Ben the big quiet house he had all to himself, though the thought of Ben's leathery vodka-numbed mother made him wince. "But don't you have a cook?"

Ben nodded. "And a gardener."

"Yeah. I don't think they're just going to stand around and smile when the little white master brings home an African man with his hands tied and locks him in a closet."

"Yeah."

"Anyway, how would we even get him from here to there?" Jesse thought for a moment, then chuckled. "Sean Connery would just fire a couple of warning shots in the air at the outdoor market and hijack a taxi."

"Yeah, that'd be cool. I wonder how many bullets are left. Do you know how to check?"

Neither of them eager to touch it, Jesse and Ben stared at the pistol, which now sat on the table in front of Nabil. Lost in thought, Nabil didn't seem to have heard the question. He looked up. "We don't need to hijack a taxi. We can get a car from my house."

"What car?" said Jesse. "What are you talking about?"

"You know we have a bunch of cars. My dad's at work. He won't notice if we take one."

"And who's going to drive it?"

"I am."

"You can drive?"

"I told you, last summer I drove our Toyota Land Cruiser on

the beach. I can shift and everything."

"Oh, yeah, you did," said Ben. "That is so cool."

Jesse said, "Wait, this makes no sense. We only wanted a car to get to Ben's house, but at Ben's house there are servants, and at your house too, and you know the mission dorm won't work, so what's the point of driving anywhere?"

Nabil said, "You have a better plan? The longer we sit around and talk, the more likely we are to get caught up here. We have no idea how far those hunters are taking Roddy before they come back for us. Do you want to be walking down the road when they drive back up?" The other two said nothing as they pictured meeting the hunters on the winding hillside road. Nabil said, "I'll run down the hill and then run or hitch a ride five minutes to the market. No one will pay any attention to me. I'll take a taxi to my house."

Ben said, "How? We didn't bring any money."

Nabil pointed at Marcel. "Yeah, but he's got some."

Jesse said, "I wonder why he was getting money just before the other guy got…"

Nabil shrugged. "Who cares? When I get to my house, I sneak in and get the car keys, and then I come back up here for you guys."

"And you're just going to drive through town like nothing's wrong." Jesse shook his head. "Nabil, I know you're tall and everything, but you're not even fifteen years old."

Nabil grinned. "But I'm white, and that still counts in Africa." He picked up the cash they'd confiscated from Marcel and headed for the door.

Ben said, "And if they come back while you're gone? What are we supposed to do?"

Though Nabil had no idea what to suggest, he made a show of stopping to ponder. It flattered him that Ben was deferring to him. Once the shock of the moment was over, Nabil had to admit he wished he'd been the one to pull the trigger on Théophile. Doing something like that made you special, and he'd been afraid Ben would take advantage of his new status to get arrogant and bossy. But once he stopped screaming and Nabil took the pistol away, Ben had been subdued and a little passive.

Not waiting for Nabil to answer, Jesse said, "We'll take him down the back stairs to the house in the forest and hide him there."

"Good." Nabil nodded his approval in a way that he felt made him still the one in charge. "And when I come back I'll honk 'Shave and a haircut, two bits,' so you'll know it's me."

He waved and walked out into the bright morning sunshine on the verandah, and as he headed for the broad steps that led down to the road he broke into a jog. He felt better with every stride he took down the hill away from the nightclub.

Watching Nabil disappear down the winding road, Jesse said to Ben, "You think he's going to come back?"

Ben didn't answer at first. Then he said, "Would you?"

They both laughed.

The clearest sign of how meek and obedient Roddy had become was that, once the kidnappers had reached Prosper's house in the new neighborhood behind the Gentleman cigarette factory, they sent Auguste back by himself to collect the rest of the boys. Meanwhile Prosper and Danton were going to write the note to be delivered to Roddy's father at the British Council, and as Auguste got back in the car they were sitting on Prosper's concrete porch having a beer to spur their creativity. When Auguste said through the driver's window there wouldn't be room in the car for the dog, Danton said, "Shoot it. We don't want a smelly dog messing up the seats anyway."

The car, a second-hand cream-colored Peugeot 404 with deep red fake-leather upholstery, belonged to Prosper, the result of some deal for which he'd acted as middleman and that he declined to talk about. But for the past year Danton had been functioning as Prosper's chauffeur—not officially or by that name or with any salary: Danton still considered himself a friend of Prosper's, on equal footing. Yet when it came time to take the Peugeot somewhere it was Danton who drove while Prosper relaxed next to him, and it was Danton who kept the car clean and fueled and running. And while Prosper didn't pay Danton directly, he did pay for the things they enjoyed together, like the beer they were now drinking.

Still, Danton often felt the urge to show Prosper he was capable of more, and both the idea of the hunting expedition to the German's hill and the idea of taking the white boys for ransom were inspired by Danton's wish to impress Prosper. And it looked as if Danton's tough-guy face-off with Marcel had worked: he was invited to stay and plan the ransom note, while Auguste got the menial job of bringing back the other boys. Even so, the thought of that German shepherd scratching the beautiful red seats of the Peugeot with his toenails brought out in Danton the protective habits of a chauffeur, one who some-times forgets that the car he cares for isn't his own.

When he got up the hill, Auguste stopped the car where the gate barred the road. He noticed the padlock holding the gate was broken (vandals had smashed it long ago, and Koeffler had never replaced it, in spite of Marcel's polite reminders to the chauffeur). But Auguste knew there was no place to turn around beyond here, and he wasn't eager to try to maneuver Prosper's Peugeot back down that last winding hundred meters in reverse without losing any paint to the thorn bushes that had grown out over the abandoned stretch of road. He walked up the rest of the way. As he approached the nightclub he called out cheerfully in Mtom, "Don't be alarmed, it's just me!"

A little puzzled at hearing no greeting in return, he walked up the wide wooden steps onto the verandah and saw Théophile lying there in the sun—another puzzle. It wasn't till Auguste was standing right over the boy that he saw the drying blood, and the buzzing flies, and the note. Kept from blowing off Théophile's chest by a solid malachite ashtray and written on creamy Club Balafon letterhead in Jesse's best penmanship, the note read in French:

Dear sirs,

This is an example of what we can do. Bring Roderick back here safe, and we will give you Marcel, also safe. When you come back, if we do not hear Roderick's voice calling to us as you walk up the road we will open fire.

P.S. A gun is aimed at you while you are reading this note.

The postscript had been Ben's idea, and something they both thought Sean Connery would approve of. Working up enough courage to drag Théophile's body outside had made them bold.

Trembling, a thousand thoughts spinning through his head, Auguste almost put the note back under the ashtray. Instead, he held it up like a flag of truce and retreated to the edge of the verandah and down the steps. Then he ran back down the road to the car. Though he drove down the hill much too fast, it wasn't the speed that almost made him miss a couple of the turns and go over the sheer edge, it was a persistent vision of the bloody mess that had been Théophile's face.

Prosper and Danton had decided, on careful reflection over another round of beer, that it would make more sense to write all the ransom notes at the same time, once they had all the boys here at the house and could get their parental particulars. So they were still sitting on the edge of the porch when Auguste pulled in much too fast, almost hitting the bottom step before he stopped the Peugeot. He seemed to be alone: had he put all the boys in the trunk?

When they'd read the note and listened to Auguste's stammering account of what he'd seen, Danton stood up. "If that's how it is, I'm going to shoot this boy right now and we'll be even."

"No, it won't be even," said Prosper. "Once they shoot Marcel in return, it'll be two to one, even though he deserves it for being stupid enough to let those children take control. Plus, you're forgetting that if we shoot this one we get no ransom."

Danton said, "Yeah," and sat back down on the porch.

As he sat down next to them Auguste said, repeating himself, "They're devils in the form of children. They shot Théophile in the face."

Prosper said, "Shut up, I have to think."

All three of them looked out at the chickens pecking the hard-packed red dirt of Prosper's yard. From behind the house they could hear Prosper's grandmother singing in Yoa. After a while Prosper said, "Clearly the general idea goes like this: We take this one back up to the nightclub and exchange him for Marcel. Then we turn around and kill the three murderers for justice and take this one back again for ransom."

Danton nodded. "And we know we're better armed than they are."

"Unless Marcel just didn't trust the village boy with a gun."

"How are you going to surprise them?" said Auguste. "Those monsters were aiming at me from hiding while I stood there."

"We know, we read the note." Danton felt ashamed of his cousin, who was behaving like a little girl in hysterics, while he himself strove to match Prosper for thoughtful cool.

"Unless it was just a lie," said Prosper, "a bluff, and they aren't there anymore."

Danton said, "Yeah, the same thought occurred to me," though it hadn't.

Prosper considered for a moment, then shook his head. "No, they have to be there. If they leave there's no way we can meet them to give back their friend. And they care more about their friend than we care about Marcel."

Danton started to nod wisely but found he couldn't, especially with Auguste's eyes on him. He could argue and fight with Marcel, and take advantage of him—he and his friends would have stolen the entire teakwood facing off the bar that time, if it hadn't been so hard to pry that first piece free—but Marcel was a fellow Mtom and a cousin of his, and Danton had to admit he was shocked to hear Prosper speak so indifferently about him.

Prosper said to Auguste, "You should've gone inside and looked around. We'd have a better idea what to expect."

Auguste stared back at him. "You're so clever, I sure wish you'd been with me to give me advice, instead of sitting around here on your porch drinking beer."

Prosper said nothing, but his face froze, and he and Auguste glared at each other. Danton, sitting between them, said, "We need to work together. We'll never recover from the shame if we let three white children beat us because we can't get along."

Prosper forced a smile. "Or for any other reason."

Nabil stopped the taxi at the corner near his house and walked past the neighbors' gates. His street seemed awfully quiet till he remembered it was Saturday morning and not even ten o'clock yet. He stopped at the big cement gatepost of his own house and looked carefully through the gate into his front yard.

The black Mercedes 280 was gone, so his father was already at the company office over the hardware store downtown. The short blue Land Cruiser Nabil had driven on the beach last summer was here in the driveway, and so was the black Citroën DS his father used when he needed to call on a local contact, like the trade minister, and subtly remind him that the Chaloubs were long-established and loyal residents of the country. Nabil was tempted to take the DS, but he had a feeling that, with all its futuristic hydraulics, it would be more complicated to drive than the Land Cruiser, and he couldn't afford to attract attention by flooding the engine in the driveway. So, the Land Cruiser.

He was just about to push open the little pedestrian gate when the gardener, Pelé, came around the side of the house uncoiling a hose behind him. His real name was something no one could remember, and he idolized the Brazilian soccer star, so the nickname stuck. He was singing an African pop song. He turned on the water and started washing the Land Cruiser. That meant he'd wash the DS next, and that meant he'd be out here in the driveway a long time. Nabil thought about Jesse and Ben waiting for him, and suddenly the nightclub on the top of the hill seemed impossibly far away and he was overwhelmed by weariness. All he wanted was to crawl back into the bed he'd left at midnight and go to sleep.

"Monsieur Nabil!" The loud cheerful voice right behind him made him jump. It was Thérèse, the cook, who'd been working for the Chaloub family for long enough that she'd fed Nabil treats when he was so small he could do no more than crawl across the tile floor of the kitchen. Normally by now she'd be inside at work on lunch, to have it ready when Monsieur came home at twelve-thirty, but she'd stepped out to get fresh herbs at the little market on the main road.

And now here was her precious motherless Nabil, not only awake earlier than she expected on a Saturday but already dressed—though not washed or combed, she noticed—and, strangely, standing outside his own yard looking in. "What are you doing?" Nabil looked awkward and embarrassed. Thérèse laughed. "Are you waiting to play a trick on Pelé?"

Nabil considered agreeing with Thérèse, and maybe getting her to play along and draw Pelé into the back yard away from the cars, but he realized that since she already knew he was here there was no sense in hiding from any of the other servants. "Yeah, I was, but never mind. It wouldn't have been that funny." He pushed open the pedestrian gate. "Here, let me carry the bag."

"Don't be silly."

They walked up the driveway together. Pelé shut off the hose as they approached. "Good morning, Monsieur Nabil! How did you get out the gate without me seeing you? You're like a Red Indian."

Nabil laughed and shrugged. As he started up the front steps and Thérèse went around back to the kitchen door, Pelé called out, "Oh, I almost forgot. As he was leaving Monsieur said to tell you he needs to talk to you at lunch, so don't go off to the American Club till after that." Nabil nodded. Pelé turned the hose on again and went back to washing the cars.

In the hallway on the second floor Nabil hesitated, torn between going one way to his own room and the other way, past his little sister's now empty room, to his father's room. He willed himself to go to his father's room. He looked through all the drawers of the dresser and the bureau, and in all the bowls on top of the bureau—loose change, cufflinks and tie pins, for some reason an entire bowlful of cowrie shells for playing mankala—but found no car keys. He went downstairs and checked the little hall table by the front door, and still found nothing.

Where did his father keep the keys to all the vehicles? Did

he really let the chauffeur keep track of them? It didn't make any sense. Besides, the chauffeur didn't drive the Land Cruiser— that was just for them, for fun. So where were the Land Cruiser keys? He couldn't ask the chauffeur, because he was with the Mercedes at the office. He couldn't ask Thérèse or Pelé, because they wouldn't know. And anyway, if he asked any of the servants it would eventually get back to his father that Monsieur Nabil had been looking for car keys.

He went back upstairs and this time went down the hall to his own room and threw himself on the bed. He could feel tears of frustration filling his eyes, and that made him even angrier and more frustrated—almost fifteen, and crying like his little sister. But he'd wanted so much to pull up to the nightclub in triumph at the wheel of the Land Cruiser. He could picture it in every detail: the nonchalant way he'd open the door and step down, the envy and admiration on Jesse's and Ben's faces. The tears finally overflowed his eyes and ran down, and he put his arm over his face both to wipe his cheeks and to hide his shame.

Why the fuck couldn't his father—an organized, meticulous, demanding man—keep the car keys in a logical place? And what the fuck did his father want to talk about at lunch? He himself would gladly never talk to his father again. He took his arm away from his face and stared up at the ceiling fan. The servants knew Nabil was awake, and Pelé would report that he'd passed on the message about lunch. His father was a busy man and didn't pay much attention to what Nabil was up to, but when he gave a direct instruction and Nabil defied it he got ugly. His father came home for lunch at twelve-thirty. It was now almost ten-thirty.

So in the next two hours he'd have to get back up the hill to the Club Balafon without a car, wait for the bad guys to show up, trade the captured guy for Roddy, get everybody home so no one would ask questions, and be back here sitting down to lunch with his hair combed by twelve-thirty. It was impossible. He'd done his best, but he was trapped here through no fault of his own, and Jesse and Ben would just have to figure things out by themselves. Nabil watched the ceiling fan go around. His eyes closed.

The old African woman with two teeth, one bottom and one top, grinned at Roddy across the narrow kitchen table. She'd never seen a white boy this close up, especially not one with red hair, and she was mightily entertained. They were sitting in the detached kitchen behind Prosper's house, a square concrete room with soot-blackened walls whose only light source apart from the low open doorway was the smoky cooking fire in the hearth.

Roddy's ankles were tied to the chair legs, but the old woman had untied his hands so he could eat. When he reached down to try untying himself, she smacked him with a plastic flyswatter, which then led her to laugh and laugh without making a sound. It was the long silent spasm as much as the two ugly yellow teeth in her gaping mouth that disturbed Roddy, and he didn't try again to untie himself. The food the old woman put in front of him in a chipped enamel bowl—fermented manioc in peanut gravy, though he didn't know it—made him almost gag on the first mouthful, but he was faint from hunger, and he thought if he rejected it she'd just laugh at him again, and he didn't want that, so he ate, very slowly.

In between bites, partly just to space out the grossness of the taste, he talked to her, explaining that by not releasing him she was taking part in a crime, and that his father was a very important man who would see to it that all the kidnappers and their helpers were severely punished. She nodded and occasionally said things in some African language—or maybe it was French but she couldn't speak properly with two teeth. Or maybe she was deaf or even retarded, like a village idiot. He gave up.

Prosper's grandmother did speak French. But she struggled to understand even pure standard French, to which she was rarely exposed in the village, and French pronunciation as bad as Roddy's was completely outside her experience. She had no idea the red-haired boy with skin as pale as an albino's was speaking a language she knew, and she nodded and encouraged him to go on because she was fascinated by watching his mouth form all those crazy sounds. He also seemed angry about something, and shook his finger in the air a lot, so she asked him repeatedly if the food was all right—she'd be happy to make him something else if not. She was sorry when he stopped talking and sullenly finished his bowl of manioc.

Prosper hadn't told her why the boy was here or why he had to be tied up and watched, and she hadn't asked. But that was normal: piles of mysterious supplies came and went in the back rooms and even on the porch of this house—car batteries, printed cloth for dresses, cured snake skins for sale to tourists, canvas army boots. She accepted that life in the city often wouldn't make sense to someone who'd spent all but her waning years in the village, and she thought of her grandson as a clever and energetic businessman who bought and sold and traded a wide variety of goods—though admittedly never till now a little white boy.

Roddy pushed aside the empty bowl and put his head down on his crossed arms. He wanted someone to talk to. He wondered how long it would be before the hunters brought the rest of his friends to the house, where he'd be the old hand who knew the ropes. He'd explain to them in just the right bored tone that the whole thing was actually surprisingly okay as long as you were careful not to look directly into the old woman's mouth.

But then he imagined telling his parents the same story, and he could hear the tone of disappointment with which his mother would remind him it was wrong to be disgusted by or to make fun of a person who, simply because of advanced age or lack of resources, suffered the probably quite painful and distressing consequences of bad oral hygiene. And then he imagined, not for the first time in the past few hours, what his parents would say to his account of breaking into the old abandoned house on the hill and smashing the window and throwing the record albums out like frisbees.

He might claim he'd just done it because the other boys were doing it, but he knew that was no excuse, and anyway it would be a lie: he'd done it because it was fun and because the house didn't seem to matter to anyone. After the kidnapping he'd persuaded himself that whatever wrong and damage he'd done was wiped out, cancelled, by the much greater wrong being done to him by the hunters. But now, as he sat facing the old woman who was gathering up the empty metal bowl and wiping the table with a dirty rag, he wasn't so sure his parents would go along with that logic.

After rinsing the bowl in a bucket of gray water and lifting the lid to poke at whatever was in the blackened pot on the fire, the old woman sat back down facing Roddy. She put her elbows on the table, folded her arthritic hands, and gave him an encouraging grin, as if to say, "Okay, I'm ready—entertain me some more."

Roddy's calf itched where the rope constricted it, and without thinking about it he reached down to scratch. The old woman tried to snatch up the flyswatter, but she'd put it aside to wipe the table, so it took her a few seconds to locate it. Then to make up for the delay she smacked Roddy half a dozen times on the offending arm and leg, even after he hastily put both hands back on the table. The whole time she was laughing that gaping, silent, two-toothed laugh. Finally she put down the flyswatter, folded her hands again, and looked across the table at Roddy with a twinkle in her eye. Today was the most fun she'd had since she came to the city, after her eldest daughter in the village died.

A brown hen wandered through the open doorway into the kitchen and looked around curiously in the gloom. The old woman called out in Yoa, "You're confused! I don't need you till dinnertime!" The hen turned around and ambled away into the yard, and the old woman laughed, both at her own joke and at the hen's obedience—still silently but so hard she had to wipe away tears. She checked to see if the boy had shared the moment with her, but he just stared back at her glumly. Roddy, who understood no Yoa, had decided anyone who could laugh that hard at a chicken must surely be a half-wit.

The room darkened as Prosper's silhouette filled the doorway. "He giving you any trouble, Granny?"

"No, no, we're getting along great. It's a shame he has to be tied up."

"That's what you think. You have no idea what these little white fuckers are capable of."

She clicked her tongue and said to Roddy—rhetorically, since she was still speaking Yoa—"Listen to how the man talks! I didn't teach him to use words like that."

Prosper stepped into the kitchen. "You can untie him now. We're taking him away."

The old woman untied the ropes holding Roddy's legs to the chair. Then, following Prosper's instructions, she used the same rope to tie Roddy's hands behind his back. Even with arthritis, Prosper's grandmother tied better knots than he did, and he knew it.

As Prosper was pushing Roddy out the doorway into the yard, the old woman tried to give the boy a banana, but with his hands tied he couldn't take it. She handed the banana to Prosper. "Give it to him later. Look how skinny he is—he needs to eat."

The three hunters, well armed, pushed Roddy to the center of the back seat of the Peugeot. Prosper sat on one side of him and Auguste on the other. As Danton backed the car out of the dirt yard onto the road, Prosper held up the banana and said, "Want this?"

Danton shook his head. "I can't while I'm driving."

Prosper threw the banana out the window. Auguste stared straight ahead, sharply aware that Prosper hadn't offered the banana to him.

Danton said, "But maybe Auguste would eat it."

Prosper said, "Too late."

Nabil woke with a surge of adrenaline. The idea that he'd just had a vivid horrible dream about the nightclub on top of the hill didn't last as long as it took him to sit up in bed. He looked at his watch—he'd only slept ten or fifteen minutes—and sighed with relief: he still had time, though he should hurry. But hurry to do what? He realized that somehow he'd figured out what to do in his sleep and was only now becoming conscious of his own plan.

He went downstairs to the kitchen, where Thérèse was washing and peeling potatoes.

"Are you hungry already, Nabil?"

"Starving."

"Lunch is hours away. You want me to make you something?"

He lifted a baguette off the counter, still warm because Thérèse had just bought it from the man who went around the neighborhood selling bread out of a big box on the back of his bicycle. "I'll just take this."

"No, you won't! That's for lunch!"

"I won't be here for lunch, so I'm having it now." He bit into the heel of the loaf, spoiling its perfection.

"Your father told you to be here for lunch!"

"Thérèse, just do your job and stop trying to be my mother!" He turned and left the kitchen, carrying the baguette. Thérèse went back to peeling potatoes, angrily throwing each one into the pan of water.

Nabil had eaten half the baguette, littering the back seat of the taxi with flakes of hard crust, by the time he got to the Quincaillerie Chaloub. Still holding the remains of the loaf, he went past the main door to the hardware store and ran up the exterior staircase and into the offices from which his father managed all the Chaloub businesses. As he'd expected, the only person visible was his father's secretary, a young African woman with an extraordinary hairdo—a pattern of diamonds all over her scalp, and the hair itself pulled up into dozens of spikes that resembled antennae—and a cleavage in her tight French dress that had been occupying a surprisingly large space in Nabil's brain for the past year or so.

She looked up from doing her nails. "Good morning, Monsieur Nabil!" she said in French. "How's it going?"

"Good morning, Cécile. It's going all right." He became aware of the half-eaten baguette and held it behind him.

"Do you have a girlfriend yet?"

He gave her the look she expected, the one that said more or less, "How could I be satisfied with any girl but you?" Cécile laughed, as always, and wagged a shiny new fingernail at him.

The formalities over with, Nabil gestured toward the inner

office door. "Is he...?"

She shook her head. "Not now," she said importantly. "He'd be very angry if I let you in."

That was exactly the answer Nabil was counting on. He did his best to look disappointed. "He wanted to talk to me at lunch today. But I can't be there. I already gave my word to my friend's family that I'd have lunch with them. And I don't have to tell you how important keeping your word is to my father."

Cécile nodded, but her raised eyebrow said, "Who are you kidding?"

"That's why I came here—so we could have our talk now." Nabil sighed, as if trying to figure out what to do next. "Oh well, please tell him I tried." He turned to go. "Thanks, Cécile!"

He ran back down the stairs to the street. So far the plan he'd concocted in his sleep was working perfectly, but of course this was the easy part: his father hated family interruptions at work, and Nabil had known he could count on being turned away.

He went around the back of the hardware store, to the loading dock area. The bay opening into the hardware store was empty, but two trucks were backed up to the next building, the deep-freeze storage where the refrigerated trucks unloaded fish from the coast and local middlemen picked it up. Nabil stopped. His father's Mercedes should have been parked here, behind the hardware store, but it wasn't.

He found his father's chauffeur, Hercule, sitting in the shade playing checkers with some friends, using bottle caps for pieces. The Mercedes needed some work done, so he'd taken it to the shop, but the mechanic had assured him it would be ready in time to get Monsieur home for lunch. While Hercule returned to his game, tossing up and catching captured bottle caps as he waited for the other man to play, Nabil considered how to adjust his plan.

He'd counted on the Mercedes, but that wasn't going to work—he couldn't afford to wait long enough for it to be ready. He noticed that this new and unexpected setback hadn't reduced him to tears, so maybe that earlier spell had just been the result of fatigue rather than childishness. By contrast, now, after even a short nap, he felt unstoppable. If he couldn't have the Mercedes he'd get another vehicle, and there were plenty here to choose from. He considered how to handle Hercule, who was the highest in status of his father's servants but the most recent hire and the one Nabil knew least well. But that meant the man also didn't know his father well, and Nabil could take advantage of that.

"My father needs to go somewhere right now."

Hercule just turned his palms up as if to say, "I already explained and there's nothing I can do."

"So he needs a different vehicle, one of these, it doesn't matter which one."

Hercule looked around at the company trucks. "Why doesn't he just take a taxi?"

Nabil said coldly, "I don't know. I didn't ask him. I just do what he says, and so should you."

Hercule's eyebrows went up and he looked at his friends across the checkers board as if to say, "Can you believe this kid?" Nabil found himself getting irritated by the man's ability to be insolent without saying anything.

Almost laughing now, Hercule said, "Monsieur Chaloub wants me to drive him somewhere in one of those fish trucks?" He looked down at his clothes in mock wonder. "In this nice uniform?"

Nabil said, "He doesn't need you to drive. He'll drive himself."

And now all the men clapped their hands and threw back their heads with laughter as they pictured their hard-faced

Lebanese boss, in his Christian Dior suit, maneuvering through the city at the wheel of a Chaloub fish truck.

Nabil said, "Shall I go tell my father you refuse to obey and you're even laughing at him?"

The men sobered up immediately: fun was fun, but losing your job was not a joke. Hercule examined Nabil carefully for the first time—till now, part of the chauffeur's studied insolence had taken the form of keeping his attention on the checkers game, as if he had more important things to do than chat with his boss's son.

"Monsieur Nabil," he said now. "Be honest with me." Nabil flushed at the implication from a servant that he wasn't telling the truth, but Hercule's tone was friendly. "Do you need a car for yourself?" Nabil nodded. Hercule went on, "Have you driven before?" Nabil nodded again. Hercule gestured toward the fish trucks by the loading dock. "Those big trucks are too hard to drive till you learn how. I myself would find them a challenge."

Hercule got up, stepped inside the back door of the hardware store for a moment, and came out holding a set of keys. "Follow me."

He led Nabil along the loading dock and around to the far side of the fish warehouse. As was the case in almost any half-forgotten scrap of yard hidden away behind a building, a couple of abandoned vehicles—cars from the Forties or the Fifties, judging by their fenders—lay there rusting, their tires long gone, elephant grass growing out through the broken windows. But next to them stood a vehicle in better shape, though still ancient: a Citroën Fourgonette—a small cargo vehicle formed by attaching the front half of a Deux Chevaux cab to a corrugated metal box.

Hercule pointed to the Fourgonette and held out the keys. "I hear this was the original Quincaillerie Chaloub truck. My friends and I use it for our own errands now."

Nabil said, "You must be joking." He could imagine what the other boys would say when he drove up in this rusting wreck instead of a Mercedes or a Land Cruiser—much less a car suitable for James Bond.

Hercule said, "I know it's a little beat up, but it works fine. And it's possible for a boy to drive. It even has gas."

Nabil, still scowling, didn't put out his hand for the keys. "Don't you have the keys to the Land Cruiser or the DS instead?"

"Monsieur Nabil," Hercule said, "I'm trying to help you, but be serious: I can't let you drive Monsieur Chaloub's good cars, his personal cars. This one he doesn't even think about."

Nabil glanced at his watch: almost eleven-thirty. He needed to move forward unstoppably. He reached for the keys. "And why exactly are you helping me?"

Hercule smiled. "Because you're the boss's son, and maybe you can help me sometime. Because now we have an understanding."

Nabil got into the car, pushing empty beer bottles and an old *Paris Match* off the seat. Hercule guided him through the primitive controls. "It can be very hard to start sometimes. If you have even a small grade to roll down when you're starting, that would help. But I hope you're not thinking of taking it outside the city. I mean, look at it—it's old!"

Nabil said, "No, no, maybe just to my house and back. It's just for fun. To show my friends I can drive."

"Why didn't you just tell me that in the first place, instead of making up stories about your father? You think I don't remember what it's like to be your age?"

Hercule stayed with him till the engine finally turned over and sputtered to life with a burst of oily smoke. It sounded like a big lawn mower. Coughing and waving his hands, Hercule shouted through the fold-down window, "The good thing is, if you're not going far, when it dies it's so light you'll be able to push it back here all by yourself."

Nabil nodded, thinking about the nightclub, far away and high above the city, up a road whose grade made ordinary cars strain. Well, what choice did he have? He released the hand brake and carefully shifted into first gear. The Fourgonette began to roll forward, shuddering enough to make all of its joints squeak.

Hercule called out, "Remember, two things: One, I didn't give you the keys, you took them yourself from the panel in the workroom—I know nothing about it. And two, if you have to turn off the engine, which I don't recommend, make sure you park facing downhill!"

3.

MARCEL LAY on his stomach, his hands and feet bound, his face twisted to the side to breathe. The moldy odor of the bare rotting mattress in the bedroom of the German's house didn't bother him as much as the idea of lying without permission in a dead man's bed.

Beyond Marcel's feet, Ben sat in a rocking chair by the window overlooking the forest, the machete across his lap, reading the liner notes from an Edith Piaf album. Both he and Jesse had wanted to stick together, but once they'd agreed on moving Marcel down here it became clear that one of them had to guard him while the other waited up at the nightclub for the bad guys to return with Roddy, or for Nabil to come back—like that was ever going to happen.

They tried to settle who went where by rock-paper-scissors, but when Ben won best two out of three by paper over rock Jesse said that was why rock-paper-scissors was stupid, because how could a piece of paper hurt a rock? It made no sense. Anyway, Jesse said he should be the one up at the nightclub, because he understood the language—they were careful not to say even the word "Mtom" in front of Marcel, to make sure none of the Africans knew Jesse could identify the language they were speaking, much less understand it—so he'd know what the bad guys were saying to each other when they showed up. And, because of course the hunters would be armed while Marcel was not only unarmed but tied up, Jesse said obviously he should have the pistol.

That left Ben with the stupid machete, and a job guarding a man who looked like he might be asleep, and a feeling that he was being pushed aside while other people had more fun: Jesse got sniper duty, Nabil got to take off for town, Roddy got a kidnapping adventure... Ben wondered if he was being punished for shooting Théophile, which wasn't fair because they'd all agreed it was an accident—and a lucky accident too, because Théophile had clearly been about to shoot them after killing Clint.

Marcel wasn't asleep, but he was happy to look that way while he considered his options. Since all of the boys' planning had taken place in English, Marcel wasn't sure whether he was being held to exchange for the red-haired boy. Even if that was the boys' intention, he doubted it would work. First of all, Marcel was pretty sure Prosper, at least, cared little enough about him that he'd rather keep the potentially valuable white boy. Secondly and more importantly, an exchange would require the hunters to come back for the other boys before they could learn what had happened up here.

Marcel didn't know Prosper, but he knew Danton, and kidnapping a white boy was a big step up from raiding a liquor storeroom and stealing some wood paneling. Marcel guessed once Danton was back in town he'd be content to ransom the one they already had, and not take the risk of coming back up the hill for more. The talk of returning for the others was just bluster, intended to make Marcel feel small and powerless on his own ground. Once the hunters were downtown even Prosper would see that fairness called for the other three boys to be considered Marcel's property, since he'd caught them first.

So no one would return, and therefore he wouldn't be exchanged. The boys would sit here all day, guarding him and getting bored and hungry and gradually realizing no one was coming back. What would they do with him then? Marcel recognized that if the boys took him to the police, the gen-darmes could quickly learn from him where to find at least Danton and Auguste, and they in turn would give up Prosper. That would be the quickest way to get the red-haired boy free, but Marcel didn't think that was the plan.

Bringing in the gendarmes would mean explaining the bloody corpse of Théophile. Marcel had heard the boys say over and over in English a word that sounded exactly like the French word "accident," but—even though he'd been in the next room when the shot was fired and therefore couldn't say for sure what had happened—nothing in their behavior afterward suggested that was what they really thought.

Could they be dumb enough to think they could just wave away the crime by calling it an accident? Did they think being white was going to protect them? Every now and then an old-time white landowner who'd adjusted poorly to the new post-independence reality was expelled from the country, his property confiscated, following the "accidental" death of one of his African workers. That made national news, of course, but did these boys or their parents even follow local events? The Peace Corps volunteer who'd spent time in Marcel's village kept trying to get his shortwave radio to deliver news of something called the Super Bowl.

Bored by Edith Piaf and stupid lyrics about love and sadness, Ben tossed the album sleeve aside and got up. Standing over Marcel, machete in hand, he asked in French, "Are you awake?"

Marcel opened his eyes. "I'm awake."

"Why haven't your friends come back?"

"I don't know. Maybe because they're not really my friends."

"Yeah, we noticed that."

"But I know where two of them live."

Ben thought for a while. Following Marcel into the crooked

alleyways of some shanty town neighborhood where the boys would be the only white people for a mile or more in any direction seemed like the worst of all possible plans. "Okay," he said without sounding interested. "That could be useful later. We'll see."

Making sure to keep Marcel in sight through the doorway, Ben stepped into the living room and sifted through the record albums on the floor for more reading matter; all the paperbacks on the bookshelves, whose cover art suggested they were Westerns, had turned out to be in German.

Watching him, Marcel indulged himself in a little fantasy of what he'd do to these white boys when he got free. The blond one here: he'd shoot him in the face the way the boy had shot Théophile. The long-haired one who'd gone back up after they brought Marcel down here: he'd shoot him too, for the brutal way these two boys had dragged Théophile's body out into the sun. The skinny red-haired one: he wasn't involved in the killing, so maybe he could go free after paying for all the damage to the German's house and the record collection. The possibly Spanish one, who'd gone away after taking Marcel's money: that was the toughest choice, because he deserved to die as much as the long-haired one, but Marcel was still convinced he was the one who'd fetch the biggest ransom.

So maybe in the fantasy Marcel would collect the ransom from the Spanish boy's parents and then kill him, and then kill the parents too—why not, since it was just a fantasy? But in reality the Spanish one had gone away with Marcel's money, who knew where and for what, and the long-haired one had gone away with the German's pistol, who knew where and for what, and the red-haired one was down in the city, probably being ransomed right now. So that left the blond one here.

As Ben came back into the bedroom and sat down in the rocking chair with another album cover to read about the legendary conducting debut of Arturo Toscanini, Marcel closed his eyes as if falling asleep, and concentrated on how to get free so he could kill this boy.

Jesse found himself shivering, though the day was plenty warm, even up here, high above the city. He wished he had something to read, so he wouldn't be so much on edge, every second on the alert for the sound of a car climbing the hill. The first few minutes—after he came back up the stairs from taking their hostage down to the house in the forest—had been the most interesting. He'd walked all around the nightclub, inside and out, looking for the best spot to hide: a place from which he could see the approaching road and the front door opening onto the verandah, and ideally close enough to hear the hunters talking.

In the end he'd chosen one of the little rooms that opened onto the restaurant area. (It was the private party room Marcel and Théophile had previously used as their bedroom.) The floor in this room was disconcertingly bouncy, but one of its windows looked out toward the city, so Jesse would hear a car coming up the hill, and the other window, at right angles to the first, looked out onto the verandah. Because the building partly embraced the outdoor dance floor, from this window someone standing outside the front door of the club would be in profile.

By the time Auguste arrived, Jesse had figured out he could close the shutters on the window and look out through the slits, so he could see visitors and they couldn't see him. He even found he could poke the muzzle of the pistol through in one place where the boards had rotted. So the note on Théophile's body didn't lie, and as Auguste read it he really did have a gun aimed at him. Jesse was a little surprised only one of the hunters had come back, but he had to admit it was a relief too. It was like a dry run of the real event, and it had gone well: he'd heard the Peugeot 404 long before it stopped at the gate down the hill, and Auguste had been so disturbed by the corpse on the verandah—indeed so obviously shaken that Jesse almost laughed out loud—that he hadn't even glanced at the closed shutters of the window off to his right.

Jesse had noticed during Auguste's visit that his own view of the last stretch of the road, the part people walked up after leaving their cars, turned out to be blocked by the verandah itself, and that was less than ideal. But luckily the note had said the boys needed to hear Roddy's voice, so that was covered, and the spot he'd chosen was in every other way the best sniper post. Jesse felt confident he was ready for the next round of the game.

He was a little surprised to find himself thinking of it as a game. After all, a dog was dead and a man was dead and a boy was kidnapped and it wasn't over yet. He certainly couldn't pretend to any kind of nonchalance about it, as if he did this sort of thing all the time. Of course all his life he'd seen men brought in to the mission hospital dying from gunshot wounds, whether from fights or from hunting accidents, and his father and mother rising from the dinner table to answer the hoarse calling and the pounding at the door, picking up a long flashlight for the walk down to the hospital before they even asked what had happened. But that was different from seeing the gun go off and Théophile fly back spraying blood, and feeling in some way responsible, since it was the boys' decision to take action that had led seconds later to the shooting.

But the shooting of Théophile had followed the killing of Clint, which had followed Ben's release of the dog, which had followed the kidnapping of Roddy. So it really was like the alternating moves of a game. When he could get away from the hospital, Jesse's father was an avid big game hunter: African buffalo, elephant, leopard. Dr. McCall idolized Colonel Jim Corbett, and one of Jesse's favorite childhood memories was of his father reading aloud to him from *Man-Eaters of Kumaon*. In fact, when he thought about it, what he was doing now, as he waited behind closed shutters for the bad guys to return, was a lot less like Sean Connery and a lot more like Jim Corbett waiting hour after hour in a tree for the Man-eating Leopard of Rudraprayag—though Jesse assumed Jim Corbett, being an old hand at this kind of thing, didn't shiver from anticipatory nerves while he waited.

The next time he noticed the sound of the engine it was already quite loud and close: either the wind had shifted or he'd let himself get distracted by leopards. It sounded like the same Peugeot—the gravelly diesel was distinctive. Making sure to stay in the shadows, he stood up and leaned out to get a view a little further down the slope. He still couldn't see the road, but, based on the direction of the sound, the car seemed to have reached the turnaround point and the gate. The engine shut off, and he could hear his heart pounding in the silence. Car doors opened and slammed. It was time.

Taking the safety off the pistol, Jesse moved to the window overlooking the verandah and the front door. He nosed the pistol into the little space between the shutter slats and focused on slowing down his breathing. Footsteps scuffed the gravel on the last stretch of road—the visitors were now in the section hidden from Jesse by the edge of the verandah. How many of them had come this time? And had they brought Roddy? He bit his lip to keep from panting.

"Guys? It's me!" It was Roddy's voice, from somewhere down there on the road, cracking into a little-kid squeak the way it still did when he was nervous or just shouting. "Hello? Are you there? It's Roddy, and I'm fine!"

Jesse waited. He hadn't thought this part through carefully: if he answered they'd know where he was, but if he didn't answer, how would they exchange Roddy for Marcel?

"Hey, is anybody there?" Roddy's voice had come no closer, presumably because whoever was holding him had stopped on the road to wait for an answer from the nightclub.

Jesse's mind raced. He had to say something soon or the men would turn around and take Roddy away again. He decided to yell to them to bring Roddy up onto the verandah, where he could at least see them all, figuring that from down there his voice would just appear to come from the verandah and his hiding place would be safe—but only till the men were closer, and then what?

But just as he opened his mouth to call out he heard voices almost directly below him, talking quietly in Mtom. The first one said, "I'm going around behind, under the building."

The other voice answered, "Okay. What should I do? Should I follow you?"

"No, stay here where they can't see you. Let Prosper handle the exchange."

Jesse began to tremble. How could he deal with all three of them if they scattered? Why hadn't he planned for something like this? Was he really that big of an idiot? And why the fuck wasn't Nabil here to help, instead of running off home like a little girl?

The sound of a man struggling through dense underbrush came up through the gaps in the floorboards below him, followed by a low "Ow! Shit!" in Mtom.

"You all right?"

"Thorns. It's nothing. You just pay attention to what's going on."

"Hey, guys! Hello?" Now Roddy sounded angry. "I thought you were my friends! I guess not, huh? Bunch of retard losers!"

Jesse wondered why Roddy wasn't taking advantage of the hunters' ignorance of English to shout out something useful about how many men there were, where they were, what guns they had. Jesse imagined he himself would have done something like that, but Roddy was a fucking little sissy and a crybaby. If they hadn't brought him along he wouldn't have stupidly bragged about his father being important and wouldn't have gotten himself kidnapped and none of this would have happened.

Plus which, it was Roddy's supposed British Boy Scout orienteering skills that had led them to take a short cut through the forest around the back of the hill in the first place— something the boys with lifelong experience of Africa would have had more sense than even to contemplate, if it hadn't been for Roddy's naive self-assurance about trailblazing. So, really, even finding the abandoned house had been Roddy's fault.

Jesse turned as quietly as he could and aimed the pistol down at the floor. The spaces between the boards were wide enough in some places that he could see the bushes moving, so if he got lucky he could fire a shot through a gap.

The voice below him said in Mtom, "Hey, Auguste! One more thing!"

The other voice was further away, under the verandah. "What?"

"Remember, even if you get a clear shot, don't shoot till we have Marcel. Not just when we see Marcel, but when we have him safe."

"Of course. I'm not an idiot, Danton. Give me some credit."

"Sorry."

"But do we kill our guy too?"

There was a pause. Jesse wanted to crouch down to get a better view through the gap at his feet, but he was afraid the slightest movement would provoke the rotting floorboards to shed wood dust and cause the hunters to look up and see him.

"What do you mean, our guy?"

"The red-haired boy. What other guy could I mean?"

"I thought for a second you meant Prosper." Both men chuckled. The first one went on. "If we can keep the boy for ransom, great. If not, oh well."

Jesse had just begun to digest that when he heard Roddy and the third man coming up the verandah steps.

"Where are your friends?" the man named Prosper was saying in French.

"I told you, I don't know! Maybe they ran away!"

Still without moving his feet, Jesse turned again to look out through the shutters. Roddy's hands were behind his back, presumably tied. Prosper had a tight grip on Roddy's upper arm, and a pistol—not part of his earlier hunting gear—pressed to Roddy's ear. Man and boy both paused on the top step as they caught sight of Théophile's body lying in the sun and the cloud of flies on the blood.

Prosper didn't look surprised, just grim, but Roddy burst into tears. The men had told him nothing in the car on the way up here about what Auguste had found on his earlier visit—in fact they hadn't spoken to Roddy at all till they got out of the car and Prosper told him to call out to his friends. But it wasn't just the shock of Roddy's first and unprepared sight of the bloody corpse that made him cry, it was that he immediately pictured himself stretched out next to Théophile, his own face erased. He shrank back, sobbing not for the African boy but for his own precious life, which was about to end here, in a few terrifying seconds, in this stupid place.

Prosper shook the boy. "You see what your little white friends did?" He was shouting—he considered himself cool in the face of violence, but the sight of Théophile had unnerved him, and he needed to release the feeling. "You like that?"

Howling, Roddy sagged so that Prosper was essentially

holding him up. Prosper swung the boy around on the verandah, still shaking him. "You want to go closer, so you can see what we're going to do to your friends when we catch them?" Roddy screamed and tried to turn away, but Prosper wrenched him around to face the corpse.

Behind the shutters, Jesse wormed the nose of the pistol back into position. If the two of them would just stop moving around out there, he could take a shot at Prosper. He was less than thirty feet away, and Jesse had had plenty of experience shooting lizards at that distance with a BB gun—and even the big lizards, the foot-and-a-half-long blue-green ones with the red throats that sunned themselves on the bare cinderblock walls of unfinished houses, offered a much smaller target than Prosper. If only Roddy would stop getting in front of him.

"What's that?" said Danton below him in Mtom, and Jesse froze and closed his eyes as though that would make him invisible. If Danton had spotted him, and even assuming Jesse survived the first shots fired up through the floorboards, the three men would hunt him down wherever he ran inside the nightclub and kill him like a rat.

"Do you hear that?" Danton called, this time in French. Prosper shushed Roddy and listened. "What?"

Auguste said in Mtom, "I hear it."

Danton said, still in French, "It's a car." He began to push his way back through the brush under the overhang of the nightclub.

Prosper was still listening. "You think it's coming up here?"

"Of course. Up here you only hear cars that are already halfway up the hill. There's no place else it can be going."

Jesse realized he could take a shot at Prosper right then, as he stood there on the verandah listening, holding Roddy at arm's length. But should he? Would Roddy, even with his hands tied, have the sense to run out of the bright sun and into the gloom of the nightclub, or would he just panic and freeze where he stood till someone shot him, either deliberately or in the crossfire? And anyway, who was coming up the hill? If it was Nabil and he was bringing help, there was no need for Jesse to die in a hail of bullets just before rescue arrived. But Nabil didn't know the hunters were here right now, so by doing nothing Jesse was letting Nabil drive into a trap. Jesse aimed at Prosper's chest, but still he waited—for what? He couldn't say.

Danton and Auguste came out from under the verandah. All three men looked at the guns in their hands, the little sniffling white boy, the bloody corpse, and finally each other. The sound of the car grew louder. Prosper turned and dragged Roddy down the stairs with him. "Let's get out of here with this one before we get caught and lose him too."

As they ran down the road toward the car, Auguste called to Danton in Mtom, "What about Marcel?"

Prosper opened the rear passenger door for the boy, then changed his mind and pulled Roddy around to the back of the Peugeot and opened the trunk. Danton, panting as he caught up, said in French, "What about Marcel?"

"What do you want me to do?" Prosper pushed Roddy into the trunk. "Obviously he's not up there. The white boys took him away, and that's probably the gendarmes coming now." He slammed the trunk lid and climbed into the front passenger seat. "Come on, let's get the fuck out of here."

Danton and Auguste hesitated, looking first at the Peugeot and then back up the hill. From down here only the underside of the outer corner of the nightclub verandah was visible through the brush. Auguste said, "And Théophile? We're just going to leave him there?"

Prosper shrugged. "We didn't kill him."

The sound of the approaching car grew louder as it reached the last couple of switchbacks. Danton and Auguste got into the Peugeot, and Danton started the engine and turned the car around. As he steered down the hill Danton eyed the pistol in Prosper's hands, acquired from a black market deal on surplus military equipment Prosper had negotiated a few months ago. Prosper was steadying the gun against the ruts and jolts and aiming down the steep road. Danton said, "You planning to shoot it out with the gendarmes?"

"No," said Prosper, "but there's a slight chance that instead of gendarmes it'll be the parents of one of those boys, coming to pick them up after their little hike. So I figure, if it's a white person we'll stop them and kill them right here on the road, as payback for Théophile."

After he heard the Peugeot start, Jesse switched from the shuttered window overlooking the verandah back to the window with a view of the hillside. He was still moving cautiously, staying in the shadows, his pistol ready, because he couldn't tell, in all the confusion and with the blind spot created by the verandah, whether or not the hurried departure was just a trick and one or more of the hunters had stayed behind to catch Jesse when he came out of hiding—or just to ambush Nabil when he got out of his car.

The overlapping engine noises, one approaching, one receding, gradually resolved, and a car that wasn't the Peugeot stopped at the turnaround. The engine shut off. There came one long blast of the horn, and then its echo returning from the next hill over. Jesse waited at the window, puzzled: hadn't Nabil said he'd honk "shave and a haircut, two bits"? Had he just forgotten in all the excitement? There was another long echoing blast of the horn. No, Nabil wouldn't have forgotten—especially knowing Jesse was listening for it, because the two of them had been using "shave and a haircut" as their joke signal ever since they saw it in some dumb Disney movie in third grade, before they were friends with Ben and long before Roddy moved here.

So who was down there if it wasn't Nabil? Another blast of the horn, and this time, after the echo faded, a man's voice shouted, "Marcel?" Jesse waited, feeling like he'd spent the whole morning just waiting hidden in this room while events he hadn't anticipated unrolled outside. But what should he do?

"Marcel? Théophile? Hurry up!" It was the voice of an African man, speaking French. Jesse waited for the sound of the man's footsteps coming up the road—to be followed shortly by his discovery on the verandah of the reason Théophile was unable to come when called. But whoever it was seemed to be staying by his car, muttering to himself or maybe listening to the car radio.

As Nabil came around the last bend in the road he was thinking about nothing except whether the feeble engine of the rattletrap Citroën Fourgonette, screaming from the effort of climbing without a break since the bottom of the hill, would have a coronary and die on the last stretch just to make his embarrassment complete.

When he saw the black Mercedes 280 parked at the turn-around his first thought was that somehow, spookily, his father had guessed where he was going and had gotten here ahead of him. He spent the next several seconds planning how he would explain away everything that had happened and that somehow his father must already know about, since he'd beaten him here: the body of Théophile, the abduction of Roddy, the vandalism to the German's house.

It was only after those several crucial seconds—during which the Fourgonette continued to chug closer to the parked car—that Nabil realized the black Mercedes must belong to the kidnappers. He tried to stop, tried to turn, tried to duck down, but the Fourgonette had spotted a place to rest its bones, and the old car summoned all of its remaining willpower to pull its driver the last few feet and expire next to the Mercedes. In the ticking, oily silence, Nabil gripped the steering wheel and thought, I'm dead.

A man in chauffeur's livery got out of the black Mercedes, and for a moment Nabil reverted to his first explanation and imagined it was Hercule—in which case he was saved and would happily and gratefully confess all to his father. But it wasn't Hercule. It was hard to be sure, since any uniform changed a man's appearance so, but Nabil didn't think this man looked like any of the three hunters from this morning. Was he still another member of the gang?

The chauffeur stood, waiting politely for Nabil to get out of the Fourgonette. When he didn't, the man came around and opened his door for him. Nabil climbed out.

Marcel, still lying face down on the German's mattress, had heard the long honks echoing around the hillside and knew what they meant, but since Ben had also heard them and Marcel felt the boy's questioning eyes on him, he remained expressionless.

Ben stood up. "What was that?"

Marcel shrugged. "I think it was someone honking."

"No shit, Sherlock," said Ben in English, since he didn't know the equivalent in French.

A few minutes later they heard footsteps coming along the boardwalk. His whole body tensing, Ben raised the machete, then relaxed when he heard Jesse's voice calling out the password, "Double-O seven! Double-O seven!"

Jesse was panting as he ran into the house, still holding the pistol. He said to Marcel in French, "There's someone out there on the road calling for you and Théophile. Do you know who it is?"

Marcel shrugged. "I'd have to hear his voice."

Jesse said, "The other guys, the hunters, they just walked

right up to the nightclub. Why's this guy honking?"

"How can I know that," said Marcel, "if I don't even know who it is?"

"What's going to happen if you don't answer?"

Marcel began again patiently. "As I already explained—"

"Yeah, we got it. Shut up."

The boys switched to English to talk to each other, but their alarm was obvious. If Marcel could delay them long enough here, Monsieur Koeffler's chauffeur would go back downtown and report that he'd been unable to pay Marcel his wages because, for the first time in five years, the nightclub was abandoned. Monsieur Koeffler, furious, would come back out here to fire Marcel and would discover Théophile.

The chauffeur himself was unlikely to find the body on the verandah, since Marcel knew the man would consider it beneath his dignity to walk up the road away from his precious Mercedes just to give a watchman his money. But Marcel's only hope for rescue—since he didn't count on the hunters coming back, and was unaware that in fact they'd already come and gone—depended on the chauffeur getting impatient and driving away to tell Koeffler. But would the chauffeur linger instead, enjoying the breeze on the hill, admiring the view of the city, smoking a cigarette, prolonging the freedom of these minutes out of his boss's earshot?

Jesse said in French, "Okay, listen. We're going to untie you. You're about to go tell whoever that guy is whatever you need to tell him to get him to go away."

Marcel nodded, considering the possibilities.

"And I'm going to be right behind you, just out of sight. And you're going to speak French, loud and clear."

Marcel nodded again while Ben began to untie his ankles. Monsieur Koeffler's chauffeur was a Yoa, so they spoke French to each other anyway.

"And if you tell him anything about us, or give him anything, or do anything suspicious..." Jesse pointed to the pistol. "I'll shoot him and then I'll shoot you. Just like you said about the dog, remember?" Jesse glanced out through the bedroom door and across the shambles of the living room to the bathroom door, where Marcel had been standing with this same pistol when he first caught the boys whipping LPs out the window only a few hours ago. "And if you don't think we mean what we say, remember we already shot one of you guys in the face."

"Hey!" said Ben in English, looking up from the ropes and reddening. "That was an accident!"

"Oh, yeah," said Jesse in French. "I forgot. It was an accident. And we don't want any more accidents, do we, Marcel?"

Marcel shook his head.

"Good morning, Monsieur," said the chauffeur to Nabil with a little salute, as a matter of professionalism keeping to himself all signs of his surprise at the tender age of the white boy driving this junker.

"Good morning." Nabil decided the man didn't sound or look threatening, and he even seemed a little puzzled by Nabil's presence here, so maybe he wasn't part of the plot.

The two of them eyed each other, each trying to understand without betraying his own confusion. Finally the chauffeur said politely, "Are you lost, Monsieur?"

Before he could decide whether or not it would be to his advantage to play lost, Nabil found himself saying, "No, no," and pointing up the hill. "This is the Club Balafon."

"Yes, as you can see," said the chauffeur, indicating the five-year-old sign Monsieur Koeffler had hung on the gate: *The Club Balafon is temporarily closed and will reopen soon. We regret the inconvenience. No trespassing beyond this point.*

Nabil nodded and studied the faded French words, lingering

over each line to give himself time to think. Why weren't Jesse and Ben coming down to give him some help—even just to let him know what the hell was going on? Oh, yeah: shave and a haircut. He reached through the window of the Fourgonette and was about to honk the horn when he stopped himself. Could he really be sure this guy wasn't one of the bad guys? He'd look like an idiot if he brought his friends out of hiding prematurely and spoiled everything. He pulled his arm back out of the car.

The chauffeur had watched with great interest while Nabil almost honked the horn. "Excuse me, Monsieur, were you going to honk for Marcel?"

Nabil nodded. How could the man have so many questions he didn't know the right answers to?

Marcel rubbed his recently bound wrists as he walked down from the nightclub. When he reached the gate he noticed another car, a rusty old Citroën Fourgonette, parked next to Monsieur Koeffler's black Mercedes in the turnaround. Koeffler's chauffeur and another person, presumably the driver of the Citroën, were leaning, each against the side of his own car, smoking and talking. Only as he squeezed around the gate did Marcel recognize the second smoker as the Spanish-looking boy who'd stolen his taxi money. Marcel and Nabil stared at each other.

The chauffeur called out, "Hey, Marcel, there you are! Bet you a thousand francs you can't guess who this is."

Marcel and Nabil continued to stare at each other. Through Marcel's head ran one explanation after another—all absurd— for why this boy who'd helped kill Théophile had come back and was now calmly standing here smoking with Koeffler's chauffeur. Meanwhile through Nabil's head ran just one question: if this guy had gotten free, what had he done to Jesse and Ben? In a sense, both of them had the same question: what the fuck was going on here?

Marcel shook his head at the chauffeur. "I give up. Who is he?"

The chauffeur laughed and snapped his fingers. "I knew you'd never get it! He's the old man's grandson!"

Nothing had become any clearer. "What old man?"

"Your old man! Your late boss! This is the German's grandson!"

Still just trying to gain time to understand what was going on, Marcel said to the boy, "You came here from Germany?"

Nabil shook his head. "France. My father's French. I'm Jean-Michel. And you must be Marcel, the caretaker." Marcel nodded. Nabil pulled out his pack of Gentleman cigarettes. "Cigarette?"

As if in a trance, Marcel accepted a cigarette and Nabil gave him a light. Marcel took in the smoke and exhaled slowly. Somewhere on the uphill slope behind him the long-haired boy was waiting in hiding with the pistol, listening.

Koeffler's chauffeur said, "Who were those people I passed on the way up here?"

Marcel shrugged. "Tourists, probably. I didn't see them." It was a reasonable guess: if it had been the hunters, why would they have left without rescuing him?

"What took you so long, anyway? I would've given up and left before now if this young man hadn't shown up."

"Sorry. I was around the back side of the hill, and it took me a while to get here after I heard you honk."

"What about Théophile?"

Marcel and Nabil eyed each other. It occurred to Marcel that if he stayed close to this boy the other boy might not dare take a shot at him. But as he edged toward Nabil, Nabil edged away.

"Théophile is… not here."

The chauffeur grunted sympathetically. "That's the problem with young people—you just can't count on them when you need them." He looked at Nabil. "If you'll excuse my asking, Monsieur, and meaning no offense at all, but how old are you?"

Nabil tried to blow a smoke ring—a skill the boys had been learning from the Matador, their favorite Marine at the American Club. The smoke came out as a disk. "I'm eighteen, but a lot of people tell me I look younger."

Marcel said, "Eighteen… And you came all the way to Africa from Germany—"

"France."

"—by yourself?"

"Sure. It's just a plane ride." Nabil worked on another smoke ring, with less success than the first. What had this fucker done with the other boys?

Marcel said, "So you must have arranged with Monsieur Koeffler to come up and see the place."

Nabil almost said, "Who?" but remembered in time that the chauffeur had told him he worked for some guy in town who was in charge of the property.

Before Nabil could answer, the chauffeur said, "That's what's incredible, Marcel—he found his way up here by himself, just using the descriptions in letters the old man sent to the boy's mother!" The chauffeur laughed and snapped his fingers again—he was beginning to get on Marcel's nerves.

Marcel said quite plainly to Nabil, "That's hard to believe."

Nabil smiled at him and then worked on another smoke ring, which also failed. "I'd really like to look around the property. After all, that's what my mother sent me out here to do, to find out if it was worth claiming."

Marcel gestured up the hill. "Please, be my guest."

So that was it: he wanted to trap Nabil here. Maybe the

other hunters had already come back, and instead of exchanging Roddy for Marcel those fuckers had somehow managed to free Marcel and capture Jesse and Ben. So now all of Nabil's friends were prisoners (or dead) except for him. Only the presence of the chauffeur was keeping Marcel from attacking Nabil—even now he kept edging toward him—so he had to make sure that when the chauffeur left, he left with him.

"No, no, I wouldn't want to put you in that position. I see now that I really ought to speak to this Monsieur Kessler first, and come back up here with him."

"Koeffler," the chauffeur corrected him politely. "Oh, speaking of which, Marcel, here's your pay." He reached into the Mercedes and got an envelope off the dashboard. Then he laughed. "Though it seems funny that I'm paying him, when it's your money, Monsieur."

Nabil waved his hand. "No, no, my mother is the one who deals with the money."

While the chauffeur was handing the envelope to Marcel, Nabil glanced up the hillside and saw Ben step out from behind a small tree. Nabil almost shouted in surprise, but Ben put one finger to his lips. In the next couple of seconds Ben made a series of signs that in his own mind represented, "Everything's okay. We have the pistol. Stay here. Make sure Marcel stays here"— but that to Nabil looked like nothing more than a meaningless flurry of pointing and waving. Then Ben disappeared behind the tree again. But even without decoding Ben's signals, proof that he was present and alive was all Nabil needed to adjust his plans.

Marcel walked away from the other two, pretending to count the bills in his envelope while he pondered his options. Was there some way he could pass a signal to the chauffeur, say by putting something in the envelope and handing it back? No, the boy hiding with the pistol would be watching for the handoff. Then what about objecting to his pay and demanding to be driven downtown to see Koeffler? No, if Marcel got into the Mercedes for any reason, both he and the chauffeur would be shot before the car turned around—a picture of Théophile's bloody face loomed before Marcel's eyes again.

Then what about grabbing the Spanish boy and using him as a human shield till they got away? But the boy was obviously wary, and seemed to be trying to keep the body of the car between himself and Marcel. Besides, if Marcel just attacked the boy without explanation, the chauffeur would of course take the side of the young white man, supposedly the old German's heir, against a mere African watchman. The boy would be free and Marcel and the chauffeur would be dead long before Marcel could set the man straight.

Then what about just taking off running, diving off the edge of the road into the brush and scrambling down the hillside to town? No, first because they'd shoot the chauffeur. And then because after that the boys would have two cars and a pistol, and they could easily catch up with him halfway down, since a straight line down the hill from here would cross the road several times as it switched back and forth on its way down, and pushing your way through the brush, even steeply downhill, was slow work.

Was it actually possible Marcel was powerless against these children? Granted, they were like demons incarnate, but could he really be standing here, unbound, with money in his hands and a compatriot a few feet away, and still have no chance of escape? Resisting the urge to crumple up the bills in anger, Marcel tucked his pay into his pocket and turned to rejoin the others.

Then he noticed that from where he stood, out in the gravel turnaround behind both vehicles, he could see the back of the boxy cargo section of the Fourgonette. Across the two rear doors, though the paint was faded, peeled, and rust-patched,

Marcel could make out just enough to reconstruct the familiar words *Quincaillerie Chaloub*. Huh, he thought, how about that. He walked back to rejoin the others.

"Well, I've stayed up here long enough, and I really have to get back to the embassy." The chauffeur gave Nabil a little salute. "Thank you again for the cigarette, Monsieur. I'll let Monsieur Koeffler know to expect your visit." Nabil nodded vaguely, and the chauffeur added, "Since it's already noon on Saturday, I'm afraid he won't be in the office again till Monday."

"That's fine, no problem," said Nabil.

"But if he wants to make contact sooner, where can he find you?"

Nabil finally blew an excellent smoke ring. "I'm at the Sheraton. Leclerc, Jean-Marc Leclerc."

"Understood." The chauffeur got into the Mercedes. "All right, as for you, Marcel, till next week—and don't keep me waiting again." He turned the big car around and began to roll downhill, then stopped. He leaned out and waved to Nabil. "And welcome to Africa, Monsieur Leclerc!" He drove off slowly, so they wouldn't be covered in too much red road dust —a courtesy he'd never thought of when it was just Marcel or Théophile standing there.

Nabil and Marcel eyed each other across the roof of the Fourgonette. Nabil smiled—and then, strangely, Marcel smiled too. From far away in the city came the long blast of the air horn at the Gentleman cigarette factory, marking twelve noon.

"I'm not going to say anything while Théophile is lying out there in the sun with flies on him."

The boys had tied Marcel to a chair, and they now sat facing him at one of the café tables. When they came back inside the nightclub, the first topic of discussion—in English—had been what to do with the dead body. Ben had said he didn't like having to step over it to get through the doorway. Nabil had said it must be his guilty conscience talking. Jesse, after calming down Ben, had said they couldn't move the body around too much if they wanted to stick to the story that it had been an accident. Unable to settle the question, they'd moved on.

Now in control again and flush from his triumph of play-acting with Koeffler's chauffeur—a performance they all agreed was worthy of Sean Connery himself, though in fact Nabil had mostly just needed to keep agreeing with the chauffeur's suggestions—Nabil said to Marcel, "All right. What do you want us to do with him?"

"At least bring him back inside and cover him."

Ben elected to guard Marcel, leaving Nabil and Jesse to pick up one foot each and drag Théophile's body back across the café area of the nightclub—detouring around the body of the dog, with the spear still in it—and into the empty liquor storeroom. They threw a balafon-stenciled restaurant tablecloth over the body and closed the door. Then Jesse threw another tablecloth over Clint. The whole time, Marcel stared at Ben and Ben looked out the window.

"Now, Marcel," said Nabil when he and Jesse sat back down again, "let's make sure we understand each other. Your friends have Roddy and we have you." Marcel nodded. "We set up an exchange, and it almost worked, but then they got scared off." That part was news to Marcel, but he nodded again. "And that means they probably think our note was a trap. So now we don't know how to find them to get our friend back. That's a problem."

"It's not a problem," said Marcel. "I already told this boy," he nodded at Ben, "they aren't my friends but I know how to make contact with them again."

Nabil said, "And why would we trust you?"

"Because I want to save my life! And I have no reason to protect those men. They're the cause of everything that's gone wrong today. If it weren't for them, all four of you would've been home with your families long before now."

The boys looked at each other and spoke briefly in English. Then Nabil said, "Even if we trust you, which is a big if, there's another problem. When the hunters were here before, we overheard them"—he was careful not to specify that it was Mtom rather than French they'd overheard—"planning to kill us all after they got you back."

Marcel almost laughed—his own plan exactly! Instead he shook his head. "That's nonsense, just big talk. Those guys act tough and walk around waving guns, but the worst thing they've ever done was steal liquor and a piece of the teakwood facing from the bar." They all looked across the room at the ugly scar. "They're a bunch of drunks. I'd be surprised if they're even capable of pulling off this ransom job."

Jesse said, "Even that guy Prosper? He looked pretty serious."

Marcel blew out his lips dismissively. "Prosper? He's the biggest blowhard of the bunch," he said of a man he'd never met before this morning. "I'm telling you, you've killed more people today than they have in their whole lives."

Ben flushed and said in French, "It was an accident."

Ignoring Ben, Nabil said in English to the other boys, "Okay, we know what the option of trusting him looks like. Do we have another option?"

"Well," said Jesse, "I'll just say it because somebody ought to say it: we could go to the police right now and tell them everything, and not get into even more shit than we're already in."

Nabil nodded. "Like, 'Hey, Mister Gendarme, um, our

friend got kidnapped, and oh by the way we smashed up a house and killed a guy,' and Ben if you say one more time it was an accident I swear I'm going to punch you."

Understanding only the words "gendarme" and "accident," Marcel watched the faces of the three boys as they glared at each other across the café table. He needed to figure out who was dangerous, who was weak, and who might be dangerous precisely because he was weak.

Jesse said, "I'm not saying we should do it, I'm just trying to make sure we think of all the choices, that's all. In fact, raise your hand if you think we should go the police." None of the boys raised his hand.

"Good." Nabil smiled. "So we're all agreed. We're going to settle this ourselves."

When they walked him back down to the turnaround spot, Marcel, his feet free but his hands still bound, did his best to lean against the rear doors of the Fourgonette at the place where the Chaloub logo remained clearest. He wanted to hide the words from the boys and at the same time to rub against them, as if he had a slight itch, to see if the sweaty back of his shirt could peel off just enough more of the flaking lettering to make the sign illegible. He couldn't tell if he'd succeeded before he was pushed into the cargo box.

Jesse climbed in after him, made Marcel sit with his back against one wall of the cargo box, and tied his arms to one of the metal ribs that ran up from the floor, across the roof, and down the other side. The corrugated roof was low enough that, even when he crouched, Jesse had to duck to avoid hitting his head. When Marcel was secured, Jesse sat down facing him.

They leaned their elbows on the wheel wells, panting, and felt the sweat coating their entire bodies. The cargo area was indescribably hot—logically enough, for a closed metal box siting in the noonday sun in equatorial Africa. There was no opening forward to the cab, so all Jesse could do was slap the front wall of the box as hard as he could—making a ringing sound that hurt their ears—and shout, "Let's go, Nabil! It's hot as fuck back here!"

Up front, Nabil tossed the machete under the driver's seat with the old French magazines and the empty bottles and got in. Then, while Ben watched enviously, he turned the key. In the first moments after Koeffler's chauffeur drove away and Jesse and Ben came out of hiding, Nabil had been dumbfounded by their reaction to the car: after all of his fears of humiliation for showing up in this rusty wreck, both Jesse and Ben had loved the Fourgonette. They thought it was incredibly cool, as good as James Bond's Aston Martin, and they wanted to hear every detail of Nabil's numerous close calls—the near sideswipes, the near stalling in intersections—on his way across the city to get here.

Nabil had had a lot to think about this morning, and he worked the starter to no purpose for more than a minute— listening to Jesse banging impatiently on the wall of the cargo box behind his head—before he remembered what Hercule had said when he first showed him the Fourgonette. Well, Nabil had plenty of downhill to give him a rolling start, but he was unfortunately parked facing the wrong way. He was going to have to turn around, and do it without help from the engine. He pushed the weird Citroën gearshift nob that poked straight back out of the dashboard to its neutral point and let off the brake.

The fully loaded Fourgonette took off backward down the steep incline at shocking speed. It was lucky for Nabil that Ben and Jesse were in awe of his precocious driving skills, and that neither of them knew enough about driving to consider that Nabil had no view straight back because of the cargo box, or that —though Nabil had practiced backing up in the Land Cruiser on the beach—his father had made sure he did it in a place where there were no nearby obstacles, so Nabil had never learned to use his side mirror.

So at first as the Fourgonette hurtled backward neither of the other boys screamed—till Nabil tried to turn and got confused and began to steer the back end of the car toward the sheer downhill edge of the road: then they screamed. Nabil twisted the steering wheel the other direction and accomplished the first part his turn—at the last possible place where the turnaround was at all wider than the road itself—by running the rear end of the Fourgonette hard up against the red dirt bank.

Moments before, Marcel had been thinking they were all going to die rolling over and over down the hillside in this stupid old car, and even if he survived he wouldn't be able to climb away from the wreck since he was tied to it. Now he wondered whether the impact against the dirt bank had scraped any more paint off the rear doors.

Chaloub was well known to be one of the richest men in the country, and it made sense that the one called Nabil—with an Arab name and Arab skin—would be his son or grandson. If the boy had claimed his parents were Peace Corp volunteers, it could only be because even he knew his real ransom value. But Marcel's chances of grabbing Nabil unawares depended on the boy not realizing that the surviving fragments of writing on the rear doors were giving him away.

The Fourgonette now sat sideways across the road, its boxy rear in the uphill dirt and its nose facing the city five hundred feet below them. Ben and Jesse had gone straight from screaming to laughing, and it was only their helpless hysterical laughter (Jesse's weirdly muffled in the cargo box) that kept Nabil from getting out of the car and throwing up—he knew how close they'd all just come to going over the edge and dying.

Marcel said to Jesse, "It isn't funny. We almost died. He has no idea how to drive. I should be the one driving."

Jesse stopped laughing. "We're trusting you to help get our friend back, but don't push us too far." He wished he had the pistol to underline his words—he missed the power he'd felt, hidden in his lookout spot, the barrel of the gun aimed at grown men, whether on the verandah or under the floor, men who had no idea what he could do to them if he felt like it. It was that power, and the resulting excitement, that he remembered now from those minutes, when in fact at the time he'd been almost sick from fear and confusion as the hunters fanned out to kill him.

But, after a long argument before they loaded up, Nabil had prevailed: putting the pistol in the cargo box was too dangerous, because even tied up Marcel might somehow get his hands on it. With no weapons at all in the back, if Marcel got loose the most he could do would be to punch Jesse some before Nabil stopped the car and opened the rear doors with the pistol ready. Jesse, unconvinced but tired of arguing, had shrugged and given up.

More cautiously than before, Nabil took his foot off the brake and the Fourgonette began to move, and this time it was rolling forward. He turned sharply and the front wheels just cleared the edge of the road where the drop-off began. Ben still hadn't stopped laughing, and now, with the car finally pointed forward down the road in a familiar way, Nabil too began to laugh.

With four people in it, the Fourgonette, still in neutral, began to fly down the steep winding road. In the cargo box Marcel and Jesse were flung back and forth as the car whipped around the turns. The rope holding Marcel's hands burned his wrists and strained his shoulders, while Jesse, doing his best to press himself against the sides of the box, still kept banging his head on the corrugated wall.

Marcel shouted in French, "Start the engine! Start the engine!"

But his voice was muffled by the metal box and drowned out by the laughter and screams of Nabil and Ben, sitting in the best seats on the best roller coaster ride of their lives. Whether or not it was true that the wheels on one side actually left the ground as the car tore around the first of the hairpin switchback turns, the bouncy suspension of the Deux Chevaux certainly made it feel that way.

Nabil screamed, "Two wheels! Two wheels!"

Ben shouted, "Just like James fucking Bond in that alleyway in *Diamonds Are Forever!*"

As they paused for breath they heard Jesse's muffled but obviously angry voice. "Hey! Cut it out! I just hit my head really hard back here!"

That made them both laugh so much that Nabil barely had the strength to hold onto the steering wheel. But right after that they came so close to flying off the road at the next hairpin turn that Ben began to sober up. "Nabil, shouldn't you turn on the engine or something?"

Nabil had in fact forgotten to do so, because he was absorbed in the challenge and exhilaration of steering down this road and because they were moving so fast it didn't occur to him the car was without power. Now, steering with one hand around a bend, he turned the ignition key and the engine rattled to life.

In the cargo box Marcel yelled, "Slow down before you put it in gear!"

Nabil heard him and began braking, and, though he was still going much too fast for the gear he chose—slamming the weird handle straight into the dashboard for second—the Citroën machinery was as solid as it was simple, and the gearbox protested loudly but held.

They drove the rest of the way down the hill at a speed still far faster than safe or normal, but by comparison sedate and disappointing to the boys—except for Jesse, whose head hurt and who was glad not to have it banged again.

As the hillside leveled out and they came to the bottom of the German's private road, where it met the paved road heading into the city from the west, Marcel realized he'd been holding his breath most of the way down, expecting to die and silently asking God what evil he'd done in his quiet life to deserve this awful end at the hands of idiotic, screaming children. When the car came to a stop at the road junction and Marcel let out a long sigh, it also occurred to him that, for the first time in five years, the Club Balafon stood unoccupied and unprotected.

AFTERNOON

1.

"IT'S THE LITTLE HOUSE all the way at the back of this alley. You can't see it from here. You have to angle a bit to the left after the water pump."

Marcel and Jesse were looking out through the open rear doors of the Fourgonette, which was parked on the bare red dirt bordering the main road where it cut through the sprawling shanty town at the western edge of the city. Nabil and Ben stood casually on either side of the rear doors of the car, ready to slam them shut if anyone came by.

"And I'm asking for Marie-Joseph, and I'm asking if she has any message from Auguste or Danton——"

"Either for you or for me. Yes."

"How could she have a message for me? She doesn't know who I am."

"If Auguste left any message for a white boy, she'll give it to you. You think any other white boy has ever been back there?"

Jesse said nothing while he thought his way through the plan again. He was the obvious choice to go in there, because anybody in Auguste's house would be speaking Mtom, so he'd catch whatever they said to each other in his presence. But even with the pistol hidden under his shirt and with Marcel kept here as a hostage he wasn't happy about it.

"Why are you looking at me like it's a trap?" said Marcel. "Think about it: how could I have arranged a trap, since I've been your prisoner all morning and I've had no chance to communicate with anyone?"

Jesse nodded, still not sure. From outside Nabil said, "Are you going or not? Because we're getting some funny looks, two white boys just standing here by the side of the road. Pretty soon someone's going to come over and ask us if we need help, and spot this guy, and the whole plan will be fucked."

Jesse climbed out of the cargo box and they slammed the doors. Then, while Ben provided a little screening, Nabil passed Jesse the pistol and Jesse tucked it into his jeans.

"It's going to pull my pants down."

"Tighten your belt."

Jesse walked away up the alley, keeping an eye on the ground to avoid stepping in the stream of pump water and raw sewage that crisscrossed the eroded red dirt.

Nabil and Ben, leaning against the side of the car, spent the next ten minutes seeing who could spot the most lizards. The nearest house, at the intersection of the alley and the main road, remained half-built, abandoned long ago with its cinderblock walls forming a waist-high maze and the room-sized spaces open to the sky and choked by elephant grass—a great place for hunting lizards sunning themselves on the unfinished walls. Normally when they played this game, if they weren't hunting using Jesse's BB gun, they aimed at the long red-throated lizards with their fingers in the shape of a pistol and made shooting noises. Today that seemed a little childish, so they just competed to claim the lizards: "Top of the wall by the papaya tree—mine."

Two women with big baskets balanced on their heads, going toward the outdoor market down the road, stopped and asked cheerfully if everything was all right.

"Everything's fine," said Nabil. "We're just looking at that house my father's building, and wondering why it's not finished."

The women laughed in disbelief. "Your father wants to live here?"

"No, no, he's building it for someone else."

"Well, nobody's done any work on that house in years, so, whoever they are, I hope they're not in a hurry."

The women walked on, still laughing. Inside the cargo box, Marcel wondered whether he should have called out to them for help. After all, while Jesse was up at Auguste's house the other boys could hardly just jump into the car and drive off, leaving their friend behind alone deep in the shanty town. Marcel realized he didn't know who had the pistol now. If Nabil had it, would he—while parked on a public street with a fairly steady flow of pedestrians even in the heat of the middle of the day— be stupid enough to open the rear doors and shoot him right here if Marcel began to raise the alarm? A normal, reasonable, thinking person wouldn't. But a thinking person wouldn't have driven down the hill the way Nabil did, and wouldn't have laughed like that while he was doing it. That was the problem with being the prisoner of thirteen-year-old boys: you couldn't depend on them to behave rationally.

Jesse came back down the alley, taking his time and exchanging greetings with the women at the water pump in a way that irritated both Nabil and Ben as they watched his gradual approach, though neither of them said so.

"Well?" Ben called as soon as Jesse was within earshot.

"Well, nothing." Jesse joined them and leaned against the hot side of the Fourgonette. "No message from Auguste or anyone else for us or for Marcel. No message, no news. The ladies were friendly and completely puzzled about why I was there."

Ben said, "It took you, what, fifteen minutes to find out there was no message?"

"They made me come in and they gave me a Fanta and some chocolate."

"Did you bring us any chocolate?"

"No." Jesse shifted to keep from leaning against the pistol, still in the back of his pants.

"If they didn't leave any message," said Nabil, "or any way to get in touch with them again, that means they don't want to trade Roddy for Marcel anymore."

Jesse nodded. "And that means they're going ahead with the ransom thing."

"What did you say when you left?"

"I said, 'Thank you for the refreshments,' and they said, 'Our pleasure. We're so sorry you missed Auguste and we'll let him know you came by.' So, nothing."

Ben said, "Did you tell them where he could find you?"

Jesse laughed. "Yeah, I said, 'We're just going to wait out there by the road in the sun so when Auguste gets home he can come out and shoot us.' Asshole."

"You're the asshole. Spastic retard. Sitting in there eating chocolate and drinking cold Fanta. You could at least have come got us."

"Yeah." Jesse laughed again. "Like, 'We'll be back in five minutes, Marcel. Don't go anywhere.' Grow up, loser."

Ben picked up a piece of road gravel and threw it at a fat lizard sunning itself on the cinderblock wall of the unfinished house, missing it by enough that the lizard didn't even raise its head in alarm.

Nabil said, "They might already be trying to ransom Roddy."

Jesse nodded. "And we're driving around with Marcel like idiots while they're already making a deal with Roddy's parents."

Knowing that saying it would make the other boys angry, and saying it anyway, Ben said, "We could call the Montgomerys and find out—if only this stupid country had telephones."

They lunged at the bait. Jesse snapped, "We do have telephones here. Don't talk about this country like you know anything."

"Oh, yeah? Where is there a phone? Have you ever used a phone?"

"There's a phone at my parents' hospital."

Ben laughed. "Have you ever seen anyone use it? Have you ever heard it ring?" Jesse said nothing. "Nobody uses phones here because they don't work. And since nobody has one there's no point in having one."

Nabil said, "My father is one of the investors in the phone system."

Ben laughed again. "Like you even know what that means."

Nabil smirked. "Like everything's so perfect in Mali." Ben's father had done agricultural advising work in Mali before coming here, and when Nabil and Jesse first met Ben he had a bad habit of comparing everything here to his old home. He hadn't done it in a while, but the other boys remembered.

Ben shrugged. "At least they have phones that work." He didn't in fact remember anything about the telephones in Mali, but there was no need to say so now.

The three of them were silent for a while, ignoring each other and pretending to care about the lizards. Since none of them knew how to end the sulking or wanted to be the first to do so, they were all relieved when they felt and heard Marcel kicking against the side of the cargo box. They opened the rear doors, crowding around to block the view of anyone who might walk by.

"It's hot in here and the rope hurts," said Marcel. "Why are you boys just standing around out there? What's the news from Auguste?"

They explained in French, and while Marcel absorbed the implications—he might have told himself Prosper would care more about the ransom than about trading Roddy for Marcel, but in his heart he hadn't really believed Danton would allow it

—the boys went back to English.

Nabil said, "We do need to find out what the Montgomerys know and how far things have gotten, so we'll have to go over to Roddy's house."

Jesse nodded in Marcel's direction. "We're just going to take this guy over there with us? And do what, leave him in the car?"

Nabil shrugged. "Is there anything else we can do?"

If, when deciding which of the boys to hold for ransom, the hunters had just looked at their houses, they would certainly have picked Roddy. The official residence of the head of the British Council was an enormous pile of stone and glass in the heart of the exclusive and mostly expatriate neighborhood that ran up the hillside just below the President's palace. Overnight stays for the boys at Roddy's house usually included a private screening of a movie from the British Council collection— sometimes an Ealing comedy, but once memorably *Lawrence of Arabia*—in the plush and heavily curtained basement screening room with its deep soft chairs and its funny smell.

The family quarters—bigger by far than Jesse's entire house at the medical mission station—were themselves dwarfed by the spaces for public entertainments: banquet and reception halls, guest wings, meeting rooms. Late at night during one sleepover, the four of them had wandered around the entire house, just counting the bathrooms. After they found two that Roddy himself had never noticed before, the total came to fourteen.

But Roddy's parents, who just lived there as part of the job, gave themselves no special airs and in fact seemed slightly embarrassed by their grand surroundings. So Nabil parked the Fourgonette outside the gate nearest the family wing—he didn't drive into the yard, since they knew he wasn't old enough to drive and he didn't want to provoke questions—and when he and Ben left Jesse in the car with Marcel and trotted up the back steps they found Roddy's parents in the kitchen in the middle of making lunch for themselves.

Mr. Montgomery looked up with a big smile. "Nabil, Benjamin! Enter, gentlemen, don't be shy! Are you hungry?"

Both boys said "Yes!" at the same time and then punched each other and said, still at the same time and very quickly under their breath, "Jinx you owe me a Coke no backsies bottle caps I talk."

Mrs. Montgomery, glancing out the window over the sink at the stairs they'd just come up, said, "Did Rod fall behind again?"

The boys looked at each other. Their first question seemed to be answered—Roddy's parents didn't sound like people in the middle of a kidnap ordeal, which meant the hunters hadn't yet made contact. So the boys moved on to their cover story. Since he was a much better liar than Ben, Nabil said, "No, Roddy's still at the dorm with Jesse. We're playing Monopoly, and they're still alive, and we both lost, so Roddy sent us over here to get a comic book from his room."

Mrs. Montgomery rolled her eyes, not just at Monopoly but at the idea of her son doing well at it. The Montgomerys were committed Labour Party people who'd met at the Campaign for Nuclear Disarmament's first Aldermaston March. One of the first things Mrs. Montgomery had done when they came to Africa a year ago was to start a women's literacy project. Now, while she and her husband fed the boys toasted cheese and British chutney and slices of avocado at the kitchen table, she did her best to explain—gently and with a sense of humor, she thought—why playing Monopoly might teach an impressionable young person to focus unhelpfully on beggar-your-neighbor competition instead of on cooperation.

From over by the stove Mr. Montgomery said, "Darling, I have the impression that's precisely the point of the game. I mean, I believe the thing was created during the Depression specifically as a satire and critique of capitalism."

"But nobody seems to use it that way—they bloody well play to win."

While Roddy's parents argued amiably, the boys put their heads down and ate. They'd both noticed it was always like this at Roddy's house—Roddy's parents talked about ideas, and made it look like flirting. Both boys wondered what that would be like for Roddy. Ben's parents were hardly ever home together: his father seemed to do nothing but work, away at one or another ag station, and his mother spent her days at the American Club, often eating lunch and dinner there. And at Nabil's house, before his mother split for France with his little sister, mealtime was for long frigid silences, or quarrels about money—too much spent, according to his father, not enough grudgingly allowed, according to his mother—or barbed messages passed from one end of the table to the other through the children sitting there helplessly. And nowadays, with only Nabil and his father left in the house, table talk mostly concerned Nabil's grades, since that was his father's idea of how to be a more involved parent.

Out in the Fourgonette, parked in the shade of the tall hibiscus hedge along the front of the British Council residence, Jesse sat on the back lip of the cargo box with the rear doors open and his dangling feet scuffing the ground. He knew Nabil and Ben were almost certainly being fed lunch, and he could imagine how Roddy's parents were entertaining them, talking nonstop about anything at all and happy to quiz the boys for their ideas. In Jesse's own home, table conversation was an extension of his parents' work: the doctor and the nurse discussed hospital business—emergency cases, community health projects, budgets —from soup to fruit.

From behind him inside the cargo box, Marcel said, "Your name is Jesse, right? Your French is very good. How long have you lived in this country?"

Jesse stopped swinging his feet and tried to decide how to answer. Was there any point now in keeping up the story about the Peace Corps? Could he account for his African-tinted French without raising even a suspicion that he spoke an African language too? He didn't feel confident enough to pull off the kind of elaborate fiction Nabil had spun for the chauffeur this morning.

While Jesse pondered, he noticed a young African woman in a bright print dress walking up the street toward him. He realized he'd been watching her approaching for a long time before he paid any attention to her, since after all an African woman walking on an African street wasn't remarkable. But this was the foreign diplomatic neighborhood, and few Africans had a reason to be out walking here, and those who did tended to be household staff and therefore knew where they were going, whereas what Jesse noticed about this woman was that she kept stopping and turning as if she were looking for something.

It wouldn't be a house number, since no house or building in the whole city had a number—mail was delivered only to boxes at the post office. But she might be looking for the plaque of the British Council, which was attached to the gatepost next to where Jesse was parked. He watched as the woman, still a hundred yards or so away, stopped to read the plaque on the gate of another house, some South American ambassador's residence. She turned and continued walking, and now Jesse could see she was carrying something white, maybe an envelope.

Without answering Marcel's awkward question, Jesse stood up casually and closed the rear doors of the Fourgonette. He thought about leaning against the corrugated metal side of the cargo box while he waited, then decided he didn't want to attract any attention to the vehicle. He ambled through the open gate: the Montgomerys always kept the gates open, as a symbolic gesture of welcome. But if he went too far into the yard he risked being spotted from the house, and he was supposed to be back at the dorm playing Monopoly with Roddy right now. And if he went too far away from the car, Marcel might take his chances and shout for help.

So Jesse walked back out through the gate and paused behind the Fourgonette where Marcel could see him through the tiny oval windows in the rear doors and would therefore know Jesse hadn't gone away. Then he sat down on the edge of the drainage ditch and pitched pebbles into the dark opening of the small driveway culvert: exactly how a boy would kill time in the middle of an ordinary Saturday if he lived here and had nothing to do with that shabby Citroën Fourgonette parked nearby.

The young woman in the bright dress, who was definitely carrying an envelope, stopped to read the British Council plaque on the post behind Jesse. Forcing himself not to turn around, he pitched another pebble into the echoing concrete culvert. The side of the pistol pressed against the small of his back, and he wondered if the woman could see it through his sweaty shirt. What would he do if Marcel started shouting? Shoot them both, then drive away? He didn't have the slightest idea how to put the Fourgonette in gear, much less how to steer. Maybe, since he couldn't get away, he'd just have to shoot himself and make everybody sorry. This whole day was fucked.

Jesse finally allowed himself to look to one side, and out of the corner of his eye he saw the woman behind him begin to walk into the yard, hesitating because it seemed so strange to her that the owners would leave the gate wide open and unattended like this. He called out cheerfully in French, "Excuse me! Can I help you?"

When Nabil and Ben came out of the yard quite a while later, carrying half a dozen old issues of *Mad* all of them had already read, they found Jesse sitting where they'd left him, in the back of the Fourgonette with the rear doors open. He waved a piece of white paper at them.

"You get exactly one guess what this is."

Nabil knew right away what it had to be, but couldn't come up with a witty reply. "Jesse, how the fuck did you get the ransom note?"

Jesse laughed. "Easy. A woman walked up here to deliver it to the Montgomerys, and I said I was their son and I'd give it to them."

"That's it?"

"That's it. She gave me the letter and she left."

Ben said, "Well, who was she? Where did she go?"

"She was just a woman from the market down on the main road. They paid her a few francs to walk up here till she got to a house with a plaque that matched the writing on the envelope."

Nabil nodded. "Makes sense. That way, if she got into trouble or was followed, it wouldn't matter, since she had no idea who they were or even what the letter said."

Ben said, "Did you ask her what the guy looked like who gave her the letter?"

"I did, and she said she couldn't remember. She's not stupid."

Nabil nodded again. "It was a great plan, and the only thing they didn't think about was that we might be sitting here waiting when she showed up."

Jesse grinned. "And by 'we' you mean me."

"Well?" said Ben. "Did you read it?"

"At first I was going to wait for you guys, but then I thought, what if it says, 'We'll be at your door in ten minutes with guns'? I'd feel kind of dumb if I was just sitting here when they showed up."

Nabil waited, forcing himself to be cool, and it was Ben who said, "Come on, Jesse, hurry up and show us the fucking letter!"

Jesse stood up and stepped away from the Fourgonette. "You weren't in such a fucking hurry while you were inside enjoying lunch, were you? Was it good? Did they make you grilled cheese sandwiches? Did you bring me one?"

Nabil said, "We're really sorry, Jesse. You know what it's like when you get in there and they start talking. Now please just show us the letter."

Jesse unfolded the grimy sheet of lined notebook paper with exaggerated drama, which the other boys endured as their punishment. Then they gathered around him to read silently. The letter was written in French, in careful grade-school penmanship.

> *Dear Mr. and Mrs. David Montgomery,*
> *I hope you are well. I regret to inform you that your son Roderick is now a prisoner. It will cost you 100,000 francs CFA to receive him safely home again. Please be so kind as to follow these instructions exactly: Put the money, in bills no larger than 1000 francs, into a child's lunch box of the clear plastic kind you can find at the Jeune Afrique department store. Leave the lunch box in plain sight in front of the main entrance of the Gentleman cigarette factory at six o'clock this evening and wait at least fifty meters away. Someone will come out with your son and, if the money is correct, will release him. If*

*you try to catch us or follow us, your son will die. If you
involve or inform the police, your son will die. If you have not
paid us by six this evening, your son will die. Please accept,
madam, sir, the expression of our very best wishes.*
Signed, Serious Men
P.S. Hi Mum and Dad! Sorry about this!
Signed, Roderick Montgomery

Though the letter certainly had its amusing aspects, and
though the boys were still exhilarated by the luck of having
intercepted it, none of them felt like laughing when they looked
up from reading it.

"Holy shit," said Ben. "They're going to kill Roddy at six
o'clock."

Nabil glanced at his watch. "And it's already after one."

"Holy shit."

Jesse said, "I feel like I'm always the one who gets stuck
saying things like this out loud, but..." He pointed through the
gates at the British Council residence. "I was thinking while I
waited: We could walk in there right now, give this note to
Roddy's parents, say, 'Hey, somebody just dropped this off,'
and let it be their problem from here on, and then come back
out here and let this guy Marcel go, and then go to the mission
dorm and play Monopoly for real." The other two stared at him.
"Guys, we're in seventh grade. We don't have a hundred
thousand francs to get Roddy back by six o'clock or by forever,
so he's going to be killed. It's not funny anymore."

Ben started to shiver, though even in the shade of the high
hedge by the road it was hot. Watching Ben give way to fear,
Nabil, who'd been almost completely persuaded by Jesse's
argument while he was hearing it, snapped back out of his funk.
"But here's what you're forgetting, Jesse. First, since it's going
take them two seconds to find out Roddy wasn't kidnapped

while playing Monopoly with me at the dorm, everything that's happened today is going to come out, and we're all going to be in deep shit, and Ben is going to be in the deepest shit of all."

Ben was opening his mouth to protest why him—till he remembered—and Jesse was opening his mouth to say that surely Roddy was in even deeper shit than Ben, but Nabil went on.

"Second, we're responsible for what happened to Roddy—if we hadn't been fucking around in that abandoned house, Roddy would be with us right now—and I still think it's our job to fix the problem we caused."

With that, Jesse could only agree, and he nodded.

"Third," said Nabil, "we can't just let this guy go: he hates us for killing the other guy and he's going to get back at us somehow if we untie him. Plus, he's the only card we have in this game."

Ben laughed. "He's like our *Get Out of Jail Free* card."

"Probably not that good anymore," said Nabil. "More like Community Chest, *Bank Error in Your Favor*. And then it turns out it's only like ten dollars. "

"But what good is he to us?" said Jesse. "He doesn't know how to find them, like he claimed he did, and obviously they don't care about him, since they don't even mention him in the note."

"I'll show you in a minute," said Nabil, aware that he was making his plan up as he went but also aware that just the appearance of being calm and in control was all he needed to stay in charge of the other boys. "But I have one more idea. I agree things have gotten serious, more serious than we can handle by ourselves. And that's why we're going to bring in..." He paused to enjoy the expressions on their faces as they waited. "...The Matador."

Ben said, "The Matador!" Even as his eyes widened at the

brilliance of Nabil's idea, he felt a pang at not having thought of it himself.

"Yup. The one and only Claudio the Matador."

Jesse laughed and pumped his fist. "Yes! The Matador, of course! Nabil, you're a genius!"

So much of what had been going on for the past hour or more, since they drove away from Auguste's shanty town neighborhood, had been mysterious to Marcel that after a while, to save himself frustration, he'd given up trying to understand. He didn't even know where they were now, though from what he could see when the rear doors were open it was obviously a rich neighborhood. So they could be parked outside the home of any of these white boys: the Chaloub boy was the most likely.

But why they'd just been sitting here on the road for what seemed like at least an hour was inexplicable. He'd heard voices a while ago without quite making out what was said (Jesse had followed the woman away from the car into the yard to talk). And now all three boys were back and were looking at some paper and talking on and on in English. Marcel thought he'd never seen anyone, not even old Mtom women, argue as much as these white boys did.

Now the Chaloub boy climbed into the cargo box and the other two leaned in the rear doors to listen. Holding up the piece of paper they'd been arguing over, Nabil said in French, "This is the ransom note your hunter friends sent. But Roddy's parents don't have the note, we do. We're going to get our friend back, and not by paying for him. And you're going to help us."

"Of course," said Marcel. "As I said before, they're not my friends."

"Yeah." Nabil waved the note. "They didn't even ask about you."

"Believe me, I'll do anything I can to help get your friend

back."

"I do believe you, and not just because those guys obviously don't care about you." Nabil waved the note again. "The other reason you're going to want to help us is, they're going to kill Roddy if they don't get their money by six o'clock. And if they kill Roddy we're going to kill you. That's a promise."

When the hunters pulled Roddy out of the trunk of the Peugeot, he found himself back where they'd started, at Prosper's house, with chickens scratching at the bare dirt of the yard and empty beer bottles scattered along the edge of the porch. While Prosper led the boy around the house to the detached kitchen in back and handed him over to his grandmother again, Danton and Auguste sat on the edge of the porch. Auguste began to check each of the bottles to see if any beer had been forgotten. "You got any more beer?" he said as Prosper returned.

"No, you drank it all."

Auguste thought about mentioning that most of the bottles had been emptied while he was up the hill discovering Théophile's body, but it didn't seem worth the bother. Instead he stood up and stretched. "I guess I'll go home for a little while. I've got beer there."

"If Marcel knows where you live," said Prosper, "the gendarmes will already be there waiting for you."

Danton said, "Marcel would never betray us. We're his family!"

"Yeah, well, you saw how much family mattered to him when we wanted to hunt up there this morning. Besides, the gendarmes will beat him till he talks. That's the trouble with you amateurs—you don't realize how big this thing is. The boy's father is obviously an important man, he knows the

President, and the gendarmes will be taking it seriously."

Auguste said, "So why didn't we choose a kid who wouldn't bring down so much trouble on our heads?"

"Because this one is worth more money!" Prosper smacked his forehead theatrically. "My God, you're even stupider than I thought!"

While Prosper and Auguste stared at each other, Danton said calmly, "Speaking of more money, maybe we should figure out how much he's worth, and then work on the ransom note, and then think about how we're going to deliver it to the boy's parents."

As before, Roddy sat in the familiar lightless and smoke-blackened kitchen, his wrists and ankles tied to the chair again. But after fussing over him for a while in a mixture of Yoa and French the old woman went away. Roddy sat there alone for a few minutes, making no attempt to get loose, at first because he expected the old woman to come back any second, and after that because, he had to admit, he was simply too scared.

He couldn't understand how the young man at the nightclub had come to be killed or even who'd done it, he couldn't understand where his friends had gone and why they'd abandoned him, and he couldn't understand how, up on that verandah, he'd been seconds away from getting shot himself and then suddenly had been rushed back here. In a way, the friendly treatment he got from the old woman was more upsetting than the brutality of the hunters: it made him feel more like a child, since she treated him like one, and instead of being comforting it just made him feel more helpless and more in need of his own mother.

Roddy put his head down on the table and began to cry. He imagined being stretched out, dead and bloody. He imagined his funeral, for some reason being held in the big reception hall at the British Council residence. He saw his parents, inconsolable, holding each other tight as they stood over his open coffin. He saw Summer, his teacher at the American School, with her peasant dress and her hippy refusal to let her students call her by her last name—a culture shock greater than Africa itself for Roddy, who till this year had attended a prestigious no-nonsense old-fashioned boys' school in Edinburgh—and Summer too was weeping great big tears down her plump makeup-free cheeks as she sat there in front of the seventh and eighth grade class and told them what a tragedy it was and how much Roddy would be missed. He got as far as picturing the unapproachably gorgeous Heather Stone weeping quietly as she confessed to Summer and the whole class that she'd secretly loved Roddy but never found the courage to tell him—and then the whole vision began to collapse under the weight of that last absurdity.

Roddy heard a sound and looked up. Someone was poking at the fire and stirring the blackened pot, but it wasn't the old woman. When she turned and then stood up to face him, he could see it was a skinny barefoot girl in a dirty shift with her hair done in short spikes. She looked about his age, but it was hard to tell with Africans.

The girl said in French, "Are you crying?"

"No! Crying is for babies."

"It's good to cry. Do you miss your mother?"

"Of course not! I'm almost fourteen!"

"I'm so sorry—you look much younger. But it's hard to tell with white people."

"How old are you?"

"I'm fourteen and a half. My name is Bijou."

That's a really nice name. I'm Roddy."

She silently mouthed "Rah...Dee." She looked a little guilty for not being able to return the compliment. "What does it mean?"

"My father says it means 'famous ruler.'"

"Oh, so that's good luck." She'd spoken without thinking, and as Roddy glanced down at the ropes tying him to the chair she went on quickly, "It means that, even if you feel like you're having bad luck right now, in the end you'll have good luck."

Abruptly reminded of the bloody corpse on the nightclub verandah, and the fury twisting Prosper's face as he forced Roddy to look at it, he shook his head. "I don't think so."

"Don't worry, Roddy, everything will be fine."

Bijou turned away and picked up a little imitation-leather school satchel with shoulder straps that she'd put down in the corner when she came in. She set the satchel on the table across from Roddy and sat down.

"Where's the old woman who was here before?"

"That's my grandmother. She went to the market."

"So are you related to the man named Prosper?"

"He's my cousin, but he takes care of me." She opened the satchel and pulled out half a dozen notebooks, each one carefully wrapped in a plastic cover protector of a different color. "My parents are no longer living."

It sounded like a formula she'd memorized, a way of talking about her loss without having to search for words every time. Roddy imagined his own parents, back in their beautiful house in Edinburgh, saying over and over to visitors, "Our son is no longer living." Then they added, with an air of mystery, "He passed away in Africa." The visitors nodded solemnly. "Och, say no more—Africa!"

Bijou fanned out the notebooks. "I have one in each color, and I don't have to label them because I've memorized what color each subject is. Here, test me."

She held up each notebook in turn and opened it so the plastic cover faced her and some random pages faced Roddy. A quick glance inside at Bijou's careful and neatly blotted fountain-pen cursive told him what the contents were about.

"Green, science," she said without hesitation. "Yellow, geography. Blue, math—do you think math goes with blue? I always think of rich dark blue when I think of math. I love math. Red, history."

He caught a name on the page she was closing. "Are you really learning about King François Premier?"

"Why not? It's important."

"It is? I mean, I don't know anything about François Premier, and I'm—"

"—And you're white, and you think I don't need to know about ancient white kings because I'm African."

"Well... no... I—"

Bijou slid all the notebooks back to her side of the table and stacked them neatly, setting the blue one aside. Then she dug around in her satchel till she found a short wooden ruler and a pencil. She opened the blue notebook to the page onto which she'd copied the problems from the blackboard this morning. Though she loved school, she also loved the feeling of only having to go to school for half a day on Saturdays, and carefully putting away her school uniform when she came home to keep it clean—but most of all she loved being done with her homework by Saturday evening. Unconsciously batting at a couple of the spikes in her hair with the end of the ruler—which she didn't need, since this was algebra, but which she still associated with the pleasure of doing math—she focused on the first problem.

Watching her across the table, Roddy waited to see if Bijou was just pretending to ignore him. She wrote something in her notebook and then erased it with little irritated grunts that suggested she'd forgotten he was there—and she had reason to be irritated, because her teacher took points off for messiness if he could see even the traces of erasing, so she had to erase in the white spaces only and take care not to erase away the blue lines printed faintly on the notebook paper. Sometimes she used a Bic pen—itself unacceptable for schoolwork—to reinforce lines she'd partly erased, but that was a desperate measure that felt like cheating, and she didn't want to think of herself as someone who cheated at math.

Feeling ignored, Roddy said, "If I get out of these ropes and run away, what are you going to do to stop me?"

Bijou looked up with a grin, their difference forgotten. "Let's see..." She glanced around the kitchen. "I'll grab the pot off the fire and throw the boiling soup at you."

"What if you miss?"

She turned to look outside. "The chickens in the yard are helping me, of course, and they surround you and trip you."

"But they can't fly, so I jump over their heads and keep running."

She laughed. "I can run faster than you, so I grab a stick out of the fire and catch up with you and set you on fire."

"But I'm running so fast the fire goes out."

She thought over her options, tapping the ruler against her hair spikes. "Then I call my cousin and he comes and shoots you."

Roddy winced and said nothing, and Bijou realized she'd spoiled the game. She'd never have said it if she thought it was possible—to her the idea of her cousin Prosper shooting Roddy seemed just as absurd as the idea of her running after Roddy and lighting him on fire. "You really think Prosper would do that? You must've done something to make him very angry if you're so afraid of him. What did you do?"

"Nothing! It wasn't me!" Tears came into his eyes again.

"What did you do, Roddy?"

The kitchen darkened as Prosper filled the doorway. Roddy shrank back in his chair.

Prosper said in Yoa, "Is he giving you any trouble?"

"No. He's crying because he thinks you're going to shoot him."

Prosper grunted and put a piece of paper and an envelope in front of Roddy. "This is a letter to your parents." He reached down and untied Roddy's hands. "Put their names properly at the top, and put the address on the envelope." He watched while Roddy wrote. "Now add one line to tell them you're okay and sign it so they know it's really you."

As Roddy considered what to put and then wrote it, he rubbed his eyes to keep the tears from falling on the paper. Prosper looked at the result. "Is this in English?" Roddy nodded. Prosper showed the note to Bijou. "What does this say?"

Bijou was studying English at school, but her spoken English was even worse than Roddy's French, and she had nowhere near enough confidence to use what she knew in real conversation. Fortunately only the last line of the letter was in English, in Roddy's scrawl—her teacher would have hit him with a ruler for handwriting like that—but while Prosper tied up Roddy's hands again Bijou quickly read the whole letter. "It's fine. It says he's sorry."

Prosper folded the paper and tucked it into the envelope. "He's sorry!" he muttered in Yoa. "Sorry changes nothing! Listen, Bijou, don't be fooled by him crying like a little baby. These white boys are evil."

"It's under control. He can't even move. What's he going to do?"

"Okay. But I'll be happier when Granny gets back."

Prosper went away to give the ransom note to Danton. Roddy and Bijou said nothing as they faced each other across the narrow table, though both of them were wondering how far away six o'clock was.

2.

AS THEY WALKED down from the parking lot toward the American Embassy Club, Nabil and Jesse debated whether or not to change into their swimming trunks. Changing would take a little more time, but not much, whereas showing up by the pool fully dressed would be weird enough to attract lots of attention they didn't want. So they detoured to the changing rooms in the clubhouse. Since they came to the club pretty much every day after school, they both had lockers here.

They came back out into the main room of the clubhouse in trunks and bare feet, with towels around their necks—and were overwhelmed by the smell of fried onions and meat from the club grill. Jesse groaned.

Nabil shook his head. "It's almost two-thirty. We don't have time."

"Fuck that shit. You had grilled cheese sandwiches and I didn't."

So, leaning into the order window of the kitchen, they both got cheeseburgers, fries, and Cokes, and put everything on Nabil's father's tab. As they left the grill with their trays, Jesse whispered, "Shit, it's Heather."

"Be cool, man."

They kept on walking, though even Nabil's tray was now shaking slightly. Out on the wide clubhouse patio they had to cross to get to the pool, two girls in bikinis were playing Ping Pong. They were both in eighth grade, and—since at the American School across the lawn from the club the seventh and eight graders were combined in one classroom, there being only five students in each grade this year—the boys spent the whole school day in the presence of these girls, but somehow meeting them after school while wearing nothing but swimming trunks was different, no matter how often it happened.

The girl at the far end of the Ping Pong table, Cheryl Larson, was of no interest to the boys, except late at night during a sleepover, when her name would come up reliably as the ultimate challenge: "If there was a nuclear war, and you two were the last humans left alive on Earth, would you do it with Cheryl Larson?" Nabil's memorable answer, "Only if the radiation had made me blind," was trumped one night by Ben— to everyone's surprise—who answered, "Only if the radiation had given her a second head."

The other girl, dashing back and forth and lunging for the Ping Pong ball right in their path, was a different story. In the catalog of graces Heather Stone had a check in every column: She was tall—at least three inches taller even than Nabil. She was slender, which meant among other things that the small breasts the boys could see hiding in her bikini weren't as grossly, alarmingly maternal as the ones a girl built like Cheryl had started toting around this year. Heather was great at sports, and could beat any of the boys at HORSE. She was the smartest kid in both grades, easily earning straight As, but she didn't make a big deal out of it. She'd just come from the States this year, which gave her not only the attraction of novelty but a dizzying collection of the latest albums by every band they knew, and she'd actually seen both Elton John and Paul McCartney and Wings live in concert. And she was the daughter of the American Ambassador, which meant—since everybody knew Ambassador Stone had gotten the job by raising a lot of money for President Nixon's reelection campaign—she was rich too.

So it was natural and normal that, as they approached this

goddess and the inevitable exchange of small talk, both Nabil and Jesse were trembling. Nabil said under his breath, as much to himself as to Jesse, "Just think about Sean Connery."

"Yeah, Sean Connery and what's her name, in the thing…"

"Exactly. Plus, remember: we killed somebody today— we're cool."

"What?!" Jesse spoke too loudly, and now lowered his voice. "That's sick! You're sick!"

"You know I'm right."

"Even if you are right, which you're not, that would make Ben cool, not us."

"Fuck off! Ben is not cool. Ben is everything that is not cool."

The Ping Pong ball skittered under their feet, and Heather bent down to get it. She straightened up and smiled at them. "Hey, guys! What's the buzz?"

"Hey, Heather." Jesse heard his voice almost squeak and kept going. "Nothing much, just hanging out, you know."

Nabil said, "I guess we're gonna swim, I dunno. You gonna hit the pool later?"

Heather glanced across at Cheryl, who stood quietly knocking her Ping Pong paddle against the edge of the table, aware that the boys hadn't even looked in her direction. Not that she wanted them to, since she thought Nabil in particular was a stuck-up creep, but still…

"I dunno," said Heather. "Yeah, we'll probably swim. It depends what Cheryl feels like."

The boys tore their eyes off Heather for a moment. "Oh, hey, Cheryl, how's it going?"

She flushed. "Hey, Jesse. Good, I guess." There was a short silence. "You gonna be here for the movie tonight?" She hated herself for asking, and hoped she sounded as indifferent as she felt—or at least as she hoped she felt.

Jesse and Nabil opened their mouths to answer, but they were both struck for the first time by the idea that, a few hours from now, happy sunburned kids in swimming trunks and their tipsy parents would be sprawled on the clubhouse couches getting ready to watch a movie and laughing and cheering, while the three of them would be trapped in a dark, desperate struggle to get Roddy back before the hunters murdered him—a struggle that seemed more likely to end badly than well.

Nabil recognized the feeling following that tempting picture of cozy normal life—the impulse just to give up and let adult events take their course, in exchange for returning to the simpler complications of childhood—as the same one that had led him to curl up for a nap at home this morning. He fought it off and said to Heather, "Oh, yeah, movie night. What are they showing?"

"*The Poseidon Adventure*. Boat turns upside down. I saw it last year in the States. I don't know why it takes so long for a movie to get out here. I mean, it comes in the diplomatic pouch." Then, seeing all three of her listeners flinch and realizing she sounded like a snob, Heather added, "But it was really good. I'm definitely going to see it again."

Nabil said, "Sounds cool. I guess we'll try to make it."

Heather smiled in a way that persuaded Nabil it was personally important to her that he be there tonight, sending a stab of adrenaline through his heart, though in fact she was smiling because she was still trying to recover from her gaffe. What was she supposed to do? If she talked about what she'd seen and done before she moved here she was a snob, and if she didn't she had nothing to say. Wishing she were back home in California, where everyone had seen the same movies and gone to the same concerts, she smiled even more brightly at both boys. "You guys are having kind of a late lunch, huh?"

Jesse looked at their trays of food. "Oh, yeah, we got caught up in some other stuff this morning. You know how it is."

"Yeah, I know. We had a sleepover and I swear we didn't wake up till noon." Heather turned back to the Ping Pong table and tossed the ball to Cheryl. "Your point and your serve." As the boys crossed behind her and walked out onto the lawn she called out cheerfully, "Don't go swimming right after eating— you'll get a cramp!"

"Right, thanks!" They heard the little ball ping-ponging again behind them. After they'd carried their lunch trays a few feet further across the grass Nabil murmured to Jesse, "A cramp in my dick, you mean." Jesse guffawed but reflected that Nabil acted a lot bolder when he wasn't face to face with the reality of Heather.

When they reached the pool they stood by the shallow end, holding their trays and looking around for the Matador. There was no question he'd be here—it was unthinkable for him to be anywhere else on a Saturday afternoon or indeed any other afternoon—but where exactly?

Claudio the Matador was one of the U.S. Marines stationed here. His entire job, at least according to him, consisted of guard duty outside the American Embassy every morning, leaving him the whole afternoon to play at the pool and the whole evening to play on the town. In the two years the boys had known him they'd never seen Claudio dressed in anything other than a pair of swimming trunks and his dog tags. He was already out of uniform and in the pool by the time they finished school and walked across the lawn to the club every afternoon, and he got dressed and slipped away to his nighttime adventures long after they were home. Not that he needed to dress before going out, since most of the lurid stories he told them about his adventures in the shanty towns seemed to involve him being more or less naked.

Among themselves the boys had debated, without resolving,

the question of whether the Matador was fundamentally cool or weird. They were thrilled by his dirty stories and flattered that he considered a handful of boys a worthy audience. But they also had a feeling, hard to put into words but real nonetheless, that there was something a little strange in a grown man telling a bunch of seventh graders about his sex life. Still, it was hard to think of Claudio as a grown man.

They agreed, guessing, that he must be in his late twenties, and some of his stories were about Vietnam, though many were about life as a teenager in a gang in East L.A. But the other off-duty Marines who used the American Club didn't hang out with him. Three or four Marines would be sharing a pizza at one of the poolside cabana tables, flirting with the Embassy secretaries or schoolteachers or aid workers tanning on the long chairs nearby, while the Matador practiced his dives off the high board or taught some little kid in floaties how to squirt water through his cupped hands.

Even the civilian adults at the club stayed away from him—or maybe it was the other way around. It might just have been that, while Claudio found most grownups and their conversation boring and artificial, he paid children the compliment of taking them seriously, even if that meant always being ready, yet again, to show a crowd of kids his bullfighter tattoo, the one that gave him his nickname—a nickname he himself had chosen and that he constantly reinforced. Every time, just as happily as the first time, with a soundtrack of swooshing wind noises that kids who'd seen the show before could imitate, he made the little matador's red cape flutter when he twitched his bicep.

It was Claudio's separation from the world of adults, the sense that he was a child in a man's body—even, often, a man's sexual body—that had struck Jesse and Ben as perfect the moment Nabil brought up his name. Claudio could do all of the many things a man could do better than a boy, but he would never betray the boys to the world of adults—he was, and would always be, on their side.

The pool area was crowded, it being Saturday, but they finally spotted Claudio perched in one corner of the deep end by himself, his tan, muscled, tattooed arms stretched out to either side on the lip of the pool. As they walked along the edge toward him, weaving around the splashing little kids, he took a breath and then just slipped into the water, sinking straight down to the bottom corner of the pool at its deepest point.

The boys stopped where he'd been sitting, their shadows on the dazzling blue water, and waited. He seemed to be squatting on the bottom of the pool in a lotus position. They waited, looking down seven feet at the top of his buzz-cut head. They waited, long enough that each of them silently wondered if someone should jump in and check on him. And then he rose gently to the surface, preserving his lotus position as long as possible. When his face emerged he didn't gasp, but took a normal breath. He looked up at the boys, squinting against the sun. "Hey, it's half of the Fearsome Foursome."

"Hey, Matador. What are you up to?"

"Deep breathing. Gotta practice your breath control, guys. You never know when you might need it, like to hide out in a swamp till the gooks go by." The boys nodded, filing away this new skill, like blowing smoke rings, as something to work on later, when their current difficulties were over.

Nabil said, "Matador, can we talk to you?"

One of Claudio's seemingly contradictory qualities was that, while much of the time he behaved like a self-absorbed attention hog who found nothing more fascinating than himself, he had a fine-tuned ear for distress in a child, and he never had to be told twice that something was wrong. He pulled himself out of the water in a single smooth motion and led the boys to one of the palm-thatched cabanas around the pool—the one nobody wanted to sit in or near, because a drainage problem in the rainy season left the ground there perpetually muddy, and then you tracked mud back to the pool or into the clubhouse.

The three of them sat around the little table, and, as they ate their burgers, the boys told Claudio the story in the form they'd agreed on while driving over here from Roddy's house.

"Here's what happened," said Nabil. "The four of us went on a hike up the hill where that nightclub is."

Claudio nodded. "Club Balafon. Heard about it. Closed."

"We found a house in the forest up there and broke in."

Claudio nodded again. "Cool beans. Too bad you didn't have some girls with you, right?" They looked at him, puzzled. He sighed. "Come on, guys—empty house, girls, everybody's excited from the danger..."

Jesse said, "You know we're still in seventh grade, right? Just like the last time we talked about this."

Claudio laughed. "You know how many girls I'd fucked in East L.A. by the time I was in seventh grade? Shit." He stole a french fry from Nabil's plate.

"Anyhow," said Nabil, "then we got caught. Some kind of watchman."

Claudio shook his head. "Fuckin' night watchmen, right?"

"Then his friends showed up, a bunch of hunters, and they kidnapped Roddy."

Claudio paused in the act of taking another fry. "Kidnapped as in take him away to beat him up somewhere else?"

"Kidnapped as in ransom. He told them his father was the head of the British Council."

Claudio laughed. "That's my little Limey buddy!"

"Well, he's Scottish actually, but yeah."

Claudio munched the fry, thinking. The boys waited. Then he looked at their faces carefully. "That's not the end of the story, is it?"

Nabil and Jesse exchanged a glance before Nabil went on with the approved version. "So then we kidnapped the watchman who caught us, so we could trade him for Roddy."

Claudio laughed and slapped the table. "That is kick-ass!" He leaned forward and squeezed their bare shoulders. "You are my boys! The Matador has raised you well! We are definitely going to get the best hooker I know—my treat! Where are you keeping this guy?"

Jesse said, "We locked him into a Fourgonette"—Claudio shook his head—"like a Deux Chevaux cargo truck, and Ben's guarding him up in the parking lot right now."

Nabil, feeling a little uncomfortable under Claudio's squeezing hand, squirmed slightly to shrug it off and said, "But it turns out the kidnappers don't care about trading for the watchman. They want a hundred thousand francs by six o'clock or they'll kill Roddy."

Claudio waved a hand dismissively. "That's bullshit. It's just talk."

"They're hunters. They had a ton of guns."

"That's not what I'm talking about. You need more than a gun to kill, you need the will to do it. I'm a trained killer, I did things in 'Nam, but I'd think twice before pulling the trigger on a kid. And these guys are amateurs. They're bluffing."

Once more, Nabil and Jesse exchanged a look, a long one this time. Jesse nodded. Nabil took a deep breath and said, in a sort of blur, "The thing is, Matador, we already killed one of them, because he killed Ben's dog." It had been hard to do, but once the words were out he felt okay.

Claudio's face went blank. He tipped back on the rear legs of his wicker chair and looked around the pool area. Then he tipped forward and leaned in close to them. "Dead for sure?"

"Yes."

"Killed how?"

"Shot in the face."

Claudio was still expressionless. "Okay, so, yeah, they're going to kill Roddy at six o'clock, if they haven't already." The boys nodded, both of them suddenly close to tears. "And now I see why you've come to the Matador."

Jesse said, "We—what do you call it—we intercepted the ransom note they were sending to Roddy's parents, so they still don't know anything about it. It's in my pants in the locker room."

"But you said they're not asking to trade for the watchman anyway." Claudio pondered, staring past them toward the pool. "Who did you say was guarding the watchman?"

"Ben."

"Then why is Ben at the pool right now?"

Nabil and Jesse whipped around in their seats in time to see Ben, in his swimming trunks, jog out to the end of the low board and execute a feeble cannonball into the water.

Ben, sitting in the open rear of the Fourgonette leafing through copies of *Mad* and wondering why nothing seemed funny anymore, had only a couple of minutes to feel sorry for himself for being left behind on guard duty yet again while Nabil and Jesse got to go down to the pool to talk to the Matador. Then he saw a reason for feeling a great deal sorrier: his mother was coming along the row of parked cars toward him. She wasn't weaving, not the way she sometimes did after a long evening at the American Club, but though she was walking in a relatively straight line she kept pausing and looking around.

Ben thought for a moment about pulling his legs inside the back of the cargo box and shutting the doors so she wouldn't see him, but it was intensely hot even in the open mouth of the box, and that guy Marcel was sweating a lot and didn't smell good, and anyway Ben wasn't eager to have to sit a couple of feet away from him in that confined space and have nowhere to hide from the piercing nonstop accusing look in Marcel's eyes.

Instead he stood up, tossed the magazines inside the cargo box, and shut the rear doors firmly behind him. His mother, now about three cars away, looked up at the sound. "There you are! Ben, where the fuck is our car?"

Ben realized with a flood of feeling that he'd unconsciously prepared an elaborate story to cover where he'd been and what he'd been doing all day, and that it didn't matter because his mother didn't even know he'd been gone and didn't care what he'd been doing. The impulse to blurt everything out—Clint is dead and I killed a man—just to get his mother finally, one time, to look up and pay attention rose and then fell away inside him.

"It's right there, Mom." He took her arm and guided her a couple of cars back the way she'd come. Then he turned and squeezed between two cars, leading his mother to their own Wagoneer, parked haphazardly in a makeshift spot on the chewed-up grass bordering the paved parking lot.

Mrs. Welsh laughed. "How am I supposed to find it way back here if all these other cars park in front of me? They weren't here when I got here this morning."

"I know, Mom." His mother was often one of the first arrivals at the club, before some of the staff, and Ben imagined if they ever started serving breakfast she might eat three meals a day here. During the rare times his father was in town and not out at some ag research station, he'd come over to the club for dinner, since that was the only way the three of them could spend mealtime together, but those occasions and maybe an early-morning round of tennis with Ben on the cement courts were as much as Mr. Welsh could stomach of the American

Club.

His mother was a big tennis player, very serious about the club's annual doubles round robin, though she and her partner, Mrs. Larson, always fell in the first round of the subsequent elimination tournament. She stood here in the sweltering parking lot, dressed in her tennis whites that were just a little too short for a woman of forty-five, her skin parched and tanned by the African sun till she resembled a piece of dark grainy furniture, and looked at the car keys in her hand.

"What did I come out here to get, Ben?"

"I don't remember, Mom."

She rattled the keys absently. "Your mom's a drunken old fool, Ben." That was nothing new or surprising—she said things like that all the time when she thought other people were thinking them and were afraid to say them. "I know! Tanning oil!" She opened the door of the Wagoneer and fumbled around in the glove compartment. "Not that I need to get any darker— my God, I'm already afraid if I walk on the beach they'll catch me and put me on a ship to South Carolina and make me pick cotton." Triumphantly she held up her emergency backup bottle of tanning oil. "But Patty Larson ran out."

It was a source of frequent embarrassment to Ben, when among his friends, that the mother of the laughably unappealing Cheryl was his own mother's inseparable club buddy. But when he wasn't around the other boys, and the Welshes and the Larsons had dinner together at the club, and Ben and Cheryl sat together at the table in the cabana, he had to admit he kind of liked Cheryl—though certainly not enough to risk defending her to the other boys. And he'd regretted the joke about her being improved by radiation as soon as the other boys laughed.

When his mother slammed the door of the Wagoneer and began to walk back toward the clubhouse, rattling away about something that, as usual, changed into something else as soon as or even before he caught on to what she was talking about, Ben looked over his shoulder at the rusty old Fourgonette and decided there was no way he could just break away from his mother and go back. And Marcel was tied up tight inside, and there was no one in the parking lot to hear him yell for help, especially no African here in the members' parking lot at the American Embassy Club.

In the clubhouse his mother wandered around in search of Mrs. Larson, then added a quick detour to the bar to get a new vodka tonic going. "The problem with Africa, Ben, and I noticed this even in Mali, which thank God was never as hot as it is here, and certainly never as humid—Jesus Christ is it ever humid— what I noticed is that the ice melts in like ten seconds, and then you're just drinking a cold fucking water tonic. And if you put more ice in, you just get a bigger cold fucking water tonic." She began to argue and laugh with the bartender, and forgot Ben was there.

It occurred to Ben, as it had to Nabil and Jesse, that it felt weird to be standing around in the American Club fully dressed. So he went to the locker room and changed into his swimming trunks to be like everybody else. He almost ordered a burger on his mother's tab, but then decided he ought to find the other boys and Claudio first. Out at the pool he didn't see them right away—they were in deep shadow in the furthest cabana—which made him feel left out all over again. Plus he was unbearably hot and sweaty from being forced to sit around in the Fourgonette in the parking lot, and from the whole day so far really. So he trotted out onto the low board and dropped into the pool.

When the voices of the boy named Ben and the woman had faded into the distance, and he was sure he was alone, Marcel tried shouting for help. After the ringing inside the metal cargo box died away he heard nothing but silence: no answering voices, no running footsteps. He had no idea where the boys had brought him. All he'd seen when the doors were open was other parked cars and a line of palm trees obscuring the view beyond. But even if he'd been free to get out and look around, Marcel wouldn't have recognized where he was, since he'd never been near the American Embassy Club before, and only the position of the hills on the horizon would have given him even a rough idea of what part of the city he was in.

As he'd done when he was alone in the cargo box before, but more vigorously now that he knew none of the boys was within earshot, Marcel began to rub his ropes against the metal framing rib to which he was tied. It felt like there was some kind of roughness in the metal, a weld maybe, that occasionally caught against the rope and in time, with patience, would fray it. When he was tired, because the repetitive movement at an awkward angle in a cramped space behind his back made his shoulders ache, he'd stop and shout for help, just in case.

He was pausing to rest and consider how he could better control his rubbing to apply the friction at the same place in the rope all the time when he heard voices and quick footsteps. Marcel opened his mouth, but something kept him from shouting: a familiar pitch in the voices, maybe, or the question of why anyone innocent would be running in the hot mid-afternoon sun.

Sure enough, it was the three boys. Marcel arranged himself to look bored and half-asleep. When they flung open the rear doors he could see in the blindingly bright light that there was another person with them, a muscular white man, and that all four of them were dressed in nothing but nylon swimming shorts.

"You see?" said Ben. "I told you he'd still be here!"

Nabil said, "I don't care, Ben. You're still a stupid, immature fuck!"

Claudio leaned into the opening and looked at Marcel. "How are you doing?" He spoke decent French, with a strong American accent plus a flavor Marcel didn't recognize. (Claudio had picked up his French at brothels in Saigon.)

Marcel shrugged. "As you see."

Claudio climbed into the box and shuffled around, trying to get comfortable. "Jesus fucking Christ this metal is hot against my bare skin!" he yelled in English and laughed. Then in French he said, "I'm Claudio."

"Marcel."

"Pleased to meet you, Marcel." Claudio turned to show off his bicep. "A lot of people call me the Matador. Check this out." He flexed to make the bullfighter's red cape flutter, and out of habit even provided the little swooshing noise. Marcel, who for a moment had imagined the boys had finally gotten smart enough to bring him a sensible adult to deal with, now realized it might be too soon to be sure.

"Anyway," said Claudio, "I guess kids like that." He straightened up, to the extent he could in the cargo box, and looked at Marcel. "So, seriously, are you okay? Tell me what you need. You must need something, locked up in this box all day."

Marcel said, "I need water, and I need to use the bathroom. And maybe some food."

Claudio nodded. "Reasonable. I'll see what I can arrange so you can stretch your legs."

He climbed out of the back to tell the boys, but they'd all heard. Ben said, "You're going to untie him? Right here at the American Club?"

"Why do you have him tied up at all? He's not one of the kidnappers, and he knows they're not trading for him, right?" The boys nodded. "So why's he tied up inside an oven? What are you guys, the fucking Vietcong?"

The boys looked at the ground. Nabil, whose idea it had been to recruit Claudio, said, "I thought you were on our side."

"I am on your side. But I think he's on your side, too—or he would be if you stopped treating him like shit."

The boys looked at each other. Not one of them was willing to go back over the story they'd told Claudio and clarify that the man Ben had killed was not technically one of the kidnappers, as they'd allowed Claudio to believe, but a youngster who seemed like a relative or at least a close friend of Marcel's, so that he had his own reasons for hating them. No one said anything.

Claudio went on. "So my plan is, we're going to release him, and feed him, and treat him like an ally, and then maybe the five of us working together can figure out how to save Roddy." The boys said nothing. "I mean, do you guys have a better plan? Because that's what the Matador has to offer."

Ben laughed. "Are you going to take him to the pool?" That made Nabil and Jesse laugh too.

"Why's that funny? Because he's an African?"

Jesse said, "Come on, Matador, don't be like that. You know it's funny."

"He wouldn't be the first African. The ambassador brought the Vice President here once."

"Ambassador Stone?"

"No, the one before him. The Democrat."

Nabil said, "Yeah, well, this guy doesn't exactly look like he's a vice president."

They all inspected Marcel, sitting there covered in a layer of dust and rust from the cargo box and a layer of shiny new sweat and a layer of already long-dried sweat, all of the layers coating and soaking through the shabby clothes he'd pulled on in a hurry when the barking dog woke him at dawn this morning.

Claudio said, "That's why we're gonna take him around the

back of the clubhouse to the kitchen. And I guess we'll figure out how to sneak him into a shower too." He held out his hand to the boys. "All right, give me the pistol and let's untie him."

Nabil and Jesse looked at Ben, and then down at Ben's swimming trunks. Ben's mouth fell open. Nabil whispered, as if Claudio couldn't hear every word anyway, since he was right there, "Ben, where's the fucking pistol?"

Ben whispered back, "I think it's in my locker with my clothes."

Claudio said, "You think? You better fuckin' know where that piece is, man!"

Ben took off running toward the clubhouse, and Nabil called after him, "Ben, you're a fucking retard!"

Ben would have shouted something back, but he could feel tears of shame in his throat, and he knew if he shouted his voice would probably crack.

Claudio called, "And don't just bring it back here waving it around! Get dressed first, and put it away securely!"

Marcel had followed nothing of the conversation except to observe that increasing the number of white people didn't reduce the amount of time they spent arguing. Claudio climbed back into the cargo box with him and smiled. "Technical difficulties, man, you know how it is."

Jesse said, "Maybe I'll go dress too, so I can show you the ransom note." He ran off. Nabil hesitated for a moment, then ran after him.

Marcel and Claudio now faced each other alone. Marcel said, "Are you in charge of those children, Monsieur Claudio?"

"Just Claudio. Or Matador." Claudio shrugged. "They're my buddies."

"And where are their parents?"

"Their parents?" Claudio laughed. "Yeah, well, the parents are definitely not in charge."

"And you know those children killed a young man this morning?"

"Yeah, I know." Claudio sounded bored.

Marcel studied Claudio's muscular build, his tattoos, his buzz cut, his relaxed graceful ease. "Are you a Green Beret?" He'd seen the movie, with a girl he was fond of at the time, at the Palais de Versailles on one of his first outings away from the nightclub after Théophile arrived to serve as his backup. For the next week, as Marcel looked out over the hilltop forest for intruders, he'd imagined being John Wayne.

"No, no, I'm just a jarhead." At least that's what Claudio meant to say, but he didn't know the French for jar, since his vocabulary was weak in the domestic arts. He thought of the French for "pot of jam" and worked from that, so that he ended up calling himself a "pothead," which he was not.

But Marcel didn't know the word pothead anyway, so he just nodded, guessing the weirdness this time was due to the language barrier rather than to Claudio himself. Marcel's previous experience of talking to a white man at length had been confined to rambling one-sided conversations with his late boss up at the nightclub, who told too many stories about the old days, before independence, before the paved roads, before the War, before this, before that... But at least the old German spoke fluent French and could express his banalities clearly.

Marcel said, "Those boys told me if they don't get their friend back they're going to kill me too, even though I'm innocent." He studied Claudio's face for a reaction and saw none. "Would you let them do that?"

Claudio thought it over. "If I felt like Roddy died because you could've done more to help and you didn't, I think I'd see their point. Beyond that," he pointed to another of his tattoos, "as the Matador says, 'Only God Can Judge.'" He leaned forward to showed Marcel the tattoo. "You understand Spanish?"

Marcel shook his head. "It's Spanish for 'Only God Can Judge Me.' I'm just a Mexican boy from East L.A., California. Livin' the dream, man."

Marcel liked the tattoo, which illustrated the words with a tough half-naked young man, rather like Claudio, his hands folded in prayer and angel wings sprouting from his back. He filed away the information, not particularly surprising, that Mexico was in California.

"Where're you from, man? You grow up here in the city?"

"I'm from a small village in the Mtom country, south of here."

"Hey, I know an Mtom girl. Real nice." Claudio laughed, and for some reason, maybe just the amount of childish dirty relish Claudio was able to pack into two words, Marcel laughed too. Still laughing, Claudio said, "I bet you know some girls."

"Not many. I don't have much money, not like you Americans."

Claudio got serious. "Maybe when this shit is over you and me should go hang out with my Mtom girlfriend. And if you're tired of Mtom girls they've got everything there."

"I told you, I don't have any money."

"I'll cover you, man. To make up for the Vietcong treatment."

"Thank you." Marcel didn't understand the last part but the overall intention was clear. "That's very nice of you."

"I think they have an Italian girl there. That interest you? You want some of that white pussy?" Marcel nodded noncommittally, sensing dangerous ground he wasn't ready to cross with this man yet.

"You know what? Fuck it," Claudio said in English. Then he switched back to French. "Lean over and let's get you out of those ropes." He reached around behind Marcel and began to untie him. "And you know what else? When this is all over and it's time to party, we're going to take those boys with us to get laid. Can you believe—the little fuckers got their first kill and they're still virgins! We gotta fix that, right?"

Marcel, pressed against Claudio's naked torso while Claudio stretched to reach the ropes behind his back, closed his eyes and admitted that this time it wasn't a translation problem: the American soldier really was just strange, and unpredictable, and a little frightening.

As he helped Marcel out of the cargo box Claudio said casually, "I understand you could make trouble for these boys. But don't embarrass them or me in this place. If you start something I'll break your neck." To illustrate the last part Claudio held up and flexed only a single hand, and that detail particularly impressed Marcel.

Prosper, Danton, and Auguste had tried moving inside the house, but the heat baking through the corrugated aluminum roof was overwhelming without the mercy of the slight breeze they'd enjoyed outside, so they turned around and came back out to the porch. Prosper brought his transistor radio out, and, while he and Danton sat against the porch posts and played cards and Auguste stretched out on the concrete to doze, they listened to Yoa-language pop, with a sprinkling of the latest hits from elsewhere in West Africa to show the D.J.'s sophistication.

The hourly news bulletin came on. Prosper held up one finger to stop card play while they listened, and Auguste rolled onto his back and opened his eyes. But, though many important things seemed to have happened in the nation and the world—at least judging by the urgency of the announcer's voice—the kidnapping of a little white boy right here in the capital wasn't one of them. When the news was over, the station switched to covering a soccer game, the local Lions playing at the Torpedoes down on the coast.

Auguste, still looking up at the ceiling of the porch, said, "Why do they bother? Everybody knows the Torpedoes are going to kick their asses."

Prosper set down the card he'd been holding during the news. "Oh, yeah? Why's that?"

"Because the Lions are a bunch of old women… even worse, old Yoa women."

Prosper said evenly, "My grandmother, a highly respected person, happens to be an old Yoa woman."

"You see?" Auguste laughed. "She's not here now because she had to go play against the Torpedoes."

Danton put down his last card, conceding the game. "If there's no report about the boy on the news," he said quickly, before Prosper could reply to Auguste, "it means the parents are following our instructions and keeping the whole thing to themselves."

Prosper nodded, reluctantly letting Auguste's insult go. "So my plan's working, and—thanks to me—very soon we'll be looking at a hundred thousand francs."

Auguste had begun to whistle, through his teeth, the last Guinean love song they'd heard. He broke off. "And then when I get my share I can go back to my house, the house I can't go to now because the gendarmes are waiting for me there—the same gendarmes who, according to what you're saying now, don't even know about the kidnapping." He started whistling again.

Prosper shuffled the cards. "If you're going to whistle, at least get the tune right."

Auguste continued to the end of the refrain. He was a pretty good teeth whistler and he knew it, and, even if he couldn't remember exactly how the song went, his version worked. "Plus, if the other boys took Marcel to the police and he told them where Danton and I live, why would they stop knowing that just because we make the trade with the parents? So maybe Danton and I can't ever go home, right?"

Danton said, "No, look, Auguste, you're confused—"

"—But, on the other hand, if the boys didn't take Marcel to the police, where did they go and what are they doing with him?"

Prosper and Danton looked at each other for the answer.

Auguste went on. "I think the police do know, even though it's not on the radio. I think the meeting at the cigarette factory is going to be a trap."

Danton said in Mtom, "You've said enough. Now stop."

Auguste didn't stop. "I think, since it's a trap and we're not going to get the hundred thousand anyway, we should take the boy back up the hill and shoot him and leave him next to Théophile. Then we all go home and we know nothing about anything and it doesn't matter what Marcel says."

Prosper said, "For a dumb fuck, you're sure full of theories all of a sudden."

Auguste smiled. "I had a nice nap on your comfortable porch. I feel refreshed." He wriggled against the concrete as if nestling into a soft bed. "Go Torpedoes! Beat those Yoa grannies!" He began to whistle through his teeth again, still not getting the tune quite right.

3.

"IT'S LIKE a submarine." As they bounced along the potholed street leading from the American Club back to the middle of town, Nabil—for whom this was the first experience of riding in the cargo box of the Fourgonette—had been struggling to find what it reminded him of.

Jesse said, "You've been in a submarine?"

"Let me guess," said Ben, "your dad owns a fleet of submarines."

"Shut up, retard. No, I mean it's like what I think a submarine would be like. You know, all metal, lots of noise but you have no idea where you're going because you can't see out."

Ben looked out the tiny oval windows in the rear doors. "We're passing the big ugly statue on Independence Square." He had his eye pressed to the glass, and a sudden lurch banged his face hard. "Ow! Son of a bitch!"

The other boys laughed. Claudio steered more consistently than Nabil, but he had yet to get the hang of the push-me-pull-you Citroën gearshift. When they were ready to leave the club and Claudio had insisted on taking over as driver, the boys had barely noticed because they were so upset at the other half of Claudio's plan, which was that Marcel would ride in the cab with him and the boys would ride in back.

"So he's going to be sitting up there with you, not tied up or anything?"

"The man has spent enough time in the hole."

"But—"

"You can do it my way or you can do it your way, in which case the Matador goes back to the pool to work on his tan." When the boys still hesitated Claudio pointed to the sun, already far in the western sky. "Time's a-wasting." And that was that.

As they set off, all three boys, though they said nothing to each other, tried to figure out how their great idea to get the Matador to help them had turned into Claudio being in charge. Was that always how it was with grownups—Claudio and that guy Marcel would hang out together like buddies while the boys got stuffed into the back, just extra weight? It didn't make sense: Claudio didn't get along with adults, he was really a kid, one of them. So what was going on? But the boys weren't ready to sound disloyal to the Matador, so for now they kept their resentments to themselves and talked about safer things instead.

"That's what we need," said Jesse. "A submarine exactly this size, so we could sneak up the river and take the kidnappers by surprise."

Ben nodded, "Sean Connery has a submarine."

But Nabil wasn't ready to play along. "The cigarette factory is nowhere near the river."

"Okay, so then our submarine can go up the water pipes and the sewer pipes—"

Laughing, Nabil began to get into the spirit. "So our submarine is coated in shit?"

"There'd have to be like a special spraying thing that cleans it off before we get out."

Ben was laughing too. "Is there a big window in front, like in *Twenty Thousand Leagues Under the Sea*, so we can watch while all the shit goes by?"

"Yes, and we can see the giant rats in the sewer!"

Now all of them were caught up in it, throwing out ideas so fast they overlapped.

"The mole people!"

"We're going so fast the mole people can't get out of the way fast enough, so we keep hitting them!"

"They bounce off the big front window!"

"They can't see, so they're all screaming in their tiny mole voices, like, 'Oh my God, what was that?'"

All three boys began to imitate the mole people of the sewers, with their digging hands as big and splayed as baseball mitts, jerking and wincing as they bounced off the nose of the speeding submarine—though none of the boys could appreciate what the others were doing, since they all had their eyes closed for verisimilitude.

In front, Claudio said, "Does it seem weird to you that the kidnappers would pick the cigarette factory at six o'clock? I mean, isn't that kind of a public place?"

Marcel braced himself as they went around another traffic circle. "No. It's Saturday. The factory closes at noon. No one will be up there. And it's a big open space, so the middle of it is far from any cover. No surprises."

Still enjoying the feeling of being clean from the hot shower in the changing room Claudio had snuck him into, and the aftertaste of the cheeseburger and large Coke Claudio had brought out to him in the little alleyway behind the kitchen of the American Club, Marcel looked out the window of the Fourgonette and noticed with a jolt of electricity that they were passing the Quincaillerie Chaloub. He was running out of time to make his move. He turned back to Claudio. "So what is our plan exactly?"

They stopped at the traffic light between the post office and the cathedral. "Can you believe it? One fucking traffic light in this town, and it's red." Claudio drummed on the steering wheel. "To be honest, Marcel, I'm not a big planning guy. I'm kind of a go with the flow, see what happens but be ready for anything kind of guy. We don't know how to find the bad guys except at the cigarette factory at six, so I guess that's where we'll be. So right now we're going to the big store—"

"Jeune Afrique."

"Yeah. And we're going to get a lunch box."

"A lunch box, but no money to put in it."

"You know, one step at a time, don't try to get ahead of yourself, that's what the Matador says."

Marcel nodded. He wondered if it was an act, or if it could really be true that this friendly tattooed sap was even more of a child than those boys riding in back, who—even though they argued constantly—at least seemed capable of making and carrying out a plan. The American military couldn't all be like this, could they? How could they have taken over the world? Though Marcel had heard the Americans were having some problems in that Vietnam place.

The light changed, and the car rolled forward. Claudio said, "And here's the thing, Marcel. When it comes to whatever's going to happen at the rendezvous—lunch box, no lunch box, money, no money—I figure however the shit falls we have one advantage."

"What's that?"

"Those guys don't know you're actually on our side. So if things get tricky, you're like our secret weapon."

As they angle-parked in front of Jeune Afrique, two dozen beggars emerged from the shade of the department store's awning and surrounded the car with welcoming cries. Claudio opened his door slowly, so he could push back a handful of tiny blind children without knocking them over. A bigger child, who led the blind tots by letting them clutch onto his shirt, held out his hand, reduced by leprosy to a blotchy palm and five smooth nubs. "No mama, no papa!" he cried.

"Me neither, man—I hear you," said Claudio in English, but his tone was friendly. He went around to open the rear doors.

Left alone in the front seat—predictably the beggars ignored him because he was African—Marcel thought about just getting out and walking away, and, once he was through the ring of beggars, melting into the stream of pedestrians hugging the late-afternoon shade next to the buildings. If he moved right now, in ten seconds he could be safe.

But then he thought about Théophile, lying under a table-cloth in the empty liquor storeroom up at the nightclub. Surely Marcel owed the boy—his kin—more consideration than just to worry about his own safety. Plus there was the Chaloub boy, back there in the cargo box. Marcel noticed Claudio had left the key in the ignition. Wouldn't that be a sweet trick—to kidnap the boy using his father's own Fourgonette!

The boys climbed out of the back and stretched, paying the maimed and deformed beggars crowding around them no attention other than just to brush them off like flies when the littlest ones, emboldened by their cuteness, plucked at the foreigners' clothes and shouted in French, from waist high, "Little white boy! Little white boy! I'm hungry!"

Claudio said to Nabil, "Clear plastic lunch box. You have money?" Nabil nodded and headed for the store, wading through beggars. Ben moved to follow Nabil, but Claudio held him back. "Just him. We don't need a whole circus just to get one lunch box."

"Well, shit," said Ben, giving up. "I never get to have fun." One of the boys' favorite games, when they were downtown together, was to wander the aisles of Jeune Afrique, gathering items off the shelves—odd things that struck their fancy but that didn't look too expensive or breakable—till their arms were overflowing, and then finally drop everything in the middle of an aisle. The original plan had been to run away afterward, back to their nearby hideout by the railroad tracks, but Roddy's impulse the first time they did it was not only funnier, it made it possible for them to return to the store and do it again: they'd get down on the floor and pick everything up, calling out, "Sorry! Sorry! Sorry!" to all the grownups—and filling their arms for yet another potential disaster. The whole game was a perfect example of what you could get away with as long as you pretended to be apologetic—and of course as long as you were white.

"You want something to do?" Claudio held out a fifty-franc coin. "Choose one beggar and give him this."

Ben said, "We never give money to beggars. My dad says—"

"I don't care what your dad says. This is my money." Claudio raised his arm to keep the coin out of reach of the children swarming and now jumping around them, though that just brought the shiny fifty-franc piece to the attention of beggars further away.

"But I can't give money to just one of them."

"You sure can't give it to all of them. What would that be, like one franc each? That's not even a penny." He pushed the coin into Ben's reluctant hand. "So pick one."

Surrounded by clamoring six-year-old beggars who had no trouble keeping their eyes on the coin as it changed hands, Ben turned slowly in a circle. Backing out of the huddle around Ben, Claudio said, "Don't just throw it away. Figure out who deserves it the most."

"I can't."

"Yes, you can. It's like you're God, or at least a small god, because you can only make one person happy. But it means you actually have to look at them, Ben."

Leaning against the side of the car, Jesse laughed. "That's it, Ben—look right into their nasty ugly yellow messed-up blind eyes and what's left of their scary nubby leprosy hands!"

"Shut up, retard!"

"Focus on what you're doing, Ben," said Claudio. "It's good

karma to give to beggars, but you've got to pay attention to what you're doing."

Irritated by the press of children around him, some of whom had wrapped their arms around his legs—and many of whom seemed to be suffering from nothing worse than dirtiness—Ben pushed his way toward the sidewalk.

Jesse said to Claudio, "What's karma?"

"It's a Buddhist thing. You do something good, so good things will happen to you."

"Could it be like making up for doing a bad thing?"

"Sure, I guess."

"Then you definitely gave your money to the right guy." Claudio waited, but Jesse said nothing more.

On the sidewalk, in the shade of the store awning, Ben looked past the beggars whose eyes were red or even white from river blindness, past the beggars who'd lost fingers, hands, legs, and even noses to leprosy, past the men born without bottom halves who scooted toward him along the sidewalk on old sheets of cardboard. Next to the entrance to Jeune Afrique—the only revolving door in the city, to keep in the air conditioning—Ben saw a young man of about Théophile's age and size whose legs were wasted down to twisted sticks by polio. He sat next to his crutches with an enamel bowl in front of him and stared expressionless into the distance, ignoring Ben and all the commotion around him. Ben pushed toward him past all the other beggars and reached out to drop the fifty-franc piece into his bowl.

"What the fuck are you doing?" Nabil had just come out through the revolving door, and Ben could feel and smell the wedge of cold dry store air he brought with him. "What are you, a tourist?"

Ben still held the coin over the bowl. The young man with shrunken legs looked past both boys as if they weren't there.

"The Matador said to give this to someone."

"So that's the Matador's money?"

Ben nodded. "He said it was good luck or something."

Nabil laughed. "What's good luck is, you just got yourself fifty francs. You can get a snack or a Fanta, or we can chip in and get cigarettes. Come on, let's get the fuck out of this freak show."

Ben lowered his hand till it almost brushed the enamel bowl, and then palmed the coin instead of setting it down. The young beggar, who knew how much money had been in his bowl before and could see how much was in it now, looked right at Ben. Nothing in his expression changed, except one eyebrow went up as if to say, "Now I've really seen everything." As Ben and Nabil walked away, the other beggars screamed at the young man with polio for his good luck.

"Success?" asked Claudio as the two boys reached the car.

Ben nodded, but Nabil said, "No. They don't have the right lunch boxes. They say they only carry them at the beginning of the school year."

"Huh. Well, now what?"

Nabil shrugged. "Now I guess Roddy gets killed because we can't trade for him."

Jesse said, "Don't be a dick. I bet one of the little kids at the mission dorm has the kind of lunch box they're talking about. We'll just take it."

"Well, let's go then." Claudio waved the boys into the cargo box and slammed the rear doors. He climbed back into the cab, where Marcel still sat patiently. Claudio reflected that Marcel could easily have walked away while they waited here, and felt again the rightness of his impulse at the club to free the man from his cage and treat him like a partner. He turned the key and heard continuous mechanical throat-clearing but no ignition. Someone pounded on the wall of the cargo box behind his head.

Outside, the beggar children who'd lost interest in them began to gather again for the show.

Marcel said, "I think sometimes you have to push to start it."

"It started fine at the American Club."

"It's not every time."

"Hell, I wish someone had told me that before I parked nose in."

"We forgot." Marcel opened his door and got out. "I'll get the boys to help." He walked around to the back of the Fourgonette and reached for the handles of the rear doors, then stopped, struck by the interesting position he was in now, about to release his own captors. The faces of the three boys were pressed against the glass of the tiny oval windows, and for a long moment they looked out at Marcel and he looked in at them. Then he opened the doors. The boys began to scramble out, but Marcel blocked their way by standing in the opening and holding onto the doors. The boys looked at him, and he looked at them, and, though no one said anything, it seemed to Marcel the same message was being communicated in both directions: "The only person here who's being fooled is the Matador."

Then Marcel moved aside and the boys got out. The African man and the three white boys gathered around the front of the Fourgonette and rolled it backward into the street with surprising ease—indeed, as his father's chauffeur had said, Nabil could probably have done it by himself. The crowd of beggars cheered and laughed.

But the main shopping district, with Jeune Afrique at its center and the cathedral and post office at its far end, ran along a flat street at the bottom of the valley. All the side streets climbed as they led away, so there'd be nothing like the long coast down from the Club Balafon to start the car. So, with a retinue of the most energetic beggar children tagging along to cheer and give advice, the four of them had to push the car a full block before the engine coughed and woke up. Panting, the boys hopped back into the cargo box. This time, just before he slammed the rear doors, Marcel gave them a slight smile.

As the car headed uphill in the direction of the Canadian mission dorm, Ben said, "Okay, did you see that? That was weird."

Nabil nodded. "Yeah, plus I wonder how many people who know us saw us. I mean, we're only a few blocks from my father's office."

"Why would it matter? It's not like you're the one driving or anything."

"Yeah, but aren't we supposed to be at Jesse's dorm, playing Monopoly?"

Jesse shrugged. "So we took a break to help Claudio start his car, and now we're going back to continue the game."

"Okay, except it's really my father's car."

"How would anybody know?"

Nabil paused while he tried to visualize the outside of the Fourgonette. "I think maybe there's something written on the back."

Jesse shrugged again, not caring much either way. "We'll have a look when we get out."

The Canadian mission dorm was just a house, but a big, sprawling old colonial-era house, with an enormous deeply shaded verandah all around it, wide whitewashed arches connecting the public rooms, high dark ceilings with huge fans always slowly turning the African air, and everywhere floors of thickly waxed blood-red concrete. The house had been built in 1905 by a missionary who lived here for fifty years, a man of God of the old school who baptized Yoa converts in the local

river—brushing aside concerns about crocodiles and bilharzia—
till he himself, as frail and white-headed as his better-known
colleague Albert Schweitzer, had to be held up by an African
servant while they stood in the river waist-deep and he per-
formed baptisms the only right way, by total immersion of
Christ-accepting adults in the warm muddy water.

The house now lodged a dozen or more children of the
Canadian missionaries who, like Jesse's parents, worked in
scattered spots around the country, far from any English-
language education. (In the grand old man's time, when people
who dedicated their lives to God held nothing, not even their
families, back for themselves, children of missionaries stationed
in the bush would have been shipped home to Canada, seeing
their parents again for a few months every seven years.)

In 1905 the mission compound stood in a clearing deep in
the bush an hour or so by forest path from a sleepy Yoa village.
Though the property had long since been surrounded by the city
that little village had grown into, the couple of acres around the
house still belonged to the Canadian mission, which by now
included a big Yoa church, a free French-language elementary
school, and a vocational training center for the handicapped.

One corner of the property, just below the house, remained
green. Here, in a little square marked off by temperate ever-
greens that had failed to thrive and had soon been overwhelmed
by bamboo and hibiscus, stood the old missionary's grave. His
headstone, cleaned once a year by the dorm children, had carved
into it his name, his birth and death dates, and the name given to
him by the Africans when he was still in his hard-charging
twenties. His Yoa name meant "Awake before anyone, asleep
after everyone" (four syllables in Yoa, four strokes on the talking
drum that would alert the next village the missionary was on his
way there), and it was written on the headstone in the alphabet
—Roman letters plus special diacritical marks—he himself

devised when his translation of the Gospel of Mark became the first document ever printed in the Yoa language.

It was through the old man's grave site that Jesse now threaded his way, giving the headstone an affectionate slap as he passed it on his way up to the dorm. The Fourgonette was parked—nose out this time—on the busy street just below him on the other side of the dense hibiscus hedge.

It was essential that Jesse get into the house, get what he needed, and get out again without being spotted—either by one of the countless little brats who would happily curry favor by telling on him, or by the house parents themselves, a couple of uptight elderly Bible thumpers named Swenson making their first trip away from Saskatchewan. Whenever Jesse got in trouble at the dorm, which was to say regularly, his friends would snap him out of his gloom with a little piece of vaudeville: "Where'd you say those new house parents are from?"

"Regina."

"Vagina?"

"Regina."

"Vagina?"

And when that had gone on long enough, and all of them were crying with laughter and begging for mercy, Jesse would say, "Maybe it was Saskatoon." And by then even Saskatoon was funny.

Jesse crossed a flowerbed, thinking more about the risk of being spotted than the certainty of trampling the flowers, and climbed over the low stone parapet onto the verandah. He crouched there, listening, trying to figure out where people were in the house and what they were doing. The third-grade girls—there were four of them in the dorm this year, insepara-ble and un-shut-up-able—had marked the verandah floor with an enormous marathon hopscotch diagram that reached at least as high as 30 before it sprawled its way in multiple chalk colors around the corner toward the front of the house. How could they even play hopscotch around a corner? Maybe they threw the beanbag to the farthest square they could see and then picked it up and threw it again. Jesse reached down next to his left foot and carefully turned a 17 into a 7: that would give the third-graders something to argue about the next time they played.

He could hear them arguing right now, because the room the four girls shared overlooked the verandah not far from where he was crouching. It sounded like they were playing Candy Land. Jesse scuttled the other direction along the verandah. The window to his own room was open, and he squatted right underneath it, next to the wall he and his room-mate Kevin had used as their soccer goal till Mr. Swenson told them they'd have to repaint it to cover up all the scuffs from the ball. It was still unpainted, pockmarked from floor to ceiling with dusty hexagons, but at least the boys had given up playing.

Kevin was a nice kid, but he was only in sixth grade, and Jesse, the oldest boy at the dorm for the past three years, felt like the age gap between them was getting bigger instead of smaller. There were things guaranteed to piss off the Swensons that Kevin was happy to take part in, like slamming a soccer ball against the verandah wall and not cleaning up, or hiding a dead snake in the room shared by the three fifth- and sixth-grade girls, but there was no way Kevin would be allowed to come on the kind of midnight expedition to the abandoned nightclub that Jesse had undertaken with his seventh-grade peers—and absolutely no way Jesse could ever share with him what had happened since it began to go wrong.

He could hear Kevin now, through the curtains swaying in the open window, half-singing and half-humming to himself, in a sweet voice that hadn't yet broken, "Prepare Ye the Way of the Lord... Prepare Ye the Way of the Lord..." At the moment, *Godspell* was the only even partway rock music the house parents would allow in the dorm—at least the only example the kids were willing to listen to: the Swensons were keen on a Christian soft rock group from Saskatchewan that had yet to find any fans among the dorm children. Jesse's attempt to slip even an early Beatles album under the wire had ended badly, with a lecture about people who thought they were bigger than Jesus.

As he crouched on the verandah, listening to Kevin sing in the plain unselfconscious way of someone who thinks he's alone, Jesse felt a weird dropping sensation in the middle of his chest, as if his heart were falling through his stomach, and he recognized it as sadness. If he'd stayed home from Roddy's sleepover last night and gone to bed, instead of sneaking off with his friends to look for trouble at the top of the German's hill, right now he too might be in his dorm room, at the lazy tail end of a Saturday afternoon, singing this beautiful song and worrying about nothing more urgent than whether or not he really believed the words.

Even more than that, Jesse realized he missed being in sixth grade—or, more realistically in his case, fifth grade—and imagining nothing more wicked in the world than making the girls in the other wing of the house run to the Swensons in their pyjamas screaming about a snake. As his heart dropped lower and lower through his stomach and he admitted to himself that what he missed amounted to the unrecoverable condition of simply being a child, the impulse Jesse felt—to climb through the window into his room and crawl into bed and pretend he was too sick to see his friends when they came looking for him —though he didn't know it, was the same one Nabil had experienced when he reached his own bedroom that morning.

Jesse took a deep breath and climbed through the window onto his own pillow. He was sorry to see that, in addition to catching Kevin in the act of singing *Godspell*, he was also exposed to the sight of Kevin—still unaware of being observed because he had his back turned—dancing by himself, his hands and hips swaying to the song. There being no way to save the poor boy from embarrassment, Jesse decided not to call out to him, and instead just stretched out on his bed with his hands behind his head, as if he'd been lounging there all afternoon.

As Kevin finally turned, still singing, Jesse assumed an expression of mild blank boredom and looked straight into Kevin's eyes. Kevin's jump and girlish scream ranked several notches better than Jesse had hoped for, and, before Kevin could think of a thing to say or even gather his breath, Jesse put his finger to his lips.

Kevin whispered, "Holy cow, Jesse! I almost died! How long have you been lying there?"

Jesse grinned. "Long enough to be grossed out."

"Shut up! I thought you were at a sleepover at Roddy's house!"

Hearing Roddy's name made Jesse sit up before he'd even realized he was going to. "I am. We are." He paused: he hadn't thought this far ahead, focusing instead on how to get into the house unseen. "Come here."

Kevin sat down on his own bed facing Jesse.

"You know how the little girls have those lunch boxes? The stupid little plastic ones?"

Kevin shrugged. "Sure."

"I need you to get one of them for me." Picturing the lunch box disappearing forever into the hands of the kidnappers, he added, "I need you to borrow one without telling them."

"Like steal it."

"Like borrow it."

Kevin paused to make it clear he didn't believe in the distinction, then said, "Why?"

Jesse waved his hands. "It's just for a stupid game we're playing, like a scavenger hunt—doesn't matter."

"So why can't you go get it yourself?"

"Come on, Kevin, you know the Flintstones"—the dorm kids' private name for the Swensons. "Once they see I'm back they're not going to let me go out to Roddy's house again today."

Kevin was torn. He resented being left out—of everything Jesse and the other seventh-grade boys ever did, of this sleepover as the latest example, and of whatever was the real reason for needing the lunch box—when he himself felt confident he was grown up enough to hold his own with those boys. On the other hand he sensed that doing the errand, getting the lunch box, could be seen as joining the big boys in a small way, putting them in his debt and making him a sharer in one of their secrets and maybe earning him the right to tag along next time. Apart from Jesse, the other boys in the mission dorm were many grades younger, and Kevin had missed Jesse so much this afternoon and been so bored he'd almost considered playing Candy Land with the little girls—the most unbearable of whom was his own sister.

"Okay. But they're all in there right now playing Candy Land. How am I supposed to 'borrow' someone's lunch box?"

"I don't know, Kevin, you can figure something out."

Feeling trusted and manipulated in about equal measure, Kevin went down the hall from the boys' wing—really only two bedrooms—into the living room, which was sparsely furnished for its enormous size, since children needed lots of indoor play space, especially during the rainy season, and they didn't spend much time in chairs. One of the sixth-grade girls had just sat down at the battered upright piano to practice. Susan and Kevin despised each other for reasons too complicated to explain or even to remember, and the two of them hadn't spoken directly in several months, not counting when it was unavoidable in their small class at the American School, so Kevin walked straight past

Susan's stiffened back and into the girls' wing. He knocked on and then opened the door to the third graders' room.

"Ew, whatta you want?" one of the little girls squawked in a duck voice, and they all screamed with laughter and fell over on their sides away from the game board in the middle of the floor.

"Aren't you tired of playing Candy Land?"

"Ew, whatta you want?" repeated the same girl, with her hands over her face, and all the girls screamed as if it was even funnier than the first time and drummed the red concrete floor with their bare feet.

"I was thinking about playing hopscotch. Anybody want to play hopscotch with me?"

Before he'd finished speaking, the four girls—flattered at any attention from this huge and scary sixth-grade boy—leaped to their feet, screaming with excitement, and scrambled through their window out onto the hopscotch diagram on the verandah.

All of their lunch boxes, thrown together in one corner of the room, looked identical—the girls had insisted on that when they dragged Mrs. Swenson to Jeune Afrique at the beginning of the school year—but they'd painted their names on them. Kevin chose his sister's, to teach her for being such an annoying baby, though he already knew he'd be sorry when she came crying to her big brother for comfort after Mrs. Swenson yelled at her for losing her lunch box.

When Kevin returned to his own bedroom he found Jesse standing there holding the BB gun he kept in the back of their closet, and that no one but Kevin—and especially not the Swensons—knew he'd brought here from home. (As for Jesse's own parents, they'd been satisfied with his explanation—which happened to be the truth—that he needed it to hunt lizards and the occasional fruit bat. "That's my boy!" his father had said.)

"Is that for the scavenger hunt too?" Kevin sounded a little sarcastic.

Jesse hadn't anticipated that Kevin would solve the Candy Land problem so quickly and had therefore expected to have plenty of time to set the air rifle out of sight on the floor of the verandah outside their window to be collected as he left, and he was caught a little flat-footed. "Uh, yeah, believe it or not." He ducked back into the closet to get the box of lead pellets.

"You want the lunch box or not?" Kevin dropped it onto Jesse's bed.

Jesse came back into view. "Oh, yeah—thanks, man." He stuffed the box of pellets into his pocket. "Wow, I can't believe you got that so quickly."

In no mood to be flattered, Kevin said nothing.

"You know what else?" said Jesse, suddenly inspired. "You know the Monopoly set from the games cupboard? Can you go get it?"

Kevin, who'd never been thanked for keeping the secret of the BB gun all year, and who'd never been invited to use it, or even to watch when Jesse and his friends had gone lizard hunting, now sat down firmly on his bed. "I'll go get it if you tell me why you really need this stuff."

"I already told you—"

"Jesse, first of all, you guys are the cool kids and scavenger hunts aren't cool. And then, you wouldn't put Monopoly on a scavenger hunt because everybody has Monopoly, and you wouldn't put a BB gun because nobody has a BB gun except you. Scavenger hunts are about things that are equally hard for everybody to find."

"Okay, Einstein, so we're going lizard hunting."

"You're lying. You would've told me that in the first place if it was true, and anyway it's going to be dark by the time you get all the way back out to Roddy's house. You gonna hunt in the dark?"

Thinking of the Fourgonette waiting on the street, Jesse was about to say, "Not if I take a taxi," but the Swensons had forbidden all the dorm kids from riding in taxis after they themselves took a ride in a dirty cab with a driver who smelled of alcohol and who cheated them of a lot of money whose value they didn't yet understand—an experience in their first week that had contributed memorably to their Africa culture shock.

It may have been true that only Jesse had been old enough or independent enough to take taxis by himself or with his friends before this year, but all the dorm children—most of whom, like Jesse, were born here or had lived here since before they could remember—felt the weirdness of being more at ease, more knowledgeable, more at home in this country than the adult couple who had parental authority over them for nine months of the year.

So instead of bringing up the taxi issue Jesse said, "Don't be a douche, Kevin."

"Ooh, a bad word, I'm telling the Flintstones."

"You're a double douche if you do." Kevin laughed. Jesse took a slow deep breath. "Kevin, please, just go get me the Monopoly game."

"As soon as you tell me what you guys are up to."

Jesse sat down on his bed, with the air rifle and the lunch box on his lap, and retraced all the events of the day in his head —the German's house, the LPs, the hunters, Roddy, Clint, Théophile, Marcel, the Fourgonette cargo box, the ransom note, Claudio—trying to figure out where even to start.

Through the curtains just above Jesse's pillow, the whiny voice of Kevin's little sister broke the silence. "You gonna come play, Kev? You said you would. We already started."

Kevin looked at Jesse. Jesse shook his head. "I really can't explain, Kevin. It's just too…"

Kevin called through the window to his sister. "Yeah, here I come!" He rolled off his bed and climbed through the window to go play hopscotch on the verandah. Jesse sat on his bed, listening to the excited cries of the little girls outside and to Susan practicing the piano in the living room. Now he could hear Mrs. Swenson lecturing the cook in her awful French, talking at the top of her voice as always, as if she thought Africans were deaf. That meant she was in the kitchen, on the far side of the sprawling old house.

So where was Mr. Swenson? Under all the other noises, Jesse could just make out the steady whine of a power tool coming from outside, like the hum of a distant mechanical mosquito. Mr. Swenson's lifelong hobby was making jewelry from gemstones, and he'd come to Africa fired up to go prospecting on romantic gravel riverbanks deep in the forest, but one visit to a local tourist shop had changed his mind— fortunately, since the crocodiles on those riverbanks would certainly have outrun him.

Having discovered to his astonishment that large crudely made knickknacks posing as "African folk art" and carved out of solid malachite were on sale for ridiculously low prices— malachite rubble being merely the tailings from the copper mines up north—Mr. Swenson had bought a stone-cutting table saw and installed it in the gardener's toolshed behind the dorm. Then he went to a wholesaler and bought hundreds of the malachite ashtrays that sat unremarked on tables in every house, restaurant, and café in the country—the cheapest pound-per-franc source of malachite he could identify—and stacked them in his shed. Now he spent many happy hours every day using his table saw to slice heavy green ashtrays into small chunks, which he then polished and made into striking African jewelry for family and friends back in Regina.

Once Jesse knew both house parents were busy elsewhere, he put down the BB gun and the lunch box and walked boldly out to the living room. Susan, whose crush on Jesse was in its second year, immediately made a dumb mistake in the piece she was practicing. She flushed but didn't look up from the piano as Jesse passed close behind her, saying nothing to her, even though he liked her, because he wasn't supposed to be here and because she seemed to be concentrating so hard. She tried to play the chord again but only made it worse, and, by the time she'd given up and retreated to the beginning of the phrase to get a running start, Jesse was already slipping back into his room and shutting the door.

He opened the Monopoly box on his bed. It was the French set, based on Paris streets and railroad stations, so the money was in francs. He just wanted the largest bills, but whichever kids had played last hadn't sorted the money before putting the game away, so instead of taking the time to go through it he stuffed the whole rubber-banded wad into the lunch box and snapped the lid shut.

As he passed the old missionary's headstone again and pushed his way through the gap in the hibiscus hedge next to the car, he was struck by how much longer the shadows seemed than when he'd left. All four of the others were sitting or lying against the grassy bank above the sidewalk, smoking. (Claudio had said people passing by would scold the boys, but Nabil had retorted that nobody cared what white children did, and he was right.) Ben and Claudio called out to Jesse at the same time, Ben saying, "Where the fuck have you been?" and Claudio, looking at the air rifle, saying "What the fuck is that?"

"I couldn't get away for a while because there were kids playing on the verandah, and it's a BB gun."

"I know that, wise guy. What I mean is, what do you think you're gonna do with it? Shoot it out with the bad guys, like the cigarette factory is the OK Corral?"

"Maybe. I don't know." Jesse was a little taken aback at Claudio's reaction to what he himself had thought was a stroke of genius. "I mean, they have a lot more guns than we do."

"Okay, true enough, and we can address that problem, but not with this pea-shooter."

Nabil took the lunch box from Jesse's hand. "This is exactly right. My little sister has one of these too... Had." As he corrected himself he imagined his sister now, walking to school with his mother every morning somewhere in France and no doubt carrying a much cooler lunch box than this piece of African-manufactured crap.

"Hey, there's money inside!" Ben took the lunch box from Nabil and opened the lid. Dropping the lunch box on the sidewalk and holding up the wad of bills, he started laughing. "Oh my God, Jesse, this is fucking perfect! We're going to pay the kidnappers a hundred thousand Monopoly francs!"

While Jesse angrily picked Kevin's little sister's lunch box off the ground, and Nabil pointed out that there wasn't a hundred thousand francs total in the whole game even if you counted all the singles, which he'd done one time when he was bored, and Claudio explained that nobody was that stupid and that giving the hunters this play money was basically asking them to kill Roddy, Marcel watched from the grassy bank, where he was still sitting, finishing the cigarette Claudio had given him.

He didn't know what all the yelling was about—white people and their arguments—and he couldn't tell at this distance in the late afternoon light what kind of money the boys were passing around and waving in each other's faces, though it didn't look like any denomination of CFA francs he was familiar with. But mostly Marcel was studying the rifle in Jesse's hand, which from here looked a lot like the kind of weapon John Wayne used when he wasn't a Green Beret. Turning the tables on these murdering little brats was going to get more complicated if they started adding extra firearms to the picture.

❖

"But, remember, your camel eats a date for every kilometer of desert he crosses."

"Then if it's a thousand kilometers across the desert, and he starts with three thousand dates, he'll reach the market with two thousand dates."

"No, Roddy, you forgot—he can't ever carry more than a thousand dates at one time."

Roddy badly wanted to scratch his head to help him think, but his hands were still tied to the chair. Bijou had been talking him through story problems for two hours now, and he was torn between wanting the conversation to go on forever and wanting the headache to end right now. She'd begun with a problem from her homework that she asked for his help in solving, and that still remained the formal pretense, though in fact she was much quicker at this kind of thinking than he was. By the time she'd finished explaining a problem to him she'd already figured out the answer—but in each case she continued to walk him through it, enjoying the born teacher's reward of light dawning on the face of her student as he finally stumbled into the clearing.

"If the camel can only carry a thousand dates, and it's a thousand kilometers across the desert, and he eats one date every kilometer..."

"Yes, that's right." Bijou watched Roddy intently, as if she could see the gears turning in his head.

But they didn't turn far before grinding. "Then he'll reach the market with no dates at all to sell."

"Plus in that case he can't get back to your oasis, so now you've lost your camel as well as a thousand dates for nothing."

"Then it's not possible, Bijou!"

"It's okay, Roddy, calm down. It's a math problem, so you

have to solve it by math, you can't just guess at the right answer. Look, let's write it down with symbols." She turned her notebook so he could read along as she wrote, $C = camel's\ rate\ of\ eating$.

The doorway to the kitchen darkened, and they both looked up to see Bijou's grandmother, with a mesh sack of groceries hanging from each hand. She looked tired and hot. Bijou pulled her math notebook away from Roddy, and there was a slight tremble in her voice as she said in Yoa, "Oh, Granny, are you back?"

The old woman just nodded. She came inside and set down the bags. "All right, Bijou, go clean up on the porch out front where the men have been. They're getting ready to leave." She gave a slight nod in Roddy's direction.

"Oh!" Bijou stood up. "What time is it?" She tried to guess by glancing out through the doorway, but the kitchen was so much darker than the yard at any time of day that it was impossible to judge the hour by the light.

Her grandmother laughed her soundless two-toothed laugh. "You're asking me, an old villager? I don't even know how to read a clock!" She bent down by the fire and picked up a machete that had been honed so lovingly for so long that its blade was only half its original width. "Maybe five, maybe six, something like that. Time to get dinner ready. Go along now." She turned and went back outside, and Bijou could hear her in the yard calling in Yoa, "Come here, pretty little hen! You were so eager to get in the pot this morning, don't start acting shy now!"

Bijou and Roddy stared at each other in silence, and each noticed the other was shivering. Bijou began gathering up all her school notebooks and pens to clear space on the table for her grandmother to cook. As she snapped shut the satisfying brass buckle of her satchel she said quickly, "The outhouse. Go up through the roof."

Roddy's "What?" was followed immediately by a chicken's scream of protest rising to outraged dignity rising to panic and ending with the whack of the machete landing in the old stump.

Bijou set her satchel on the floor in the corner of the kitchen and went out without looking back at him. All the hair on Roddy's neck was standing up and he had goose bumps on his arms and legs from the hen's death scream. He tried to stop shaking but couldn't.

The old woman came back into the kitchen, the headless body still twitching and spouting blood from its neck as it hung by its feet from her hand. She dropped the hen into an enamel basin to finish bleeding, and washed the machete with a ladleful of clean water. The hen's wings beat against the lip of the basin.

"Excuse me," Roddy stammered, his voice cracking. "I have to go peepee."

The old woman stopped and looked at him. Finally a sentence she could understand—so the strange red-haired boy spoke some French after all. She said slowly in her best village French, "Wait. The men are coming to get you very soon."

"No, I have to go now! Please!"

He sounded so desperate that the old woman asked thoughtfully, "Caca?"

"Yes! Yes! Now!"

She put down the machete just long enough to untie his right hand, then stepped back and watched, machete ready, while he himself untied his left hand and then both feet. Having heard Prosper describe what the boys had done to Théophile, she was no longer in the mood to play flyswatter games with even this harmless-looking white child.

Free of the ropes, Roddy stood up and then bent forward and held his hands over his lower abdomen to suggest an imminent bout of diarrhea—and indeed it was true he felt far from well. The old woman gestured toward the doorway with the machete, and its clean sharp edge sparkled in the firelight. As Roddy came around the table she pointed to the hen now finally motionless in the basin. "I can take your head off that skinny little neck with one swing." She spoke in Yoa, but somehow he understood her meaning perfectly.

Roddy walked out into the yard with the old woman behind him. He gave up the idea of simply running away from her as soon as he felt the pain in his cramped, protesting, long-immobilized legs. The sun must certainly be low—the entire yard was in deep shade from trees and neighboring houses. The old woman tugged on the back of his shirt to turn him away from the main house toward a flimsy-looking outhouse in the far corner of the dirt yard.

They passed the chopping block, coated in fresh blood and surrounded by a coiling pattern of blood spattered in the dust that reminded Roddy of the tie-dyed T-shirt he'd bought when he and his parents first arrived here at the beginning of sixth grade, eager to throw their arms around the enchanting exotic complex reality of Africa. As he stepped around the blood his knees bumped against each other and he almost fell, but the old woman didn't catch him. When they reached the outhouse she explained, more in gestures than in words, that she would wait right here for him to come out. She rested the machete on her shoulder.

Roddy opened the plywood door, and a wall of stench hit him in the face. Willing himself not to gag, he stepped inside, pulled the door shut, and rotated the chunk of wood on a screw that served as the latch. Now he had to turn and face the hole. So little daylight remained, and the wood floor of the outhouse was so dark from the stains of use, that he had some trouble distinguishing the rim of the hole from the pit itself. He wanted to believe the floor was clean, that all the smell was rising out of the hole, but the stench was so strong, so fresh, so immediate, he couldn't stop himself from imagining that the floor all around him was punctuated by piles of carelessly deposited shit—and the more he fought the image the stronger it grew.

He still hadn't dared move his feet, and he'd lost all desire to contribute either peepee or caca to the abundance he imagined to be on display here. Again he felt the gag rising, rising, rising—and then he remembered to drive it back down by whistling, a trick Jesse had taught him on a field trip on one of the first days Roddy felt he might be able to make friends with the other boys in sixth grade who'd lived in Africa their whole lives and who seemed to have nothing in common with him.

So now—without having to make any noise, because it was just the position of the muscles at the back of the throat that held back the vomiting impulse—he whistled the first thing that came into his head, which was "God Save the Queen." And whether it was because of the muscular action, or the memory of befriending Jesse, or the idea of the dear funny old queen herself, or a combination of all three, Roddy began to feel better.

He looked up at the roof of the outhouse, which was low and easily within his reach. It was made of palm thatch, and there was a fairly small gap positioned more or less over the shit hole, maybe for ventilation (but it wasn't working, if so) and maybe to let the rain do some of the cleanup (but it was the dry season). Could he fit through there? If not, he thought it would be easy enough to enlarge the hole by pushing aside the thatch. But how could he climb up there without first taking his chances on standing right in what he expected would be the worst and thickest shit piles around the rim of the hole? Could he find some toehold on the walls? He pressed against one of the plywood walls, shuddering at its sliminess, and the poorly attached plywood bowed outward. It would never support his weight. The roof itself, resting on the posts that formed the corners of the outhouse, looked much stronger. So he'd have to grab hold of the sticks that spanned the top of the walls and on which the thatch rested, and pull himself up through the gap. And if he was wrong and the roof couldn't support him, he'd probably fall straight through the hole into the pit.

But the alternative was to turn around, walk out into the blood-spattered yard, and put himself back into the hands of Prosper and his friends. He couldn't allow himself to think about it any further, so instead he took hold of the middle pair of cross sticks as far forward as he could reach. Noticing that they too were slimy and telling himself it couldn't possibly be urine way up there, he began to whistle again under his breath. "Send her victorious, happy and glorious..."

He heard Bijou's voice behind him in the yard, calling to her grandmother in Yoa. The old woman answered, and a loud discussion followed. It sounded like the old woman was stepping away from the outhouse to talk to Bijou. He wondered whether Bijou was doing it deliberately to help him, since scrambling up through palm thatch would make quite a lot of noise, and if the old woman were still waiting quietly outside the door she'd hear him. If so, he couldn't hesitate any longer.

He jumped up and forward toward the gap in the roof. His head immediately hit the thatch, which was a lot firmer than he'd expected, and his left hand slipped off its cross-stick. As he dropped toward the pit his legs went out automatically and slammed against the plywood walls, which bowed out but slowed his fall just long enough for him to stab his left arm through the gap in the roof, and then his head, and then his right arm. The thatch scraped his back and chest as he dragged himself through the hole. In continuous motion from the time he'd first committed himself and jumped, he saw nothing around him and was never fully on top of the roof, since he began to tumble headfirst down the back side of the outhouse even before his legs were clear of the hole.

Like a well-trained Boy Scout, Roddy curled as he landed, but when his legs arrived, flipping over his head and slamming into the ground, the impact knocked the wind out of him. As he lay there looking at the sky, fighting for breath and so disoriented by his somersault that he no longer knew which way was forward, he listened for the voices of Bijou and her grandmother but heard nothing. Was the old woman already back, waiting by the outhouse door? How long would she give him before she got suspicious and demanded to hear his voice answering from inside as he crouched over the hole?

He rolled over and staggered to his feet, his head still spinning, his lungs fighting for air. The outhouse had been built against the back fence of Prosper's property, and rolling off the roof had put Roddy on the other side of the fence. Ahead of him, cut up unevenly by rainy-season erosion, the ground sloped down into a wasteland gully, one of many that separated the neighborhoods and shanty towns of the city. Doing his best to be careful of his footing on this uneven ground in the fading light, he ran down into the darkness of the gully.

After blundering painfully straight through bushes for a few seconds, he found himself on something like a path and followed it as it zigzagged down the slope. The gully wasn't deep, and in less than a minute he reached the bottom. Here the path ended at a stream, which spread out and turned the last few yards of the path into mud. (People in Prosper's neighborhood used a spot slightly upstream of here to do laundry and to get drinking water when the communal tap out by the main road failed.)

The taller bushes crowded out what little afternoon light remained down here in the gully, and in the premature dusk it was hard to tell whether the path really ended here or if it resumed somewhere on the other side of the stretch of trampled mud. Roddy stopped to consider and listen: aside from his own panting he could hear only the comfortable conversation of frogs and the trickle of the stream falling over stones nearby—no angry voices behind him, no sounds of pursuit. He had escaped.

The skin on his back and sides and stomach stung where sweat now ran into the long scratches he'd gotten forcing his way through the thatch roof, and the fetid smell of the mud here at the bottom of the gully recalled the foul air in the outhouse, but, as he stood at the edge of the stream, panting, the reality of his sudden freedom spread like a shock from the pit of his stomach to every finger and toe.

At that moment, absurdly, unaccountably, Roddy realized he had a fiercer, more urgent erection than he'd ever experienced in his short pubescent life. In his mind's eye he saw Bijou in the firelight of the kitchen: the shining line of her neck from her earlobe to her clavicle, slightly exposed at the opening of her dirty shift as she bent over her math notebook, the curve of her wrist and her palm as she tapped her head with her wooden ruler, deep in thought, the flash of her eyes and mouth when she laughed, looking straight at him across the table.

While his brain knew that without wasting another second he ought to run across the stream and through the mud and up the other side of the gully and keep on running till he was far from Prosper's house and this whole section of the city and maybe not stop running till he was all the way home, his groin knew he had to masturbate—right now.

His fingers trembling, Roddy unbuttoned his shorts and dropped them and his sweat-soaked underpants to his ankles and began to pump. As aroused as he was, as full of long-pent-up intense emotion and the urgent need to release that emotion, he knew it was only going to take him a few seconds to finish. Out of some habitual sense of tidiness he turned to aim toward the bushes, so his semen wouldn't just fly out all over the path.

Now his awareness of the very danger he was courting by not running—even his inability to run if he needed to, with his pants and underwear hobbling him—added to his arousal, and he pumped harder, his breath coming faster.

Something moved in the gloom in front of him, and before he had time to be alarmed his eyes resolved the image in the near-dark and he realized he was looking at Bijou and she was looking at him. He gave a little cry of surprise, but his pumping hand didn't let go or even stutter in its rhythm. As Bijou stepped fully into view, her eyes dancing from Roddy's flushed face down to his pale skinny naked torso and the erection sprouting from his fist, the infectious sparkling mischief in her grin made him laugh—short, rhythmic bursts of laughter that were little more than intensifications of his panting.

Bijou crossed the few feet between them, the beads in her hairdo rattling as she pulled her dirty shift off over her head. In that one move she was completely naked, without even flip-flops on her bare feet, and, as Roddy instinctively let go of his erection to reach out and put both hands on her hips, as bony as his own, she in turn took hold of his penis. It had crossed her mind to explain to him that she'd followed him down into the gully as soon as she could get away, to make sure he was okay—and clearly he was a great deal more than just okay—but as soon as she had the heat of him in her hands she knew it would be better if neither of them said a word.

And so in the next few minutes of urgent silence Roddy became the first among the four boys in his seventh-grade class to have real sex with an actual female person—such an unexpected, astonishing turn of events, considering where Roddy stood in the pecking order with either boys or girls at the American School, that even while it was happening he knew there was no point in ever telling the other boys about Bijou, since they'd never believe him.

NIGHT

1.

MARCEL DIDN'T HAVE a watch, and from the passenger seat he couldn't read the one on Claudio's left wrist, but as the Fourgonette rolled up into the big empty square in front of the Gentleman cigarette factory he could see the sun, far away across the whole smoke-hazy city, setting behind the German's hill, and he imagined that with binoculars he might be able to make out the nightclub—his home for five years now—silhouetted at the top against the red western sky.

Claudio stopped the car. They were alone, and—in what at this hour on a weekday would have been a busy, crowded square—there was nothing to see but the long blank concrete wall of the factory, its whitewash right now pinkish orange as it reflected the last of the light. Behind them a couple of acres of scrub land separated them from the edge of the nearest shanty town: the land belonged to the factory, for future expansion, and the company periodically bulldozed the squatter shacks that sprang up among the weeds. There was no sign of the kidnappers, and this wide-open meeting place had been well chosen to make sudden or surprise arrivals almost impossible. So either the others were running on what the old German had taught Marcel to think of as "African time," or they themselves were early.

If so, it was a miracle, considering the nonsensical and time-wasting detours Marcel's captors had indulged in on the way here—and Marcel was amused to notice he still thought of the boys riding in the cargo box as his captors, though the big

American soldier next to him went out of his way to treat him like an equal. After the stop where the long-haired boy, Jesse, had come back with some kind of pump-action rifle, and after the endless argument there, they drove to a nice neighborhood and the blond boy, Ben, went up a driveway and into a house and came back a few minutes later holding a couple of thousand-franc bills. Marcel couldn't follow what was said, but, considering how pleased Ben and the other boys seemed to be with themselves, he'd guessed Ben had stolen the money from his own house. Marcel wanted to make a mental note of exactly where they were, so he could come back later and carry out his plan of revenge on the parents of Théophile's killer, but there'd been a couple of distractions.

First, a gardener watering the flowers at Ben's house noticed the unfamiliar car parked outside the gates and gave them all a long, careful look—and Marcel felt a strange awareness of being the only African in this group. He wanted to get out of the car and say, "You don't understand! I'm not with them, I'm not their guide or their servant—I'm their prisoner!" But the gardener was almost certainly a Yoa, so Marcel would have to use French, and the whites would understand what he said—and now, especially, was not the time to raise their suspicions. No, he had to be docile and cooperative just a little longer. But how much longer? When would the time be right for action? It frustrated Marcel that his entire plan amounted to waiting in readiness for the right moment to strike.

The second distraction was that, while he and Claudio waited in the front seat for Ben to come back out, Marcel could hear the other two boys standing behind the Fourgonette, talking excitedly in low voices and maybe rubbing or scratching the rear doors. Had they finally noticed the telltale remnants of the *Quincaillerie Chaloub* sign, and were they trying to erase the rest of it in case Marcel himself hadn't yet spotted it? There was no mirror on the passenger side of the car, but Marcel shifted in his seat so he could see into the mirror on Claudio's side. He caught a glimpse of the Chaloub boy gesturing and pointing, maybe at the rear doors, but then he moved and was concealed from view by the corrugated side of the cargo box.

Marcel looked away and pretended to be half asleep when Nabil came around to Claudio's window and said something quietly that made Claudio get out and hold a long conference with the boys behind the car—a muttered discussion in English that ended only when Ben came out of his house waving the money. Then the boys laughed and laughed while they slapped the two real CFA bills over and under the whole stack of odd-looking bills, the ones Jesse had brought back when he showed up with the rifle and the plastic lunch box, and put a rubber band around the wad and stuffed it into the lunch box.

Claudio looked thoughtful when he got back into the car, but as they drove away he cheered up and explained to Marcel that they needed to make one more stop. "We're going to my favorite whorehouse!"

Marcel's jaw dropped. "You need sex?"

Claudio slapped the steering wheel and laughed. "Yes, dammit, I need sex! Who doesn't, right?"

Marcel laughed too, but he found himself wondering yet again whether it would be wiser to give up his hopes for revenge and just open his door at some intersection and run.

"No, seriously," said Claudio, "the sex is for later, remember? When we have the little English bugger back and we're gonna get all those boys laid to celebrate." He chuckled. "And if any of those kids are too scared to get some pussy of their own, they can just watch the Matador do his thing, right? You know what I'm saying?" He clenched his bicep, and the bullfighter tattoo rippled its red cape while Claudio made that whooshing noise again.

Marcel laughed nervously, having no idea what to say.

"Don't tell me you don't like to spice it up a little, man." Claudio punched him in the arm. "Have an audience, a cheering gallery while you get it on with that Italian girl?"

Marcel couldn't even laugh anymore, but he found his face was conveniently frozen in a laugh, and that seemed to satisfy Claudio. They drove on for a while, lost in their own thoughts. When they passed the street leading toward the cigarette factory and didn't turn, Marcel said, "So, if we're not going to the whorehouse, where are we going?"

"No, we are going to the whorehouse. Just not for sex." Marcel waited to hear more, and noticed Claudio seemed conflicted about whether to go on. Could he be weighing what the boys had told him about the paint on the back of the Fourgonette and deciding whether or not he could still trust the African? Marcel said nothing, and finally Claudio seemed to settle his internal debate and said, "I'm going to borrow a gun they keep there."

"Another gun? Don't we already have two?"

"Two? Oh, you mean Marshall Dillon back there with his Daisy? Yeah, right."

Marcel didn't understand what Claudio meant, but he said, "And doesn't the American army issue you with weapons?"

Claudio laughed. "Well, I'm Marine Corps, not Army, but in any case there's no way I'm involving a traceable government-issue firearm in this thing. It's bad enough I'm spending my off-duty getting involved at all, but at least if it's not my gun I can say I was at the pool the whole time."

And then he told Marcel a long story about a stolen gun he used to keep at a brothel in Saigon, which seemed to end with Claudio shooting a customer who was mistreating his favorite hooker in some way, but Marcel couldn't be completely sure, because Claudio kept sprinkling in brothel-related words he must have thought were French but that Marcel assumed were actually Vietnamese, and because Marcel's own attention was divided as he tried to calculate how the addition of yet another gun would affect his plans. If the boy Jesse used his rifle and Claudio used the gun from the whorehouse, who'd get the German's pistol? Might Claudio give it to Marcel himself? Was trusting him enough to tell him about the extra gun a sign that, in spite of the boys' suspicions, Claudio really believed Marcel was on their side against the kidnappers—and believed it enough to hand him a pistol?

Claudio's favorite whorehouse stood in the middle of the shanty town bordering the swamps downstream of the artificial lake built twenty years ago by the colonial French governor—a lake legendary for both its waterskiing and its crocodiles, or as everyone called it, "Lake Don't Let Go of the Rope." Like its neighbors in all directions, the whorehouse was a low one-story shack made partly of mud and wattle, but its roof was tin instead of palm thatch, and after early success the owner had doubled its size by adding a wooden extension to the front, which ended in a low roof overhanging a few cheap tables and chairs. Citronella candles marked the divide between the seating area and the dusty lane where the Fourgonette parked. Two unlit neon signs, one for a Nigerian beer and one for Gentleman cigarettes, hung against the porch posts. A fat woman in a pagne and a head scarf sat at one of the outdoor tables smoking a pipe and watching the new arrivals without expression. It was, in other words, like every other brothel Marcel had ever been to, if you didn't count the handful of white children along for the ride.

He had no great desire to go inside—indeed, he imagined for just a moment he could take advantage of Claudio's absence to switch seats, drive away, and steal the whole carload of boys, to be ransomed or killed at his leisure—but Claudio insisted Marcel go with him. Was he just being friendly, or was this a sign of lack of trust? After letting the boys out of the back of the Fourgonette to get some air, Claudio waved to Marcel to follow him and ducked under the low porch eaves, nodding to the woman in the pagne as they went by.

Inside the whorehouse, Marcel got a sense of what Claudio's ordinary life was like when he wasn't driving murdering little boys around town. For a solid ten minutes, from the moment they pushed through the bead curtain into the darkness of the bar area, Marcel heard nothing but screaming and shouting in French and Yoa.

Some short whore, too dark-skinned to be from this part of the country, was beating Claudio, slapping him over and over, while the skinny bartender, who seemed like he was feverish from a bout of malaria or something worse—constantly mopping his face with a hand towel and fanning himself—just laughed and bantered with Claudio over the whore's head, and the madam, who looked like she might be the twin sister of the woman outside with the pipe, yelled at Claudio that he couldn't have her gun because of what he'd done the last time, and the bartender put the pistol—one of those odd-shaped German things that looked ancient, maybe even from the First World War—out on the bar just to tantalize Claudio, and the madam eventually relented and said he could borrow the pistol, but only if he left his watch as collateral, and then to get the watch back he'd also have to pay his entire bar tab when he returned the gun, and while Claudio argued with the madam the short whore, still slapping him, tried to pull him into the back room, and a few seconds later the two men were out in the dusty shanty town lane again, with the watch still on Claudio's wrist and no First World War pistol in his hand.

Marcel reflected that even in 1973, even in a proudly independent African nation, even in a roomful of Africans, an African man accompanying a white man was invisible—no one had said a word to Marcel or even directed a curious glance his way the entire frantic ten minutes. Maybe they took him for the American's chauffeur.

"Yeah, well, fuck that shit." Claudio grinned. "I'd never see my watch again if I took it off in there." He glanced up at the setting sun. "So I guess we'll just go to the meeting with the firepower we have." As he closed the boys back into the cargo box he said to them, "And we'll go to a different place to celebrate afterward. They won't have an Italian chick like this place, but I bet you boys are more curious about a hot little chocolate number anyway, aren't you? Don't worry, the Matador understands."

When it became clear they were alone in the big square in front of the cigarette factory, Claudio let the boys out of the back and they milled around, stretching their legs. Marcel got out too, and he watched while Claudio ambled out to the middle of the square and set the lunch box on display on an upturned cracked green plastic bucket he'd found in the windblown litter near the parked car. Then Claudio came back, and he and Marcel each sat on one of the old-fashioned front fenders of the Fourgonette, smoking and saying nothing. A gust of sunset wind slid the green bucket a few feet but didn't tip it over. A stray dog passing through the square noticed the group and came over to beg, and the boys called him closer to get him within range before pelting him with stones.

The last sunlight faded from the square, and the electric lights along the factory wall flickered on. Claudio glanced at his watch. "Almost six-thirty. Your friends coming?"

"They're not my friends."

Claudio seemed not to have heard. "According to the

ransom note, your friends said they were going to kill the boy if we weren't here to make the trade at six. We got here about ten after, by my watch anyway. So have they killed him?"

Marcel shook his head. "It's Africa—ten minutes is nothing."

"Let's hope so, for the kid's sake and for yours."

Marcel exhaled his smoke carefully. "What do you mean?"

"You know what I mean."

The three boys had gathered a little distance away to listen, though the two men spoke as quietly as one could across the hood of a car. Marcel felt a slight chill when he noticed the boys still had their hands full of stones, though the dog was long gone, yelping away across the square with his tail tucked.

Nabil said, "Hey," and they all looked up as the cream-colored Peugeot 404 came into view at the opposite end of the square. The car paused when the men inside spotted the Fourgonette, then turned and parked at the foot of the factory wall. The entire diagonal expanse of the square separated the two groups.

Claudio said, "Here we go," but so much under his breath that he might have been talking to himself. Though he'd gone from embassy guard duty in Saigon to the same detail here, there was no question the former involved more adrenaline than the latter, and right now he realized how much he missed it. But he stayed seated on the fender of the Fourgonette, waiting.

Marcel felt his heart pounding—whatever he was going to do, it was coming soon now, and if he let the moment slip away he'd forever be shamed by the memory of having failed Théophile—but he took his cue from Claudio and stayed seated on the other fender.

The three boys came forward, stones dribbling from their hands, and stopped at an invisible line level with the front bumper of the Fourgonette. None of them spoke.

The doors of the Peugeot opened, and Prosper and Auguste

got out, while Danton remained at the wheel. Auguste stayed by the car, and Prosper began to walk slowly out toward the lunch box.

"That's the leader," Nabil said to Claudio, "definitely the scariest one."

"Okay, but where's your buddy? Do you see him in the car?"

Though almost no light remained in the sky, the square was fairly well lit by the fluorescent lights on the factory wall, but the angle of the artificial light around the Peugeot left the interior of the car in deep shadow. Squinting, Jesse said, "I don't think he's there."

"Well, fuck," said Claudio, sounding annoyed as he stood up and took a step forward. He called out loudly in French across the square, "Hey, you! Stop!" Prosper continued to walk slowly toward the bucket in the center of the square. "I said stop! Where's the boy?"

Still walking, Prosper called back calmly, "When I see the money's there, you'll get the boy."

"That's not right!" Ben hissed. "That's not the agreement!"

"Relax, kid, the Matador's got this." Claudio pulled the German's pistol—Marcel's pistol—out of the waistband at the small of his back and held it up, aimed at the sky. He called in French, "I am a U.S. Marine Corps sharpshooter, and if you take another step I will shoot you through the eyeball." He wasn't in fact a sharpshooter, especially not in this light and with a handgun, but he'd just remembered the French word for "sharpshooter" and couldn't resist using it.

Prosper, however, stopped where he was, about twenty feet from the lunch box. "We said no police."

"I'm not police, and I don't give a damn about arresting you, and I will shoot your ass if you don't produce the boy."

Prosper stood still, considering. Auguste's voice came across the square, calling in Mtom. "Marcel? Is that you?"

Marcel stood up and called back. "Who else could it be?"

Auguste laughed. "Are you all right?"

"I'll be fine in a few minutes."

"Listen, Marcel..." While Auguste hesitated, Nabil edged closer to Marcel to reduce the chances of him just walking away from them across the square to his friends.

Auguste laughed nervously. "There's a complication..."

Claudio turned to Marcel. "Okay, that's enough talking in your lingo. From now on you talk in French so everyone can understand, you get me?"

"Yes, sir," said Marcel in English—amounting to about half of his total English vocabulary picked up from the movies. Ben laughed at the look on Claudio's face.

Jesse went around behind the car and took Claudio's sleeve. "Shit, Matador," he murmured, "you should've let them talk. I can speak their language, and the other guy was about to tell him something important."

"About what?"

"I don't know—you cut him off. He said there's like a..." Jesse searched for the right translation for the Mtom word. "Like a problem, a muddy situation."

"Muddy?"

"Not real mud, it's an image. It's hard to translate."

"Does it mean they killed him already?"

"I don't know, man! It just means there's a problem. If you'd just let them go on talking..."

From the middle of the square Prosper called out in French, "Mister American Army!"

Claudio called back, "What?"

"We need to discuss the agreement. But there's no reason to be shouting at each other. Why don't you come out here and talk it over with me?"

Claudio laughed. "Yeah, right. Where's the boy?"

"That's exactly what we need to talk about. Put your gun down and come out here unarmed." Prosper stretched out his arms and turned in a slow circle, reaching back to flip up the tail of his shirt to show he was hiding nothing. "As you can see, I myself am already unarmed." Since from the Fourgonette Prosper was little more than a silhouette against the factory lights, his display proved nothing.

Ben whispered, "When they took Roddy away that guy had a big hunting knife."

Hearing Ben but not responding, Claudio thought it over for a while but finally shrugged. He held the German's pistol up so Prosper could see it, then reached across the hood of the Fourgonette to hand it to... to whom? Marcel, standing right there, was so struck by the unlikelihood of getting his own gun back that it took him a second to put out his hand—and in that second Nabil, still crowding him to keep him in line, moved faster and reached past Marcel and took the pistol. He'd seen Marcel's aborted reach, and now he gave him a long hard look in the eye while he said to Claudio, "Okay, Matador, I got you covered."

"Terrific." Claudio laughed, his sarcasm mixed with affection for Nabil. "All I ask is, for fuck's sake don't shoot me."

As Claudio strolled out to the center of the square, Prosper drifted almost imperceptibly closer to the lunch box, so that, by the time Claudio stopped, the two men were separated only by the upturned plastic bucket. They took a moment to size each other up in silence.

Prosper couldn't confidently place the age or status of the soldier facing him. "Are you the boy's father?"

"No, they're friends of mine, and I'm helping them out."

"Congratulations. You have nice friends. Do you know what your friends did this morning to my friend Théophile?" No one would have been more surprised than Théophile to hear Prosper describe him as a friend.

"Cut the crap. Where's my friend Roddy?"

Prosper began to laugh. "It's a little embarrassing."

"What, you're embarrassed you killed him already?"

"What?" Prosper stopped laughing. "What are you talking about? You think we're cold-blooded murderers, like those children over there?"

Back by the Fourgonette, Ben shivered. "What are they talking about? And why's it taking so long? And where's Roddy?" Having answers to none of those questions, Nabil and Jesse ignored him.

Claudio waited in silence, and Prosper went on. "As I say, it's embarrassing. The boy is... well, in fact, the boy is sick."

"Sick?" Claudio leaned in. "What do you mean, sick? What kind of sick?"

Prosper smiled and patted his stomach. "He has the runs. Something we fed him today disagreed with him."

"So you're taking him to the hospital."

"No, no, don't exaggerate—you white people are always overreacting. Maybe he just found my grandmother's village spicing a little too strong for him, that's all."

"A kid who's sick needs to get home to his own bed and take some medicine. So where is he?"

Prosper laughed again. "Honestly? Right now he's probably squatting over the shit hole in my yard." He couldn't resist saying it, though he immediately regretted giving away where Roddy had been kept. "Even if the boy had wanted to come, I would've been concerned about the upholstery of my car."

"Who's taking care of him? He's just a kid."

"Don't worry, my grandmother is with him, and she knows exactly what to do. She'll make him a medicine from the leaves of a certain plant... I don't know the name in French." Prosper was beginning to enjoy himself. "Anyway, we decided we should come here at six even without the boy, because we knew you would worry."

Claudio said, "Thanks, very kind of you." He felt a little at a loss. The story rang true: it was exactly the kind of thing that had happened all the time in Vietnam, and it was certainly embarrassing to explain to your CO that you'd failed to do this or that because at the critical moment you were squatting behind a bush evacuating liquid shit. The only part of Prosper's story that didn't fit in Claudio's mind was that, if he was telling the truth, he ought to have announced right away that Roddy was sick, rather than strolling over to the money without saying anything.

Claudio glanced back at the boys and Marcel, waiting in an uneven line by the car, then turned to Prosper again. "So now what?"

"Now we wait."

"Why don't we just agree on another rendezvous time, and meet again in an hour or two, when the boy feels better?"

Prosper chuckled. "You're a very clever man, Mister American Army. Now that you've seen me, and my friends, and my car, and you know my grandmother is taking care of the boy, of course you want some time to go get the police or the Green Berets—or even just to follow us yourself. No, no, my friend, the boy will feel better very soon, and till then nobody leaves."

"So we just wait?"

"That's right, we wait. Be patient: it won't be long. The boy wants to see his friends as much as you want to see him." Prosper reached down for the lunch box. "And in the meantime I'll check the money."

Claudio slapped his big hand down onto the lunch box. "Stop right there." At both ends of the square the onlookers leaned forward, startled that after all the talking the two men had suddenly come to grips, like contestants getting ready to arm wrestle.

Their faces now inches apart, Claudio and Prosper eyed each other. Prosper said, "Your side of the bargain is the money. Our side of the bargain is the boy. I've explained about the boy, and his absence is no fault of mine. Is there some reason I shouldn't count the money?"

"The reason is, I'll stick this whole lunch box up your ass before I let you touch the money without seeing the boy first."

Neither of them moved, Claudio holding the lunch box down and Prosper resting his hand on the upturned base of the bucket an inch away from the lunch box. In his peripheral vision Claudio kept track of Prosper's other hand for any sign that he might reach for a knife.

Over by their car, the boys watched as Auguste, far across the square, lifted something up from behind the open car door he was leaning against.

"Holy shit," said Jesse, "He has a rifle." He ran to the back of the Fourgonnette and returned with his BB gun. Now Marcel had Nabil on one side of him and Jesse on the other, both armed. When the time came to get a weapon, which should he choose? Jesse would be the easier one to overpower—Nabil had a year's height advantage over the other boys—but Marcel had spent five years caring for and taking target practice with the pistol now in Nabil's hand, and, if he needed to fire off a quick shot when seconds mattered, familiarity was essential.

Claudio said to Prosper, still just inches away, "Listen to me. Being surrounded by all these amateurs with guns when you and I are at close quarters like this makes it more than likely that we're just going to get shot by our own people. I recommend that you and I slowly disengage." Prosper nodded but didn't move. Claudio said, "All right, I'll go first."

Taking his hand off the lunch box, he straightened up. A

moment later, Prosper did the same. Everyone at the edges of the square breathed.

Ben called out, "Hey, who's that?"

From around the furthest corner of the cigarette factory wall, about equidistant from both groups, a small figure came loping into view. It passed into and out of the pools of fluorescent light from the factory walls, but before it had crossed even a quarter of the distance toward them the boys knew who it was by its familiar, awkward, somehow peculiarly British knock-kneed run.

Jesse screamed, as loud as he'd ever screamed, "It's Roddy!"

It was indeed Roddy, and he had an enormous dreamy grin on his face.

Before Bijou left Roddy, when it grew so dark they could barely see each other in the dense brush at the bottom of the gully, she explained that she'd tell her grandmother and Prosper she'd gone looking for the escaped prisoner down there and hadn't found him—he must have run the other direction, along the fence and out to the road, when he got away through the outhouse roof. She showed him the path he should follow, across the muddy stream and up the other side of the gully, then gave him one last, long kiss—in truth a little fumbled, since neither of them had much experience at this—and ran back through the brush toward her house. They'd said nothing stupid about trying to meet again.

In the gathering darkness the twists in the path and in the contours of the gully itself would have confused even a clear-headed person, and Roddy's head was spinning as he relived every astonishing moment of the past few minutes while he stumbled along. So when at last he came out of the gully into a built-up neighborhood again, the first lane he found didn't immediately lead, as Bijou had said it would, to a busy street where pedestrians would provide safety in numbers and a taxi would whisk him home. But Roddy was so full of euphoria that he had no room left for anxiety, and he jogged for quite a while without concern along featureless unlit lanes that led nowhere in particular.

At certain spots he could see a vista of other hills and other neighborhoods, and if he'd known the city as well as Nabil or Jesse did he could have oriented himself by the characteristic lights of the Presidential palace or the Sheraton Hotel in one direction or the unmistakable green-yellow-red of the lone traffic signal downtown in the other direction. But he saw nothing beyond the ecstatic fire inside his own head, till a glow of fluorescent lights a few blocks away to his left drew his attention as he crossed the intersection of a couple of dusty lanes. Those lights overlooked the cigarette factory walls and not the busy commercial street Roddy expected, but even as he jogged into the large paved square and toward his friends he had no idea he'd inadvertently delivered himself to the place named in the ransom note, since he'd never been near the factory and didn't recognize its walls and he was in any case still lost in a joyful daze.

As the other boys jumped up and down and screamed Roddy's name and waved him frantically toward them— unnecessary, since that was where he was headed anyway—no one was more surprised or had to work harder to hide it than Prosper. When he'd come to fetch the boy he'd found his grandmother waiting patiently, machete in hand, by the outhouse. Forcing open the door and finding the place empty and the roof mostly caved in, he'd known right away it was too late to recover the prisoner. The gully that wound along behind his neighborhood was densely overgrown, and night was falling, and not even a child would be foolish enough to hang around at the bottom waiting to be caught. There was no point in shouting at his grandmother—inconceivable disrespect in any case—and even before Bijou returned empty-handed from searching the gully Prosper had moved on.

While Danton and Auguste swore and kicked things and moaned theatrically about fate or the gods or whatever it was that wished them ill and conspired to foil all their schemes and keep them poor, Prosper quietly made a new plan. He saw a way to dangle the boy's arrival in front of his parents—for that was whom he expected to meet at the rendezvous—long enough to put his hands on the ransom money and get away. Confronting the stubborn and wary American soldier, instead of the frightened naive couple he expected, had been a complication, and Prosper was only a few moments away from giving up the whole job as an honorable failure when the boy ran into view and solved all his problems.

Now, as he reached down and took hold of the lunch box, Prosper said to Claudio, "You see? You were wrong to doubt me, but I won't take offense. The boy is yours, exactly as promised, and the money is ours."

Claudio, confused by the surprising arrival of Roddy on foot from the direction opposite to the way the kidnappers' car had come, strained in the gloom to see whether Roddy was really okay as he rejoined his friends in a hail of backslaps and head noogies. As a result in all the excitement he forgot for a moment that his own side of the bargain was not exactly as promised, and that his plan had been the same as Prosper's in reverse: he hoped to retrieve Roddy before the kidnappers noticed they were getting Monopoly money. All he could think to do as Prosper backed away with the lunch box was to nod in agreement.

Marcel had no idea he was about to do anything, and certainly no plan. But the excited victorious laughter of the four boys was unbearable, and he heard himself shout across the square in Mtom, "Auguste! The money! Tell Prosper the money's not right!"

The next moment he was shoved hard, so that he lost his balance and fell against the fender of the Fourgonette. Steadying himself there and turning, he saw the boy named Jesse standing there with his fist raised. "We told you no more talking in Mtom!" But Jesse, first of all furious at Marcel's sudden betrayal and then flooded by the disturbing, even violating sensation of knocking over a grown man—something he'd never done before, and indeed couldn't physically have done till his growth spurt this year—had slipped up and yelled at Marcel in Mtom. He knew from the look on his face that Marcel had noticed, and they stared at each other. Nabil stepped up next to Jesse and glared at Marcel, the pistol obvious in his hand.

"Prosper!" Across the square Auguste shouted in French, his voice high and urgent. "Something's wrong! Marcel says to check the money!"

When Prosper first leaned over the lunch box he'd seen, through the clear plastic lid, the face of a thousand-franc bill. Now he opened the box and took out the money, throwing the box aside. The thickness of the wad felt right. He noticed the American soldier backing away from him.

Roddy's high piping voice screamed out, "Why are you paying them anything? I escaped!"

Still watching Prosper and warily backing away—his forgetfulness about the Monopoly money cured by Auguste's shout—Claudio yelled back to Roddy, "What did you say?"

"I said I escaped! I got away! Don't give them any money!"

After a first confusing riffle through the stack of bills, Prosper fanned out the money more carefully. Between the top bill and the bottom bill, both of them real CFA currency, lay an array of bills in extraordinary colors, with denominations ranging from one to five hundred, each bill featuring nothing more than a tiny cartoonish picture of a train engine. With quick strides Prosper advanced straight at Claudio, screaming, "You cheated us!"

Claudio stood his ground. "And you cheated us!"

Out of habit, Prosper reached behind his back for his pistol, but it wasn't there. "You fucking white bastards! You think you can go on doing this shit to us forever? That time is over!" Anger and humiliation overcoming his normal better judgement, and with the whole wad of bills, good and bad, still clenched in one fist while his other hand reached for the hunting knife he'd made sure to keep with him, Prosper threw himself on Claudio—a mistake, since Claudio was not only bigger and more fit but, as a Marine, had abundant training in hand-to-hand combat. He slapped the knife aside, then knocked Prosper off his feet, and was poised to drop on him and apply a choke hold, when a shot rang out and Prosper screamed.

Little was clear at that moment, including who'd fired. Even later, when Auguste was known to have shot first, his intentions remained in dispute. He said he was trying to protect Prosper because he thought the American soldier was about to kill him with his bare hands. But, though he was steadying his hunting rifle across the top of the open doorframe of the Peugeot, his aim was off—and possibly Danton moving in the driver's seat, in response to the fight in the middle of the square at the moment Auguste pulled the trigger, bounced the car enough to account for what happened. In any case the bullet didn't hit Prosper, but it ricocheted off the paved ground close enough to him to cause a spray of tar and dirt to sting the top of his head, and the scream expressed more his startled expectation of death than even the transient pain.

The deflected bullet rose and smacked into the hood of the Fourgonette, and it was that loud metallic ding right next to them that the boys heard first, before the report of the gun or Prosper's scream. Ben shouted, "Jesus Christ!" and they all ducked.

Nabil fell flat on the ground like the rest, and then realized that, as the one entrusted with the pistol, he ought to be doing something to protect Claudio. He rose onto his elbows and extended the pistol in front of him, looking for a target. Out in the middle of the square Claudio was crouching down and looking around, trying to figure out who'd fired and whether the bullet had been meant for him or for Prosper, and Prosper was rolling over and realizing he was not in fact dead. Over on the other side, Danton, inside the car, was yelling at Auguste, outside the car, for having shot Prosper.

An enormous weight struck Nabil from above and crushed him flat against the ground, knocking the wind out of him and jamming his chin hard into the dirt. Twelve hours ago Marcel had been ready to spend his own money on taxi fare to deliver four trespassing vandal children back to their parents for punishment. Starting with the murder of Théophile, those twelve hours had been filled with violence, humiliation, imprisonment, and insult, and through all the abuse Marcel had waited and watched for his moment, unsure what he would do when the time came but determined to be ready for it. And now, with the hood of the Fourgonette still ringing from the ricochet of Auguste's bullet, Marcel saw the moment had arrived, and he threw himself with all his weight onto Nabil's back.

The impact knocked the pistol out of Nabil's hand, and Marcel pushed the boy's face into the dirt while he reached over him and got the familiar grip of the German's gun back into his own palm. With his fingers locked in the boy's hair and the muzzle pressed to his ear, Marcel rolled off to one side and into a sitting position, pulling Nabil up with him. His plan, to the extent he had a plan, was to shoot the other boys for Théophile and keep the Chaloub boy for ransom—and hopefully Prosper and his friends would have learned enough from the fiasco of the first kidnapping that the second one would go more smoothly.

In all the excitement and the shouting and the darkness in the square, it took a moment for the other boys to notice what was happening right next to them, and by the time they did it was too late. So when Marcel sat up with Nabil and aimed the pistol at them, they could do nothing but stare helplessly. Jesse was the closest, but something in Marcel resisted—the part that couldn't help feeling in some way connected to a boy who spoke Mtom like his own brother—and he shifted his aim to Ben, the worst of them, the real killer. But the last boy, Roddy, was in the way, and, in the moment Marcel hesitated over shooting Roddy, Nabil shouted, "Matador, help!"

Marcel swung the pistol and smacked Nabil on the side of the head, knocking him down, but it was too late. Claudio had already spun around and was sprinting flat out toward them from the middle of the square. Auguste fired again from far away, and, though this shot also missed Claudio, at least this time it didn't hit the ground first but ricocheted directly off the fender of the Fourgonette. Undeterred by the gunshot behind him or the metallic ding in front of him, Claudio ran straight for Marcel.

As Marcel watched Claudio coming closer every second, running in some kind of posture Marcel assumed was the product of American military training in how to advance under fire, he remembered how this odd man-child had befriended him today, how he'd freed him from the hellish cargo box over the objections of the boys, how he'd fed him and given him a shower at the American Club, how he'd looked forward to treating him to a celebratory night at a whorehouse, even the innocent glee with which he showed off his bullfighter tattoo—

and Marcel was surprised at how clear it was to him that none of that mattered.

Regardless of how friendly and open he could be with an African and a man of his own age, in the end the American soldier was on the side of the white boys and would always be on the side of the white boys. Seeing in his mind's eye the Matador's less famous tattoo, the one that showed a man like Claudio with an angel's wings, Marcel thought, "Yes, 'Only God Can Judge Me.'" And then he braced himself to shoot Claudio from twenty feet away.

But before Marcel could pull the trigger, Auguste fired again from across the square, and this time there was no ricochet, because the bullet hit Claudio and stayed in him. Auguste fired once more, as if to prove the previous shot was no fluke, and that bullet too hit Claudio squarely. It could just have been his momentum, but Claudio kept on coming, and when he was ten feet away Marcel thought he himself might have to finish the job. But then Claudio's legs gave way and he slumped to his knees, staring in surprise right at Marcel, and then, with a whooshing exhalation much like the sound effect he provided when he flexed his matador's cape, he fell face first in the dirt.

Maybe it was the reality of close-up violent death, after so many hours of threatened violence looming just out of sight—or maybe it was the realization that nothing, no protector, now stood between them and the Africans' revenge—but seeing Claudio brought down charging like a big-game animal unfroze the boys, and their instinctive recoil from his collapsing body turned directly into flight. In the moment it took Marcel to decide he didn't need to pump still another bullet into the American soldier, three of the boys scrambled to comparative safety behind the Fourgonette. Marcel still had the fourth one, the Chaloub boy, the only one he wanted to keep alive, but Nabil began to squirm like a cat in his hands and bit him hard.

While Marcel wrestled with Nabil, slapping him when got a chance with the big, open-handed slaps that would have been sufficient punishment for everything twelve hours ago, Prosper got up off the ground in the middle of the square and ran back toward the Peugeot to get his rifle. He met Auguste running out toward him, and stopped him and tried to wrestle the rifle from Auguste's hands.

There were more rifles in the trunk of the Peugeot, but Prosper wanted this one: because it was his own and he didn't want to have to use Danton's while Auguste went on using his, and because in the time it would take him to run all way to the car and fumble around in the trunk the action on the other side of the square would be over, and because he couldn't quell the small suspicion that Auguste had almost killed him not quite by accident and he didn't want to give him another chance.

Auguste, in turn, saw nothing wrong with his own shooting so far—the right people were down and the right people were safe, after all—and therefore saw no reason why he should just hand over his weapon to Prosper like a servant. So the two of them stood there in the square, pulling the rifle back and forth between them and cursing at each other, and Danton climbed out of the Peugeot and shouted at both of them to stop behaving like children.

Marcel finally pinned the squirming Nabil face-up to the ground by putting his knees on the boy's shoulders. He rested the muzzle of the pistol on Nabil's forehead and shouted, "Do you want to die, Chaloub?" It would have been simpler just to pull the trigger, but Marcel really wanted to subdue the boy and keep him alive. Even a fraction of the wealth of the Chaloub family, handed over in ransom, would make it possible for Marcel to send some kind of compensation to Théophile's parents, and still have enough left over to give up guarding the nightclub, to get married, to start a business of his own, and—

from what he could earn by his own care and labor if only he had the seed money to make a start—to build a house, a good house, made of concrete blocks, plastered and painted, with a tin roof, next to his father's house in the village.

Then Marcel heard a strange pop nearby and felt a sharp pain in his left eye. When he put his hand up to find out what was wrong it came away covered in blood, and then he realized he could see nothing with that eye, nothing but blood. As he stepped back, trying to wipe the blood away to see if he still had an eye, Nabil scrambled away to the Fourgonette.

Looking up with his still good right eye, Marcel saw Jesse, who was standing up in the rear opening of the cargo box, facing him across the corrugated roof of the car and holding that strange John Wayne pump-action rifle. Marcel raised his pistol, but Jesse ducked behind the cargo box, and anyway the blood must have spread to his right eye too, because Marcel now realized he could see almost nothing.

While the kidnappers across the square argued over Prosper's rifle at the tops of their voices, and Marcel, hunched over, blindly spun in circles trying to wipe the blood out of his eyes on any surface—skin or clothing—that wasn't already soaked in blood, Nabil turned the key and tried to start the Fourgonette. Marcel could hear the ignition firing over and over, with no result, and while Nabil called to the other boys for a push Marcel screamed across the square, "You idiots! Stop fighting and help me!" But he wasn't sure they could even hear him.

There was no point in wasting bullets when he couldn't see to aim, so, following the sound of the engine turning over and over and failing to start, Marcel threw himself against the front bumper of the Fourgonette. Leaning so far over that he was almost parallel to the ground, he dug his toes into the dirt. He knew a strong man could hold back a Deux Chevaux this way, even if the engine was running, and the Citroën Fourgonette was nothing but a Deux Chevaux with a cargo box, and till Nabil got the engine started it had no force to oppose him except the other boys pushing from behind.

Nabil shouted out his window, "He's pushing back! Push, you motherfuckers!"

But, instead of pushing, Jesse stepped around to the side of the Fourgonette and raised his Daisy rifle again. Marcel heard that odd little pop once more, and this time it felt like someone had struck a match on his left cheek. He reached up to find out what had happened, but there was still so much blood on his face from the earlier shot in the eye that it was impossible to tell. He heard another pop, but this one seemed to have missed him completely, and he put his head as far down as he could, hoping to use the curve of the hood to shield his face.

Now blinded by blood and relying on nothing but sounds to follow what was going on, Marcel heard a real gunshot behind him—it was Prosper's rifle, going off harmlessly into the air, as he finally pulled it out of Auguste's hands—and then Prosper shouted, "Hold on!" and began running toward him. With the struggle over the rifle now ended, Danton, never more than a noisy spectator, jumped back into the Peugeot and started the engine. He meant to drive across the square and stop in front of the Fourgonette, blocking its escape.

Marcel heard Prosper shout, "Marcel, look out!" But before he could do anything—and what could he have done, not knowing what to look out for?—Ben had run around the side of the Fourgonette and shoved Marcel hard enough that his hands, slick with his own blood, lost their grip on the bumper, and—since he was already stretched almost parallel to the ground—he fell flat on his face.

Now, with a cheer, the boys pushed harder than ever before, and, having suddenly nothing to oppose it, the Fourgonette rolled right over Marcel without touching him. The engine coughed, coughed again, and came rattling to life. Without waiting for Nabil to brake, in fact while he was accelerating, each of the boys jumped into the car by the nearest way—Jesse and Roddy into the cargo box, and Ben into the front passenger seat.

Thinking, in all the confusion, that the Fourgonette had actually crushed Marcel rather than merely passing over him, Prosper recoiled in shock as he ran. While the boys were hopping in, the car was still moving slowly enough to catch up to, and Prosper sprinted on a diagonal to intercept it—and was himself almost run down. Danton honked, Prosper dodged the wrong way, and the fender of his own Peugeot brushed him staggering aside while Danton hit the brakes.

Having lost those precious seconds, Prosper and Danton could only watch as the Fourgonette picked up speed, with nobody but Auguste left to chase it. Even Auguste, unarmed and out of breath, gave up when Jesse, sitting in the bed of the cargo box with his legs dangling outside and the rear doors flapping, aimed the BB gun back along the road at him. The Fourgonette rattled away out of the square and down the road into the neighborhood around the factory, its rear doors still flapping as it went out of sight.

Auguste walked slowly back to the others, holding out his palms in futility. Danton got out of the Peugeot, and in silence the three kidnappers went over to Marcel, who'd pulled himself up to his hands and knees but was still looking down at the ground.

"You all right?" There was no answer, and Danton squatted next to him. "Hey, Marcel? You all right?"

"I think they shot out my eye."

Danton turned Marcel's chin toward him. "Fuck, that's a lot of blood." He got out the big bottle of water he kept in the trunk of the Peugeot for topping up the radiator and poured it over Marcel's face. "Well, you've got a big scratch on your cheek."

"No, it's not that, it's my left eye."

Danton poured more water over the eye, and Auguste aimed a flashlight at Marcel's face. Danton used his fingernails to pick at something. He laughed. "Look at this, Marcel. This airgun pellet hit you right above the eye, under the eyebrow, and stayed there. Your eye's fine."

Marcel blinked and looked around, shutting his right eye to test his left. It was true: his eye ached and stung, but he could see. "Thank God... And thank you, cousin." He squeezed Danton's hand.

Prosper looked up from his examination of Claudio's body. "This American soldier has nothing on him except his I.D. tags —his pockets are empty."

"Then I guess I saw him give his last fifty francs to a beggar downtown."

Prosper laughed and shook his head. "Stupid Americans."

"Take his watch at least," said Auguste. "It's a good one."

Marcel, not knowing he was going to say it, said, "I want the watch."

Prosper shrugged and handed it to him, and Marcel put what for some reason he thought of as the Matador's whorehouse watch on his own wrist. Prosper lifted Claudio's head and pulled the chain off his neck. He examined the dog tags in the palm of his hand, then held them up for the others to see.

Auguste laughed. "So that's what we get for our whole day's work: a watch and a tin necklace. Nice kidnapping job, guys."

Prosper thought of a hundred retorts, but in the presence of his kill Auguste had gained some rank, and anyway he knew Auguste would just bring up, yet again, Prosper's foolish decision to let his grandmother and the little girl guard the prisoner, so he said nothing and instead threw the dog tags as far as he could into the vacant scrub land across from the factory.

"Okay," said Danton. "Now what?"

Prosper nudged the body with his toe. "Well, first, we get the fuck out of here. People in this neighborhood know better than to get curious when they hear shooting in the night—but still, no point hanging around till someone catches us with a dead American soldier."

Danton nodded. "And then?"

"And then..." Prosper shook his head. He wanted to remain in charge, to be the one the others looked to for instructions, but he was at a loss. Twelve hours and nothing to show for it.

"And then," said Marcel, massaging his eye, "we go find the white boys. I know where they live, because they were stupid enough to show me their houses. So we go find the boys, and we kill them, and then this is over."

The other men looked at each other and then at Marcel. It was hard to believe this could be the same man who'd confronted them by the bar of the nightclub early this morning with high-minded notions about poachers and trespassers and the wishes of the old dead German. But they had yet to hear how Marcel had spent his day.

2.

"SO, RODDY, you gonna tell us what happened or what?"

Nabil had driven without stopping from the cigarette factory to this overgrown vacant strip wedged between the railroad tracks and the back side of the downtown commercial block that included the Jeune Afrique department store. It had been an almost instinctive choice of hiding place: Nabil and Jesse had started coming back here after they found it in fourth grade— slipping through the alleyways between the buildings into their own private land, a world of garbage, feral cats, and a hundred scattered termite mounds at the center of downtown—while their parents thought they were safely occupied sitting on the floor in a back corner of the nearby French bookstore reading *Tanguy et Laverdure* comic books without buying anything. But back here was better than any comic book, and they could pilot their own Mirage III jets around the termite mounds, refueling in midair before the next raid.

Letting anyone else into the secret had been a big step, and they'd known Ben for more than a year before bringing him back here. When Roddy moved here in sixth grade his invitation had come more quickly, and if they thought about it Nabil and Jesse would have admitted it wasn't so much because of any special quality in Roddy but because the place itself had lost some of its magic: maybe it was Ben who'd already spoiled it, by stubbornly not understanding the fighter pilot game, or maybe it was just a part of growing up, and as they got older they needed a place with stronger magic, like the Club Balafon.

Roddy kicked thoughtfully at the base of the eight-foot-tall termite mound behind which they'd parked. "It was nothing much. They tied me to a chair and made me eat gross food."

"That's it? The whole day?" Jesse picked up a stone and flicked it toward what might have been a feral cat or maybe even a cane rat—it was hard to tell, since the only illumination came from the street lights a block away, and the termite mounds threw long overlapping shadows. "You sounded like you were scared shitless when they brought you back up to the nightclub."

"No." Roddy fought back a quick picture of Théophile's fly-covered corpse on the verandah. "I was just worried because I thought something had happened to you guys."

"Oh, right." Nabil laughed.

"There was a creepy old woman with only two teeth." Roddy kicked the termite mound again. Though Prosper's grandmother had been a lot tougher on him at the end than at the beginning, Roddy felt an odd discomfort, a small betrayal, as he mocked her—and he was certainly not even going to mention Bijou's existence. "And then I pretended to be sick and went to the outhouse and climbed out through the roof and ran away."

"You're James fucking Bond." Ben aimed for sarcasm, but even he could hear the envy in his voice—he desperately wished he'd been the one chosen to be kidnapped.

"I guess. But right now I just really, really want to go home."

"Home?" Nabil snorted. "Claudio the Matador just got shot right in front of us like an animal and all you want to do is go home?"

"Well..." Roddy felt a lump rising in his throat and was grateful the darkness hid the tears in his eyes. "It was awful, and I definitely think we should tell the police, but I'm really tired of people being dead, and I'm tired of being told it's my fault when it isn't."

"Don't be a fucking crybaby," said Ben. "The Matador was there to help you. "

"And you fucked the whole thing up by showing up again like a retard instead of really running away." Nabil shook his head.

"But I feel like you guys started it when you killed the watchman's friend, and——"

"What? You shut the fuck up, Roddy!" Ben shoved Roddy, and Roddy shoved back.

"He's right, you know." They stopped in surprise and turned to Jesse, who sounded solemn. Looking gravely at the ground and assuming the round oily tones of one of the preachers in the Canadian mission—his roommate Kevin's father, actually— Jesse said, "Claudio died for our sins... Praise Jesus... Amen." They stared at him, still not sure he was joking. He laughed and did a little jig on a low termite mound. "And, if it was all our fault, that means all the more that we need to avenge the Matador's death to make it up to him."

Nabil ran up the side of Jesse's termite mound and howled, "Revenge!"

Ben ran up the other side and beat his chest like Tarzan. "Revenge!"

Still putting on the voice of Kevin's preacher dad, Jesse bellowed, "Vengeance is ours, sayeth us!"

Roddy said nothing, but he knew there was no point anymore in talking about going home.

They pushed the Fourgonette out of the vacant strip of termite mounds and through the alleyway between Jeune Afrique and the bookstore to get the car started: their second time today doing that at the same spot, but at this hour on a Saturday night the stores were closed and the street was deserted, the beggars having gone home when the shoppers did. As the engine caught and sputtered, each of the boys pushing decided the cargo box was dark and unappealing and had bad associations, and without planning to, one by one all of them hopped into the front seat. So there they were: Ben sitting on top of Jesse in the passenger seat with his head out the window, and Roddy half sandwiched between Ben and Jesse and half in Nabil's lap. Every time Nabil hit Roddy in the chest when he reached for the weird push-me-pull-you gearshift knob in the dashboard, they all howled with laughter.

It felt good to be together again, no matter how much they bickered, and—though they'd never have admitted it, out of loyalty to the dead—it felt good to be in control again, instead of being thrown around from side to side in the cargo box while up front Claudio and his new buddy Marcel made all the decisions. They didn't have the pistol anymore, but they had the nightclub's machete, lying on the floor at Nabil's feet, where it had been all day—forgotten in the face-off at the factory because the boys had been riding in the back when they got there—and they had Jesse's BB gun.

Jesse, trying to hold the Daisy rifle between his knees in a way that didn't poke either Ben or Roddy, kept repeating, "I shot him in the face!" and as they drove through the quiet downtown streets the others answered in chorus, "You shot him in the face!" It felt a lot better to be angry and triumphant about Marcel than sad for the Matador and afraid for themselves, and sometimes Ben, overcome with bloodlust, screamed out the window all by himself, "He shot him in the face!"

The lone traffic light was red, but there were no other cars in sight, and Nabil sped up and drove right through it, rattling over the railroad crossing just beyond it while they all hooted with laughter. But as they approached the next intersection, where the streets fanned out toward different parts of town, he slowed down. "We're going to that guy Prosper's house, right? I mean, that's where they were all day, so that's probably where they'll go now. So, Roddy, which way?"

Roddy scratched his knee where the gearshift knob was tickling it. "Um…"

"Come on, retard," said Ben. "You went there in a car and you left there on foot, and you don't where it is?"

"Um…" The last thing in the world Roddy wanted now was to find his way back to Prosper's house, where not only the kidnappers but Bijou would be waiting, but he didn't feel smart enough or strong enough to deflect his friends.

Jesse said, "We know it was in the neighborhood behind the cigarette factory, because you didn't run that far before you found us." He pointed. "So let's go that way, and when we get into the area you'll remember."

"I don't want to go that way." Nabil drummed on the steering wheel. "We'd have to drive right by my father's store, and that bastard Marcel knew my name—he called me Chaloub. They might be waiting for me there."

With his arm outside the window, Ben slapped the side of the car. "I knew it! That son of a bitch read the sign on the back!"

Nabil said, "What do you mean, you knew it? You didn't know it. I was the one who said it. You said I was being paraloid."

Ben laughed. "The word is paranoid, dumb fuck!"

"Whatever."

Ben was still laughing. "He said paraloid!"

Nabil somehow reached through the tangle of bodies and shoved Ben. "Shut the fuck up, asshole!"

Ben shoved him back indirectly by pushing Roddy at Nabil. "You're the asshole! Paraloid asshole!"

"Shrimp!"

"Mongoloid!"

"Mongoloid shrimp!"

"Paraloid mongoloid!"

"Paramongoshrimpaloid!" They were both laughing now.

"Hey! Knock it off!" Jesse turned his head to get some air. "Every time you shove each other something bony digs into my ribs."

After a detour to avoid passing in front of the Quincaillerie Chaloub, they drove back out toward the cigarette factory without further squabbling. As they reached the turn that led up to the factory itself—where, like Roddy when he was running, they could see the indirect glow of the fluorescent lights on the factory walls over a rise at the end of the narrow side street— they grew quiet.

Jesse said, "I wonder if we should go up there and get the Matador's body."

"What the fuck?" Ben gaped. "We're not going up there again!"

"So you want to just leave him lying there in the dirt?"

"What, you want to drive along with him rolling around in back?"

Jesse had no answer, but Nabil had already turned up the side street. They drove into the big square in front of the factory, airgun and machete at the ready, but it was deserted. There was no sign of Claudio's body. (Prosper and Danton had pitched it deep into the overgrown vacant lot before they left.) All the boys in the car were silent as Nabil made a wide turn around the square and drove back down to the main road.

Though he knew only that Roddy had come through the gully and wound up on the side of the factory where they first saw him, Jesse quickly navigated them to within a few blocks of Prosper's house—much too quickly for Roddy's liking. As they rolled along more slowly now, staring at every house and up every lane, all the houses looked to Roddy like Prosper's house, each female pedestrian picked up by the headlights looked at first like Bijou, and his heart thumped unbearably. At one point he felt sure this next one was the house—convinced beyond doubt, he could almost taste the fermented manioc again—and he felt his body twitch and imagined, crammed in as tight as they were, that all the others must have felt it too. But he said nothing, and a few minutes later they reached the big street that marked the edge of the neighborhood. Nabil stopped the car at the intersection.

"You're a lame-ass fuck, Roddy." Ben spat out the window. "If I'd been kidnapped, I'd have know how to find my way back there."

"Sorry, guys."

Nabil said, "Well, with luck maybe next time they'll kidnap you, Ben. But don't count on me to come get you."

"I won't need your help, retard." Ben opened the door and got out of the Fourgonette.

As Ben walked away without looking back, Nabil called out, "Hey! Come back!" But Ben kept on walking, down the street and around a corner. "Fuck, now what?" Nabil got out and hurried after him, leaving the engine running.

Left alone in the car, Jesse and Roddy said nothing for a while. Then, feeling they were still uncomfortably close to Prosper's house, Roddy said, "Seriously, Jesse, can't we just go home?" He'd thought Jesse would be the reasonable one in the bunch, but it was Jesse who'd led the screams for revenge in the termite field.

Jesse said nothing. He stared out at the nighttime street, though all he could really see was the look on the Matador's face as he fell, and all he could hear was his own voice, stupidly shouting at Marcel in Mtom.

A few moments later Nabil and Ben came back around the corner, grinning. Nabil was carrying a brown paper bag, and Ben was munching on something that proved on closer view to be a greasy, sugar-coated beignet. Holding up the bag, Nabil called out, "Dinner!" and Jesse and Roddy climbed out and helped themselves.

Through his beignet Jesse said, "Ben, why'd you just take off like that?"

Ben shrugged. "Sorry. I smelled food."

"He was just getting one for himself, the little asshole." Nabil laughed. "I used the rest of that son of a bitch Marcel's taxi money to get enough for all of us."

Jesse said, "Because Nabil's not a selfish little oinker like some people."

"Hey, all I had was fifty francs!" They could barely understand Ben as he stuffed the rest of his first beignet into his mouth and reached into the bag for a second.

Nabil pulled the bag away. "Wait, that was the fifty francs the Matador gave you downtown." Ben nodded. "The last thing the Matador ever gave us, and you just spent it on a greaseball?"

Ben nodded again. "I was hungry." He reached in and got his second beignet while the rest of the boys avoided looking at each other.

"Hey," said Jesse, wiping his mouth. "We know where one of the other guys lives. The third guy, the one who shot the Matador. What's his name... Auguste. Marcel took us to his house in the shanty town—it was the first place we went."

Nabil wadded up the empty paper bag and threw it into the street. "Let's go." They headed back through downtown and out to the last shanty town on the road that led west to the coast. Parking in the same place they had that afternoon, next to the abandoned half-built cinderblock house, they got out and looked up the winding alley. For some reason—probably just Saturday night—there seemed to be much more activity here now than in the afternoon: African pop music blared from several competing radios, strolling couples hopped over the rivulets of sewage and greeted older people sitting in their doorways enjoying the cool of the evening, and, way up in the wider space by the public pump, children were dancing by the light of kerosene lanterns.

Jesse said, "So, your idea is we just walk in there, carrying a BB gun and a machete, and kill the bad guys and leave."

"Yeah. We're white. We do what we want." But Nabil himself didn't sound as sure anymore.

Ben crowed, "Shoot 'em in the face!" but the others ignored him.

"Okay," said Jesse, "but I can tell you, since I'm the one who went to the house before, it's at least a five-minute walk in, and a five-minute walk back, and that's with nobody getting in the way." They all nodded and thought silently about their chances of getting out alive. "Plus, this afternoon the Mtom ladies there gave me chocolate and a Fanta."

Ben laughed. "What's that supposed to mean?"

"It means they were nice to me and I don't feel like hurting them, which makes it even harder to get the bad guys if they're all in the same house."

"You spastic, they were only nice to you because they thought you were a friend of what's his name. Once they find out what we did—"

"—What you did—"

"What some white boys did, they'll turn on you just like that Marcel fucker did. He was acting all nice for a while too."

Thinking about the change in Prosper's grandmother between morning and afternoon, and, even more, about the shocking contrast between the Marcel who tried to protect Roddy from the kidnappers up at the nightclub this morning and the almost unrecognizable Marcel who attacked Nabil at the factory just a few hours later, Roddy realized he agreed with Ben for once, but he decided to stay out of it.

Jesse shook his head. He felt like he'd been playing Roddy's customary role all day—being the reasonable, cautious, principled one—and now that Roddy was back Jesse shouldn't have to do it for him, so why was Roddy saying nothing?

Ben said, "I thought you wanted revenge."

Jesse persevered, but without much enthusiasm. "I do, but on the right people, not on random people just because they're Africans."

"Oh, I'm sorry," Ben smirked. "I didn't realize we were in Sunday school."

Nabil said, "Here's an idea: how about both of you just shut up?"

Three girls about their age came along the road and turned up the alley, then noticed the boys and stopped. They said something to each other that was too quiet for Jesse to follow over the music playing nearby, but even from the fragments he knew they were speaking Mtom. The boldest girl stepped right in front of the boys and said in French, "Hi, guys." The other girls behind her giggled.

After a tiny pause, because her greeting had been directed at all of them, Nabil said, "Hey. How's it going?"

She focused on Nabil. "Pretty good, thanks. In fact better than good—excellent." She looked around at her friends. "Right?" They just giggled.

Nabil felt it would be cooler to lean against the fender of the Fourgonette—and why didn't he have his father's sleek black Citroën DS at a moment like this?—so he did, taking his time. "You live around here?"

Her arms crossed in front of her, the girl pointed up the alley with pursed lips. "Up there." She looked Nabil over carefully. "Are you French?"

"Lebanese."

The other boys watched, enjoying the spark and heat of the

girl even though it wasn't directed at them. Jesse tried to catch the eye of one of the other girls, but they were too shy to look at anyone but their friend. Roddy allowed himself to think of Bijou and didn't realize a huge stupid grin had spread across his face again.

The bold girl said, "Your French is really good."

"I was born here." Nabil laughed. "Just like you."

She took a tiny step closer. "So you're really African."

Nabil shrugged, knowing it wasn't what he said that mattered. "Okay, sure."

"Then why do you call yourself Lebanese?" she mock-scolded him. "Are you ashamed of being African?"

"My parents, you know how it is." He shrugged again, as if to imply only parental pressure could keep him from declaring his allegiance to Africa.

She nodded, knowing he was bullshitting and liking him the more for it. She released Nabil from her gaze and looked around to include the whole group. "We're going dancing up there." She nodded up the alley in the direction of the pump. "You guys want to come?" The girls behind her burst into screams of laughter and snapped their fingers.

The four boys looked at each other, each thinking his own thoughts, which revolved variously around a BB gun and a machete, chocolate and a Fanta, the astonishing softness of Bijou's breast, being caught unarmed in a shanty town crowd when the kidnappers showed up for the dance party, Claudio's face smacking into the dirt for the last time, a hot shower and a soft bed...

The girl laughed. "Don't tell me you don't know how to dance!"

Nabil said, "Oh, I can dance."

"So what are you afraid of, African boy? We won't bite!"

If Nabil had said "we" instead of "I," if he'd made any effort to include the other boys, it might have bothered Jesse less that Nabil had missed several opportunities to point out that he wasn't the only one of the group born here. It went beyond mere pride: Jesse's African birth—at the little mission hospital in the bush, and not at some fancy French clinic here in the city—was an essential part of himself, more important than even he knew. And when the girl cooed over Nabil's French, Jesse had to stop himself from breaking in and telling her casually in his fluent Mtom that speaking French didn't make you an African— any idiot who went to school could do that—but speaking Mtom like a native certainly did.

But he held back, partly from his all-day caution about giving up the advantage by letting people know what he knew, but mostly from a feeling that the way to impress a girl was to be cool and nonchalant, like Nabil, and showing off his Mtom skills would come off as trying too hard. Instead he said in English, "Wait, guys, I've got it! We're idiots!"

Nabil wasn't ready to be so easily distracted, but Ben said, "What are you talking about?"

"Why didn't we think of it?" Jesse laughed. "We keep trying to figure out where they live, but we know exactly where one of them lives—at the nightclub!"

Now he had Nabil's attention too. "That's true."

"And there won't be other people in the way up there, like here, and he's the worst one—the traitor."

Ben said, "Fuck, yeah! It's because of the traitor that the Matador got killed."

"Wait," said Roddy, "You're talking about going up to that nightclub again? With the dead body and everything?"

Nabil straightened up. "Like Ben said, fuck, yeah! Don't be a little sissy fraidy-cat, Roddy."

Jesse said quietly to Roddy, "Anyway, we moved the body out of sight."

Nabil gave the bold girl a little courtly bow. "Thanks for your kind invitation, but we have to run."

She said nothing and watched in confusion as the boys all piled into the car. Jesse held back, partly so he could avoid being on the bottom of the pile this time. As he got in on top of both Ben and Roddy, he turned to the girl and said in Mtom, "Maybe we'll be back later for some dancing. See you then, I hope." Without waiting for her reaction he pulled his leg in and slammed the door.

Nabil turned on the ignition, and the starter gave its unproductive dry cough, again and again. "Fuck this piece of shit," he said. "If we have to get out and push in front of those girls I'm going to be so pissed."

Jesse said, "Yeah, and you're not even the one who has to get out."

The bold girl reached through the window and put her hand lightly on his arm. "You speak Mtom?" Jesse smiled modestly and nodded, but before he could say anything more the engine came to life and Nabil put the rusty old Fourgonette in gear and, after a few lurches, drove away along the westward road toward the turnoff to the German's hill.

The cream-colored Peugeot 404 came to a stop in front of Ben's gate. "This is where the worst one lives, the one who murdered Théophile." The bleeding had stopped and the stinging in his eye had lessened, and while Marcel leaned forward in the back seat and navigated for Danton he rolled the souvenir BB pellet around in his fingers.

"It's all dark," said Auguste. "No one's home."

Prosper said, "Or they're all asleep. Only one way to find out." He opened the front passenger door, then chuckled. "At least I know I don't have to worry about a watchdog." He got out, found the gate locked, and climbed over it.

The other three men sat in the car, smoking in silence. After a while Danton said, "Should we worry about a neighbor spotting the car, if something happens?"

"Nothing's going to happen," said Auguste, "because there's no one here."

A couple of minutes later the gate opened from the inside and Prosper got back in the car. "There's no car in the driveway, and if there's anyone inside they aren't responding to stones on the windows."

Auguste said, "Like I said—"

"Yeah, we heard you." Prosper got comfortable. "So, where to next?"

They drove back toward the center of town. Even from where they parked, on the street below the Canadian mission compound, they could see several lights burning in the rambling old colonial house above them through the trees. As the other men gathered their weapons and began to open their doors, Marcel said, "Wait." He held up his BB pellet. "I want this one for myself."

He'd never been inside the mission compound, but he remembered where Jesse had pushed through a break in the hedge, and he followed the path that led up past the grave of the old missionary, whose name, even if Marcel had had enough light to make out the letters, he wouldn't have recognized in either English or Yoa. Just like Jesse before him, he crossed the flower bed and climbed quietly over the low stone parapet onto the verandah.

The shutters were closed, but in three different rooms with lights on—and even in two rooms that were dark—Marcel could hear the voices of children: small children, in the rooms whose lights were off, older children in the other rooms, and three or four different voices in each room. Could the boy Jesse possibly come from such a large family? In one of the dark rooms, the one with the littlest girls, he now heard the loud, scolding voice of a woman, followed by the sound of a child answering in tears.

From the other direction Marcel heard a man's voice, and he moved quietly toward it along the verandah. At the last window on this side one of the shutters wasn't fully latched, and, because the loud voices in the room would cover the sound of his movement, he crouched down and crept to the window to peek in. A boy a little younger than Jesse sat on his bed, looking down at the floor. The man lecturing and waving his finger at the boy looked old, old enough to be Jesse's grandfather, with silver hair and deep wrinkles and heavy hands.

Out of Marcel's confusion an idea emerged—an idea whose simplicity and boldness made him smile. He backed away from the window, straightened up, and tucked the pistol into his waistband, under his shirt at the small of his back. Then he followed the verandah around to the front of the house and lifted the heavy English brass knocker on the front door.

Nothing happened, but he knew the house was full of noisy children, so he knocked again, louder this time. After a while the big door opened and the silver-haired old man stood in the doorway looking at Marcel under the porch light. Marcel smiled brightly and said in Mtom, "Good evening, grandfather, I apologize for disturbing you at this hour."

Mr. Swenson smiled and shook his head. "Sorry, fella," he said in English, "I'm new to the country and I don't speak the lingo."

Marcel switched to French. "My mistake, sir—we can speak French."

"I do speak some French," admitted Mr. Swenson, and paradoxically it was the stumbling badness of his French, learned without much enthusiasm late in life, that made him comprehensible, because if he'd spoken the fluent French of a native Québécois Marcel wouldn't have understood a word.

"Perfect," said Marcel. Since the old man spoke French not only much worse than Jesse but with a different accent, and since he'd already demonstrated his complete ignorance of even a simple greeting in Mtom, Marcel knew the answer but asked anyway, "Are you the father of my young friend Jesse?"

"You know Jesse McCall?" The old man flushed with anger. "Where is he? He's supposed to be getting ready for bed now."

"Are you his father?"

"No, I'm not his father. His father's far away in the forest, I forget the name of the place. I'm his..." But Mr. Swenson didn't know the French word for house father, or even for dormitory. "I take care of him. I take care of all these children." He stepped out onto the verandah and pulled the door shut behind him to keep out the bugs. "Where is he?"

Marcel backed up, out of automatic deference to an elder rather than from any fear of this old man with liver spots on his deep-veined hands. He smiled to turn aside the man's anger. "Then it seems we're both looking for him."

His French unable to contain his thoughts, Mr. Swenson switched to English for an extended burst. "I tell you what, if that boy's parents had the slightest bit of backbone and any sense at all about keeping him on a shorter leash when he was younger —but there's been no parenting, at least what I'd call parenting, what with him growing up here in a dorm most of the year and I guess doing what he pleased since he was yea high—I mean just look at the kid's hair! Like a hippie or a girl, and the parents say nothing." He saw Marcel nodding politely, understanding nothing but his anger, and went back to his slow, makeshift French. "Are you a praying man?"

"Excuse me?" The question was so unexpected Marcel

assumed he must have misunderstood.

"My friend, are you a Christian?"

Marcel answered uneasily, "I was sent to the Catholic mission school for six years, and sometimes I go to Mass at the cathedral here."

"So you're a Catholic." Mr. Swenson nodded. "That's something at least. You say you're a friend of this boy Jesse McCall. I'm asking you now, if you would, to pray for him. Join your prayers to mine."

Marcel stammered, "I don't understand."

"I know this is not a good time to be a young person, with the whole world going crazy and turning away from God. But I feel Satan has a strong hold on this particular young man, and I pray to bring him back to God, and I'm asking you, as a Catholic, to join my prayer for this boy—heck, I'd even say yes to a juju or a gri-gri prayer, or whatever you people call it, if that's what it would take to save him, because that's what matters most to me."

Having no idea what to say, Marcel just nodded. But instead of going on, the old man stared at the ground and shook his head. He knew he'd spooked this African man—he was used to having that effect on people. But the way he saw it, it didn't matter if you were a roofing contractor in the middle of Saskatchewan or a semi-retired mission volunteer in the middle of Africa: your faith was only real if you lived it. Even the oldest of these dorm kids were younger than the Swensons' own grandchildren, and he and his wife had known that would be a challenge before they got here, but somehow he'd trusted that the strength of his lived faith, and the love that flowed from it, would be enough to help a troubled boy like Jesse straighten up and fly right. He continued to trust in his faith—what choice did he have? What else was there?

Marcel cleared his throat and said, "Well, since he's not here

I'll look for him elsewhere."

Mr. Swenson smiled at him. "You seem like a nice person. Maybe he'll listen to you. And when you find him, tell him to come home."

Marcel shook the old man's hand and went down the front steps. Because he couldn't duck around the side of the house while he was being watched, he walked down the gravel drive toward the tall brick Yoa church at the front of the mission property. When he felt sure he was beyond the reach of the porch light, he looked back. Seeing the front door closing as the old man went inside, he stepped off the driveway and doubled back around the house to the shortcut through the private cemetery.

He pushed through the hedge to the car and sat down heavily in the back seat. Feeling the pistol jammed painfully against his waist, he took it out and put it down next to him on the seat. There was a short expectant pause.

"We didn't hear any shots." Prosper flicked cigarette ash out his window.

Marcel took a deep breath. "He's not there, and his parents don't live there."

"Lots of lights on." Prosper looked up through the trees at the house. "So who lives there?"

"Some other white people. An old man. It doesn't matter." Marcel slapped the back of Danton's seat. "Let's get out of here." He noticed he was still rolling the BB pellet around in the fingertips of his left hand.

When they got all the way downtown, Danton drove slowly past the Quincaillerie Chaloub. They weren't aware the company offices were above the store, but in any case the whole building was dark. The only light on that block came from the loading dock behind the refrigerated fish warehouse next to the store.

Marcel said, "Must be nice to be the owner and go home on a Saturday night and leave your Africans to make more money for you." The others all nodded, imagining that life. "Anyway, I don't think we want to tangle with those guys."

Danton laughed. "Yeah, they'll come after us in their big Chaloub fish truck and flatten Prosper's poor little 404."

As Danton drove on, Auguste said, "Yes, it must be nice to be rich like Chaloub." The others nodded. "Too bad we'll never know what it's like. Too bad somebody was a fucking imbecile and picked the wrong boy to kidnap this morning."

In the front seat, Prosper felt the blood rush to his head, but he reminded himself the time for payback would come. He said coolly, "I don't remember anybody objecting to my choice."

Danton looked over and laughed. "Except the red-haired boy —he certainly objected."

"And you know," said Auguste, "I think it might've been the same fucking imbecile who allowed even that wrong, useless boy to escape!"

Prosper was now so angry his lips were almost too stiff to articulate the words. "Go ahead, keep on talking, enjoy yourself."

Auguste was untouchable now, the sight of the big American soldier as he flopped down into the dirt playing over and over in his head. He went on, giggling at his own wit and daring, "Tricked by a snot-nosed child! Incredible!"

Next to him Marcel said in Mtom, "Auguste, stop, that's enough." He added in French, "Both of you, knock it off or we'll stop the car right here and make you get out and walk!" Then he laughed. "What is that from? That's from some French movie. No, an American movie, dubbed in French. I saw it at the Palais de Versailles maybe a year ago. Ah! With a girl—such a girl. A sweet girl…" Marcel smiled as he remembered her, and they drove on in silence.

When they reached the rich neighborhood on the hillside below the President's palace, Marcel guided Danton along the quiet streets till they came to the vast place he thought was the Chaloub residence, but that was in fact Roddy's house. Here the neighborhood was anything but quiet: luxury cars were parked on the grass shoulder on both sides of the street for more than a block in each direction, and the chauffeurs leaned against their cars, smoking, or gathered in small groups to talk.

The house itself and the large garden around it blazed with light, and people in evening dress—tuxedos or African or Asian drapery—strolled out of the house onto the wide balcony to look out at the lights of the city or down at the African jazz combo in the garden, a local group Mr. Montgomery had discovered and was doing everything in the power of the British Council to support.

"See what I mean?" said Marcel as they drove slowly by, all of them feeling that Prosper's second-hand Peugeot 404 seemed a little shabbier than usual. "These Lebanese merchants are loaded."

Prosper said, "And you think the boy, the Lebanese one, is in there now, walking around eating hors d'oeuvres and wearing a nice suit and with his hair all slicked down?" It didn't seem likely, when put that way, but where was Nabil if not here? Marcel shrugged and said nothing.

"If he is here," said Danton, "he's in the safest place he could be right now. Look at all these chauffeurs and bodyguards watching us go by. I don't even feel comfortable slowing down here. And you want to walk in there with hunting rifles and stroll past a hundred people and find the Chaloub boy and kidnap him? We'll have to go get tuxedos first."

Auguste laughed. "And a black Mercedes instead of this old thing."

When they got a safe distance beyond the party they pulled

over to the side of the road to think. Marcel felt all the others looking at him. "Well," he said without much conviction, "at least we know where the Chaloub boy lives now. We can come back and get him another day, when there aren't all these people here."

Prosper laughed, with that insulting edge he used. "So that's it? We all just go home now and have a drink of milk and go to bed? Except for poor Théophile, of course—he doesn't get any milk tonight."

Marcel said nothing, but he imagined how much fun it would be to slam Prosper's face over and over against the hood of the 404. Danton gave a little grunt, nothing more, but somehow it was enough to suggest to Marcel that Danton was picturing the same thing. But Danton just said, "Let's not give up yet. Where else did those boys take you?"

"The American Embassy Club."

"Right—the soldier bought you a hamburger."

Auguste said, "I still can't believe you got into the American Club! You should at least have asked to go swimming. I would have."

Marcel laughed. "No blacks in the pool, stupid."

"If the boys went there," said Prosper, "they're safe. That's where all the off-duty American soldiers go, like the one the boys hired today. We'd have no chance."

Auguste shrugged. "He wasn't so tough."

The others said nothing but wondered privately how long they would have to endure the new Auguste, smug and full of himself.

Danton said, "Where else, Marcel?"

Marcel remembered the shanty town brothel he'd visited with Claudio, but he couldn't picture the boys going back there by themselves. Where else had they stopped? The Jeune Afrique department store—irrelevant. And then he remembered the first stop of the day, at the end of the wild death-defying ride down the German's hill: Auguste's house. How to explain to the other men that he'd led the boys there? How indeed to explain it to himself? He tried to reconstruct his own thoughts at noon today: the sense that the other men had abandoned him in favor of ransoming the red-haired boy, the calculation that, if he was on his own, he had to do whatever was necessary to arrange a trade and get free. It all made sense, but that didn't make it any easier to explain now.

Marcel cleared his throat and said, as casually as possible, "We did go to Auguste's house."

The whole car was silent, but somehow the silence seemed deepest right next to Marcel on Auguste's side of the back seat. Then Auguste said, not as a question, "You went to my house."

"Yeah, I thought that was the most likely place to arrange a trade."

"You took those boys to my house."

"Well, I was their prisoner, but I showed them where it was."

"You exposed my family—my wife, my mother, my child— to those murdering—"

"Yes."

While Auguste drew in a long breath, Prosper said, "Well, that answers the question of where those boys are right now. Especially since Auguste was nice enough to shoot their American army friend in front of them."

Danton started the car and turned around, and they drove back down the hill past the big diplomatic reception fast enough to draw the attention of several lounging chauffeurs and body-guards. To break the silence in the car, Marcel said, "You knew the boys wanted to trade me for the red-haired boy, and yet you abandoned me. I was on my own after that. What did you expect me to do?"

Prosper sniffed. "I don't really understand your logic, but I certainly do understand why your little visit to Auguste's house slipped your mind tonight, and I'm beginning to understand why, even though you say you were their prisoner, when we saw you outside the factory you seemed to be a free man."

After that no one in the car said another word till they pulled up at the foot of the alley leading toward Auguste's house. The whole shanty town seemed to be outside now, enjoying the cool of the evening and dancing to the music blaring from a dozen radios. The four men pushed their way up the alley through the crowd till they reached the house. Auguste's mother was sitting just outside the door of the mud-and-wattle hut, sharing a short bench with three other elderly ladies, all of them beaming, shiny with sweat from dancing, and drinking beer while they recovered.

"Hey, Auguste, there you are!" She passed him her beer. "You're back in time for the party!" She waved greetings to the other men.

Auguste held the bottle absently. He put his mouth next to his mother's ear so she could hear him over the music. "Did some white boys come here?"

"Sure, a white boy came here, this afternoon. He was nice— very well brought up."

"That's all? No one since then? You're sure?"

She laughed. "Auguste, you think I wouldn't remember something like that?"

He noticed the beer in his hand and drained the bottle. Giving the empty back to his mother, he waved to the other men—who'd heard nothing over the noise—to follow him back down toward the road. As they squeezed through the space around the public water pump, where the music was loudest and the press of bodies was thickest, Marcel watched while Auguste exchanged words with a girl who talked and nodded without ever quite giving up dancing.

Out at the street the men gathered around the front of the Peugeot. Auguste said, "My daughter says the boys were here, but they didn't go into the neighborhood. They've gone up to the nightclub to find Marcel or wait for Marcel up there—in any case, to kill him."

"Okay," said Marcel with a dry laugh. "And now I hope all of you are done thinking I'm on their side."

Prosper kicked at the tire. "And they told your daughter their whole plan, just like that?"

"No, they were talking amongst themselves in English." Auguste grinned proudly. "My daughter is first in her class in English."

3.

SINCE THEY WERE only in seventh grade, and hadn't yet reached the end of their first day in the world of violent crime, the boys continued to make the beginner's mistake of preparing for the best possibility instead of the worst. Somehow they expected Marcel to come home by himself: to be cheerfully dropped off by his friends and left alone on the hill with his enemies.

They knew the Fourgonette would give them away, so they had to hide it. They opened Monsieur Koeffler's *No Trespassing* gate, and, after first turning the car around to face downhill for an easy getaway when the job was done, they half-drove, half-pushed it in reverse up the unused and overgrown last hundred yards of the road. The top of the cargo box just fit under the edge of the big verandah, so they carefully backed the car up as far as they could, till it was hidden partly by the overhang, partly by the stairs.

An almost-full moon hung in the cloudless dry-season sky over the city, and its cool rays reflected here and there off the curving hood of the Fourgonette, so Jesse used the machete to cut a few palm branches, which they laid over the front of the car as camouflage. And then they all stood on the verandah and looked out at the lights of the city, twinkling far below them in the haze of wood smoke, and waited for Marcel to come home.

Roddy said, "What if he doesn't come back? How long are we going to wait? Tomorrow? Monday? Don't we have to go home sometime?"

"He's the night watchman." Nabil was getting tired of explaining things to Roddy that were clear to everyone else. Somehow missing out on the killing of Théophile, and everything that had followed from it, seemed to have deprived Roddy of common sense. "It's night. It's his job. He has to come back."

But Roddy kept returning to questions they'd already settled. "And he has a pistol, and what do we have?"

Jesse counted off on his fingers. "We have a BB gun, and a machete, and he doesn't know we're here, and he's gotta be half blind after the cigarette factory, and there's four of us and one of him."

"But what if the other guys come with him?"

"What for, retard?" said Ben. "They don't live here, he does. They're not the night watchman, he is."

"Stop calling me a retard, I'm just trying to help."

"You wanna go back and be kidnapped?"

Roddy thought of Bijou and said nothing.

Nabil said, "All I know is, we came up here this morning for an adventure, and, no matter what, we're going to have a fuck of an amazing story to tell about how we spent Saturday."

Jesse laughed. "You're kidding, right? We can't ever tell anyone about this."

"Hmm." Nabil smiled into the darkness. "Not even Heather Stone?"

"Are you nuts?"

"I don't know—I bet she'd be impressed."

"Okay, yes, we all know she's hot, and we're still not telling her, and Nabil, even if you do I'll deny every word of it, and then you'll just be a big fat liar, and she'll think you made this shit up just to look big, and that's not very impressive."

"You wouldn't! What a jerk!" Nabil laughed.

Roddy said, "Maybe before we spend any more time figuring out what we're going to tell people, we should make sure we know how to get out of this alive."

At exactly the same time the three others all said, "Fuck you, Roddy!" and then laughed and turned around to punch each other in the arm and mutter, as fast as possible, "Jinx you owe me a Coke no backsies bottle caps I talk."

When they finally heard the sound of the Peugeot 404 coming up the steep road, the boys retreated to the positions they'd planned. Jesse had chosen the front room again, the one that overlooked both the hillside and the verandah. This time he had his Daisy rifle instead of Marcel's pistol, and since it was plenty dark inside he'd opened the shutters. He thought he might be able to pick Marcel off by moonlight before he even walked through the front door of the club.

The Peugeot came around the last bend and stopped at the turnaround spot by the gate. Jesse heard car doors opening, and then the distinct sound of four different doors slamming shut, and right away some of the reckless fighting spirit began to leak out of him. After that he heard no voices, and if there were footsteps coming up the path they were so quiet he might have imagined them.

Then he heard a low chuckle from somewhere near the verandah. Shrinking into as small a space as possible—though he felt sure he was safe in the darkness—he listened while below him the men swept the palm fronds off the Fourgonette, then reached in and released the hand brake, then rolled the car out from under the verandah and down the path to the first sharp turn.

There was a short silence, during which Jesse tried to move a little to see better by moonlight, though he knew it was hopeless because of the overhang of the verandah. Finally he heard the surprisingly gentle sound of the Fourgonette being pushed off the edge of the path and crashing through brush and small trees and over rocks as it bounced and tumbled end over end down the steep slope into the forest far below.

Over the thump of his heart Jesse heard a man say in Mtom, "Sorry about your vehicle, Monsieur Chaloub. But you've got so many nice cars I'm sure you won't miss that ugly old thing."

Another voice said, still in Mtom, "Be quiet. We need to keep them guessing."

And after that Jesse heard nothing—no voices, no footsteps, nothing. He told himself not to worry about the loss of the Fourgonette: after all, they weren't trapped up here, since they could just run down the road and into town when this was all over. But somehow the fact that the men had taken the trouble to get rid of the car was itself alarming—as if they were sending the boys a signal: this ends here and there's no escape, no running to mommy now.

The more Jesse thought along those grim lines, and the longer the silence lasted, the harder he found it to bear the idea of the four men fanning out around the club to hunt the boys— this time without the casual chatter that had given them away in the morning. He told himself to calm down, reminding himself that now, with the shutters open, this room wasn't the trap it had been this morning: he had two ways out—through the door into the main room of the club, or out the window onto the verandah. And he reminded himself he was a good enough aim with his trusty Daisy to have hit Marcel in the face twice, and maybe even to have put his eye out. Again he summoned the memory of Jim Corbett waiting for the Man-eating Leopard of Rudraprayag: Colonel Corbett wouldn't have given a moment's anxious thought to a handful of natives who couldn't even pull off the kidnapping of a seventh grader.

Jesse could hear low voices now, but they came from behind him, inside the club. Adrenaline shot through him for a moment, till he recognized the sound of Nabil and Ben arguing in a half-whisper. When they first went inside after they heard the

Peugeot coming up the hill, Nabil had pulled all of the fuses out of the fuse box in the storeroom—something he'd watched his father do at home when they had electrical problems—to keep the men from just switching on the lights and catching the boys cowering and blinking in the glare.

After that he began moving around the main room, choosing and then rejecting one hiding place after another. He had the machete, and crouching down behind a cluster of café tables to wait for Marcel if somehow he got past Jesse seemed like a smart idea—till he heard the Fourgonette tumbling over the edge and drew the same conclusion Jesse had about the symbolic meaning of that sound.

As he got up from behind the tables to look for a better spot, he heard Ben calling to him in a whisper. "Nabil! Turn on the lights!"

Nabil followed the sound into the business office at the rear of the nightclub before answering. "What the fuck, Ben?" he whispered. "They're right outside. They can probably hear you."

"Just turn on the lights for a second!"

Since he'd scattered the fuses across the floor of the storeroom, Nabil couldn't have restored light even if he'd wanted to, which he didn't. "No fucking way! Why?"

"The door to the stairs is locked. We need a back way out!"

It was true: at Marcel's insistence, they'd locked the little door leading to the stairs down to the house in the forest before leaving the hill that afternoon. Since they had more than just Marcel to cope with now, they definitely needed another escape route, but where had they put the key? Nabil set the machete down on the office desk and pulled out his cigarette lighter, and the two of them began to search the room by its tiny flame.

Nabil, his temples pounding with his pulse, was painfully aware not only of the light—as faint as it seemed, it was the only artificial light on the entire hillside—but of the inevitable noise he and Ben made as they shuffled around the office, feeling every flat surface for a small key. What had they done with it? Was it possible one of them had pocketed it? How long could they keep this up before the men caught them? Would it be wiser to give up trying to unlock the door and just hide somewhere?

Then Nabil had a sudden memory picture of Jesse putting the key on the shelf behind the bar. He clicked shut his lighter, went out into the main room, and felt his way over to the bar by faint moonlight. As his fingers found and closed over the key, right where Jesse had left it, he caught sight of Roddy crouched in the back corner behind the bar, tucked in as tight as his skinny frame would go.

Nabil had thought about and rejected that spot as a hiding place—it was a dead end with no escape route, except maybe by vaulting over the bar itself, and it was where Marcel had put the boys this morning when the hunters first showed up, so they'd certainly remember to check there now. Roddy stared up at him, his eyes huge, his lower lip caught between his teeth to keep them from chattering. Nabil thought, "Poor kid, he's really not old enough for this kind of thing. We probably shouldn't bring him along next time." But he said nothing and went back to the office.

Here, at the rear of the nightclub, almost no moonlight came through the windows, and Nabil had to click his lighter one more time to find the keyhole. The instant the little door was unlocked Ben opened it and rushed out, and in the moment before Nabil snapped the lighter shut he saw Ben had taken the machete with him down the rickety stairs.

That asshole! Now what was Nabil supposed to use to defend himself? And how was Ben going to help them fight the men if he ran away? Hoping against all realistic expectation there might be another pistol, or a knife, or something—anything— here in the office, Nabil flicked on his lighter and began a frantic hunt through desk drawers and file boxes.

Jesse, at his sniper post in the front room, could hear all the shuffling from the office, and, without the slightest idea what Nabil and Ben were up to, he wished they'd cut it out—not just for their own sakes, since if he could hear them the men probably could too, but because the constant low-level rustle from the rear made it almost impossible for him to hear what was going on outside and around the nightclub.

But now he distinctly heard something new nearby—maybe a creaking board on the verandah itself. Making sure to stay in the shadows, he peered out through the window overlooking the verandah. A dark figure was creeping up the big main stairs, hugging the front wall of the club, holding a hunting rifle that caught the moonlight. Jesse moved his BB gun into position, reassuring himself for the hundredth time that he'd already racked the air pump to charge the cylinder. He had a clear shot now, but he knew the BB pellet would do the most damage from close up, so he waited. After all, the man, whichever one he was, would have to come about twenty feet closer along the verandah to get to the front door of the club, and Jesse decided to wait till just before the man turned to go in, so he could hit him in the face rather than in the ear.

But when the man reached the first window overlooking the verandah right by the head of the stairs, the one furthest away from Jesse, he hopped over the windowsill and disappeared from view with no more noise than the slight scrape of a chair leg by the café table nearest to the window. So now there was a man inside—a man who could make it to the door of Jesse's room in twenty seconds without even hurrying.

Jesse froze, willing himself to stay calm, but his brain was screaming at him, "Get out, get out, get out!" He began to straighten up and lean forward to go out through the window, then stopped as he saw first the head, then the shoulders, of another man coming up the stairs onto the verandah. So now he was surrounded. If the man already inside the building didn't come to this room first, Jesse might have time to hide behind something, though there wasn't much furniture in this room. He turned carefully to look around, remembering not to move his feet because of the creak and bounce of the floor.

The sounds from the office had stopped, and Jesse could hear the man in the main room bump into something and curse quietly in Mtom. Then he heard the sound of a light switch being flipped on and off repeatedly—in vain, of course—followed by a low chuckle. The second man, outside on the verandah, had paused at the top of the steps, maybe trying to decide whether it was really necessary to go through the window like a commando or whether he could just walk in through the front door, since his companion was already inside and obviously having more trouble with the furniture than with the boys.

Jesse made his decision: he would shoot the man standing out there like a great big target on the verandah, and in the confusion that followed he'd go through the window and jump off the verandah into the bushes. Turning back toward the window, he raised his air rifle to aim at the second man's face— and then he heard the door to his room open. He felt, more than saw, that the first man was standing in the doorway, looking around.

Danton, for it was he, didn't see the boy in the shadows, but he saw a slight glint of moonlight on the BB gun as Jesse aimed it out the window. Danton sprang across the room, and as he landed on Jesse with his full weight the bouncy termite-hollowed section of floor they were standing on collapsed and they both fell through. Still entangled, crashing through thorn bushes, they hit the ground hard, and both of them cried out in pain.

The second man, still waiting on the verandah, knew what

had happened, because he was Marcel, and it had been clear when he and Théophile moved out of that room that the floor would give way someday. Marcel raced back down the stairs and turned to run under the verandah to reach Danton, but the brush was dense under there and not enough moonlight came though the gaps between the boards overhead to help him find a clear way through.

Jesse, lighter than Danton and not as winded by the fall, heard the sound of the second man approaching from the front. He tore himself free of a thornbush and scrambled past Danton, who was still doubled over in pain. But a moment later Jesse realized his hands not only stung from a hundred scratches, they were empty—he'd dropped the Daisy rifle.

He turned back, saw Danton's hunting rifle lying there, and reached for it. Danton, still recovering, grabbed the other end of it and began using it to pull himself to his feet. As Danton's hand approached the trigger Jesse realized he himself was holding the wrong end of the gun—the muzzle was pointed right at him, and he'd already seen how a struggle like that had ended this morning—and the sound of the other man crashing his way through the brush toward them was getting closer. Jesse let go, and, while Danton staggered backward to recover his balance after the sudden end of the tug-of-war, Jesse scrambled away, around to the back of the nightclub, through the thorn bushes.

He'd gained a lead of only a few seconds, however, and, by the time he reached the little staircase at the back and allowed himself a moment to pause and decide whether to run up the stairs into the office or down the stairs to the house in the forest, he could already hear Danton coming after him. Jesse knew he'd locked the door in the afternoon, and he guessed Nabil and Ben might have opened it during all the shuffling and whispering, but he wasn't sure and he couldn't afford to be wrong: by the time he turned back from a locked door Danton would be waiting for him right here on the stairs. Besides, he knew the men were already inside the club, and he knew what it was like to be trapped in there with them and had no urge to go through that again. He turned and ran down the staircase into the forest, wishing he had a weapon of any kind.

Danton came around the side of the building in time to see Jesse disappearing down the steep stairs into the darkness where no moonlight penetrated. Since Marcel had kept the secret of the German's house from him, Danton had no idea this back exit from the nightclub even existed, though he'd spent several days here as the substitute caretaker that time he and his friends had stolen the teak plank off the facing of the bar.

He looked up the stairs, trying without success to picture where in the club they emerged, then decided he'd solve that mystery later, when he'd settled the bigger mystery of what in the world these astonishing steps could lead to as they dropped into the ravine in a direction where no village lay for many kilometers through dense forest.

Holding his hunting rifle ready, Danton followed Jesse down the steps at a jog. After a couple of slips on broken boards and a couple of missteps on boards gone entirely, he slowed down: he knew the ache all over his body from the fall through the floor had only just begun and would get worse, and he wasn't eager to add to his bruises by foolish haste.

When he reached the bottom of the stairs and saw the boardwalk stretching away into the darkness, winding around the contour as it clung to the slope, he took his time, testing each board, watching for gaps to step over, holding onto whatever branch or shrub he could reach on the cliff next to him. The more amazed he grew at the ambition of the original construction—impressive even as it rotted—the more sure Danton became that he didn't have far to go to find Jesse: no one, not even the crazy German who built the Club Balafon, could have hoped to push this folly more than a little distance into the forest.

The collapse of the floor in the front room, and the shouts of surprise and pain that went with it, were Nabil's first clue that the men had entered the nightclub. (He'd heard the tables and chairs scraping as Danton stumbled around, but assumed they were caused by Jesse or Roddy looking for a better hiding place.) Giving up his search for a weapon, he snapped shut his lighter and waited in the dark, crouching behind the German's big desk.

Through the small back window of the office he heard first one person and then a second come running around the outside of the building, pause below the back door, then head down the stairs into the ravine. It might have been Jesse followed by one of the men, but if so why didn't the man call to his friends to join the pursuit? Instead Nabil began to imagine it might have been Jesse and Roddy, running away from the nightclub just like Ben as the men came in the front. But if that was true, it meant Nabil was now alone, one against four. He held his breath and listened. The door between the office and the main room was closed, and he waited for what seemed like a long time before he heard anything.

Then it was unmistakable: someone tripped, cried out in surprise, and fell heavily against the bar, knocking a few glasses off a shelf. Right after the sound of shattering came a voice in French. "Jesus, what kind of sick person leaves a dead dog just lying around for people to trip over?"

After a short laugh, a second voice said, "Hey, dumb fuck—do you do shit like this on purpose?"

The first voice answered, "Fuck you, Prosper."

Another laugh. "Wow, that's a really witty comeback."

"Fuck you double—how's that for wit?"

Nabil now felt sure he'd been right: it must have been the other boys he'd heard running away before, because the men were working their way from the front of the nightclub to the back, and if they'd now reached the bar it meant not only that they'd long since passed Jesse's hiding place but that they would have found Roddy if he were still there.

After furious thought, Nabil saw a way out. Making sure his body and the desk hid the glow, he flicked on his lighter and pulled a sheet of paper—some old letter or bill—out of the nearest open drawer. The paper lit easily enough, but when he held it to the leg of the desk, or even the nearby wicker chair, nothing happened. Why wouldn't the furniture catch fire? Yes, of course this was equatorial Africa, but still, it was the dry season—it hadn't rained for weeks, maybe a month. The useless paper torch flared up in his hand, and he dropped it before it could singe him. It fell between the gaps in the old floorboards, leaving him in darkness again.

"Did you see that light?" It was the second voice again, the unpleasant mocking one.

"No."

"Of course—why did I even ask?"

If the first part of Nabil's plan—to set the nightclub on fire and burn the men alive inside it—had failed, he could still move on to the second part—to go out the back door and down the stairs and run like hell and keep on running and not stop till he was safe in his own bed in his own house, and tomorrow, though he would certainly not tell his father what had happened, he might write to his mother and his little sister and tell them.

If one of the men thought he'd seen the flame under the door, he didn't have much time. Nabil stood up, crossed the office, opened the little door that led to the back stairs, and found himself face to face with Marcel, whose hand was reaching out for the doorknob at that moment.

They both froze in surprise, but Marcel recovered first. He held up his pistol, and, pushing Nabil back into the office, stepped in through the doorway after him. "Young Master Chaloub—this is the second time today I find you trespassing!"

When Ben escaped with the machete, after Nabil finally found the key and opened the back door, he too meant to run away as fast and as far as he could—though for Ben that was Plan A and not a desperate last resort, and he intended to leave all his friends behind, whereas Nabil thought he was the last of the boys still in danger. No great fan of heights but driven by more than ordinary desperation, Ben made it down the ruined staircase and even along the wobbling boardwalk—suspended over night-shrouded forest depths he had to force out of his mind—and at the far end he ignored the little house and tried to find the path the boys had taken to get here in the morning.

But what had started then as the appearance of a clear path when they left the road on the front side of the hill, facing the city, had gradually faded into something almost imaginary, till, by the time they'd wrapped around the hill to the forest side, the path amounted to not much more than Roddy, Mr. Boy Scout, picking his way from one relatively clear foothold or firm handhold to another, and the others following his lead one by one. So now, as Ben stood at the end of the boardwalk staring at the forest ahead of him, trying to find any trace of the boys' last steps before they came out onto the mysterious boardwalk and discovered the little house, it wasn't just the darkness that kept him from spotting the head of the trail—there really was no trail.

But Ben had the machete, and why not? Why should Nabil and Jesse always get the cool weapons? He'd just resolved to start using the machete to hack his way through the steep forest and back around the hill—back to a normal, sane world where four grown men weren't trying to kill him and he was just a seventh grader—when he heard someone running toward him along the boardwalk. In fact he felt the shaking of the whole structure long before he heard anything.

Creepy though it was, the house standing right next to him offered more cover than just waiting here like an idiot at the end of the boardwalk. Ben pushed open the door and went in. The darkness inside was even deeper than on the boardwalk, and after he slipped on a couple of scattered record albums he paused to let his eyes adjust. He could clearly hear someone running on the boardwalk, getting closer.

There was no place to hide in the living room, so he turned to the right, to the bedroom where he'd spent the morning guarding the prisoner—just sitting here while Jesse, and Nabil, and even Roddy had all the fun. He got down and slid under the nasty old bed, keeping the machete in his hand. Maybe if whoever was chasing him came in here and stood by the bed he could take a swing and cut his feet off at the ankles.

The person Ben heard running along the boardwalk was Jesse, still smarting from his fall through the floor with Danton. He had no idea Ben was down here—the plan had been for all four boys to ambush Marcel inside the nightclub—and he had no reason to call out the Double-O Seven password or anything else. He took one look at the wall of forest where the boardwalk ended, regretted not having a machete (Jesse prided himself on his machete skills, which he mostly used to chop down termite mounds), and ducked into the house.

He too found the living room unpromising. He stepped into the bedroom, but—fortunately for his ankles—he didn't have to approach the bed to decide this room gave him the creeps. He turned around, crossed the living room, and went into the bathroom, where all the trouble had started this morning. He stopped to listen, but heard no one running after him. Had he escaped down the stairs without Danton seeing which way he went?

Danton, of course, had seen him, and was coming, but he was taking his time. There was no need to run or get out of breath: Danton had grown up in the village, and he knew a white boy wasn't going to move fast in the forest, even by moonlight, even if there turned out to be a real path at the end of this crazy boardwalk.

The German's house, when he finally saw it as he came around the last bend in the boardwalk, did disconcert him a little, he had to admit. Though he quickly decided it must be a place the old German had built for himself—and not, as it appeared in this doubtful light, some kind of witch's house magically produced here overnight like a giant toadstool—it was still, for all that, the house of a dead man, and needed to be approached with caution and respect.

Up at the nightclub, Prosper came through the door from the main room into the owner's office with his army-issue pistol raised and Auguste close behind him. He turned on a flashlight and shone it in Nabil's blinking eyes. "Ha! I wondered who you were talking to in here, Marcel."

Marcel nodded, his eyes and his pistol still on Nabil. "This is the one I was talking about."

"Oh, yeah?" Prosper sounded bored. "Which one is that?"

"You know, the Lebanese, the Chaloub boy." Prosper just shrugged. Marcel said to Auguste, "This is the one we should've taken this morning."

With his hands in the air Nabil said quickly, "My name is Nabil Chaloub, and my father is one of the richest men in this country. You know, Chaloub—the hardware store, and the fish trucks, and a bunch of other things."

Far below, Danton pushed open the front door of the little house and stepped inside. There was no obvious path leading away from the end of the boardwalk, so it seemed likely that Jesse was in here. If so, he was trapped, and Danton knew the boy was unarmed. He waited in the living room, letting his eyes adjust and examining the floor with the toe of one shoe, trying without success to figure out what the hard flat things were that kept sliding around underfoot.

"Danton!" It was the faintest whisper, coming from his left. The whisper came again, in Mtom. "Danton, it's Théophile!" Danton began to shake, and was angry at himself for shaking, and still shook. "Danton! It's Théophile! I cannot rest! I am unburied! Unburied and unavenged!"

Danton thought, this is my own fault—what fool enters the house of a dead man uninvited? He wiped cold sweat off his face. He took a step back toward the front door, then stopped. Marcel had told them in the car, as they drove away from the cigarette factory, that the long-haired boy, Jesse, spoke good Mtom. So this whispering voice might just be Jesse, trying to play him for an ignorant superstitious African.

Up in the office, Prosper kept his flashlight aimed at Nabil's eyes. "We already know who you are—we're not stupid. But you told us your parents were in the Peace Corps."

"I was lying, because I didn't want to be kidnapped."

"You lied to us?"

"Come on, Prosper," said Auguste, "don't act so offended. He lied to protect himself, and you would've done the same thing."

Prosper didn't turn around. "Keep out of this."

"My father will pay a lot of money to get me back. A lot of money! I'm his only son. I'm all he has, because my mother went to France with my little sister. He'll pay you anything you want, anything you ask. Please, I beg you, believe me! Look, I have a photo with my family, and it has our names on the back. I'm Nabil Chaloub."

As Nabil was bringing his hand down to reach into his pocket for the photo, Prosper lifted his pistol, pressed the muzzle against Nabil's heart, and fired. Blood sprayed across the desk, and Nabil dropped to the floor at their feet.

Danton took a step toward the bathroom—toward the voice he now felt sure was actually Jesse—then paused again as he heard a shot from up at the nightclub. What if he was wrong, and it was the ghost of Théophile calling to him after all? Danton tried to sort through his family relationship to Théophile to figure out how close they were, but it was complicated and in his present state of mind he couldn't do it. But they were certainly related, so what did he have to fear?

Now he sifted through the half dozen interactions he'd ever had with the boy after Théophile came to the city. He was forced to admit he'd always been to some degree sarcastic and condescending to a kid he saw as a village yokel, and their last exchange, that morning, when he'd led the mockery of Théophile's homemade wooden spear, was at once typical and the worst example. That was the trouble with making fun of someone, Danton reflected: you never knew when they might turn up dead and hold it against you.

The killing of Nabil had happened so fast that Marcel found he was still aiming his own pistol at the empty space where the boy had been standing. All he could say was, "What?" He looked down at the body and saw his own future hopes—business, family, house in the village—fading as the boy's eyes faded to blankness.

"What the fuck, Prosper?" said Auguste. "He was only

reaching for a photo!"

Prosper shrugged. "I don't care what he was reaching for."

"But he was the rich one! We would've been rich!"

"Grow up, Auguste." Prosper nudged the body with his toe. "Can't you see we're past the point of taking hostages and holding people for ransom and playing pirates like little children?"

The second shot somehow made Marcel jump more than the first one. Auguste's hunting rifle might not have been as good as Prosper's, but at close range it was good enough to blast Prosper across the small office and smack his entire body against the far wall. Marcel, feeling more and more like a spectator, turned and watched Prosper slide slowly to the floor, pulling a five-year-old Gentleman Cigarettes calendar down with him.

"Well, Prosper," said Auguste to the body as it settled, "I guess even Mtom villagers eventually get tired of arguing."

Shortly after the first gunshot Danton heard a second shot. Were the boys shooting back? Now he saw his own dilemma in a different light. How could Théophile's spirit focus on a little thing like some friendly teasing, when he had far greater causes for anguish? The white boys had shot him in the face! What ghost would waste its time on a family member's little jokes after that? Danton walked firmly toward the bathroom, convinced the voice belonged to Jesse but ready if need be to face the spirit of the unburied and unavenged Théophile.

He stepped through the doorway, still not sure in his heart whether to expect Jesse or Théophile, flesh or wraith. He saw no one, but by the window there was a face—a round black face, with a single eye. His heart pounding, his legs protesting, Danton crossed slowly to the bathroom window, and finally realized he was rattled enough to have mistaken an unsleeved propped-up record disc for a person, with the faint light coming through the center hole passing as the eye. He picked up the LP, being careful not to touch the jagged broken glass all around it where those stupid boys must have smashed the big window this morning. To think—those little animals had just been throwing the old German's music into the forest!

Jesse stood up from the bottom of the bathtub, where he'd been curled, and—just as Danton began to turn toward the sound behind him—shoved him hard. Danton overbalanced, tried to catch himself but just sliced his hand on jagged glass, and fell out the window with a scream. The scream ended abruptly, quite a ways down, when he struck a big tree branch. He dropped further, struck another tree, dropped again, struck something else, and kept on dropping into the impossible darkness of the ravine.

Jesse stood at the window, trying to breathe but unable to, as if he were deep underwater, like the Matador in the corner of the pool practicing hiding from gooks. He was sorry Danton had taken his hunting rifle down with him, but he knew getting it away from the man without himself being dragged out the window would have been a matter of sheer luck, and he decided —considering he'd just killed one of their enemies unarmed, by his wits alone—he ought not to be too hard on himself.

While Auguste was prying the pistol out of Prosper's dead hand, Marcel noticed something glowing between Prosper's outstretched feet. As he crouched down to peer through the office floorboards he heard a long, awful scream that ended abruptly, as if chopped off. He looked at Auguste, who'd clearly heard it too. "That came from down in the ravine—the German's house."

Auguste stood up. "Danton... I think."

"But there's a fire under the floor. We have to put it out."

"I'm going now—maybe they're torturing him."

Marcel nodded and turned his attention back to the fire, which seemed to have grown even as they spoke. When he looked up again, Auguste was still standing there, looking confused. "How do you get down there?"

Marcel pointed to the little door that looked like a closet. "I'll catch up with you as soon as I put it out."

The shots in the distance had been scary, but the hideous scream from right nearby, preceded and followed by silence, had so unnerved Ben that he lay for a long time under the German's bed, trying not to tremble but feeling the floor tremble with him, trying not to cry but feeling his nose run and not daring to sniff it back in. He needed to pee desperately, almost badly enough to go right here in his pants, but he closed his eyes and told himself no, no, no, no, no...

Then he heard footsteps on the boardwalk again, the sound of someone slowly approaching the house. After that, nothing for a while, and it was too dark to tell whether the person had come inside. But then the whispering started again, the same whispering as last time, and Ben had the answer to the question he'd been avoiding asking: it was Roddy or Jesse or Nabil who'd gone screaming out the window, and it was the African man who'd stayed behind in the bathroom, waiting to find Ben and kill him. As the whispering went on and on, he fought a rising desire to scream, till he knew either he had to do something right now or he had to go ahead and scream and let out his fear and give away his hiding place—and he wasn't willing to die like a cockroach cornered in the dark under a bed.

Abandoning even simple caution, Ben slid out from under the bed without taking much care to be quiet. Then he groped his way across the living room and into the bathroom. All he wanted to do right now was to make the whispering stop. Seeing no one, he moved slowly past the bathtub toward the window— unable, even with his fear of heights, to stop himself from looking out to see if he could spot whoever had fallen.

As Jesse sprang up out of the tub he recognized Ben at the

window. Ben heard the sound of rustling behind him, and, whirling around reflexively, swung the machete across Jesse's throat. Before he even felt the pain, thinking Ben had swung and missed, Jesse said, "Ben, it's me." But then blood sprang out and flooded his shirt front, and he stepped back as if to get away from it, and his foot slid on the smooth curve of the bathtub, and he felt lightheaded and couldn't see, and he fell, curling into a fetal ball as he fumbled for his throat, trying to hold the two halves together, the bottom of the tub around him filling with his blood.

When he told Marcel he was going on ahead, Auguste had been full of the righteous adrenaline that came from finally popping that asshole Prosper. But the further he went down the ruined staircase into the ravine and along the fragile boardwalk as it wound around the hillside, the less eager he became. And when he caught sight of the little house hanging over the forest his reaction was even stronger than Danton's had been: the place gave him the willies.

He stopped at the end of the boardwalk and decided to wait for Marcel to join him. After all, even if this wasn't what it so clearly looked like—the house of a witch—then it was still a house where at least one of the boys was waiting to ambush him and do to him whatever had been done to Danton to make him scream like that.

As he waited there on the boardwalk, facing the front door of the German's house, Auguste listened to the familiar sounds of the African forest night all around him, but he didn't hear Jesse inside calling to him in the voice of Théophile's ghost—fortunately for him, because Auguste was precisely the kind of credulous, superstitious villager Danton looked down on, and he would have done exactly what any restless spirit told him to do and walked to his death.

After a few minutes Auguste heard some vague noises from inside the house, but with Marcel still not here to help him he stayed where he was. Then the front door flew open and someone, one of the boys, burst out and ran straight at him. In the instant Auguste recognized Ben and saw he had a machete, Ben swung the machete at him—an awkward, flailing stroke that Auguste easily dodged—and sprinted away along the boardwalk.

Auguste wiped blood off his face—but the boy had missed, hadn't even come close, so there was someone else's blood on the machete, enough blood for drops to fly off when the boy swung it: Danton's blood. That little son of a bitch—the same one who'd killed Théophile and started all this—had killed Danton, ending his scream with a pitiless chop, and now he was racing up to the nightclub to do the same to Marcel, who wouldn't be on his guard because he expected Auguste to have handled things down here.

Auguste took off after Ben, puffing after a few steps but determined to shoot the boy before he even got to the stairs. But the boardwalk curved so much as it followed the hillside that Ben kept disappearing around the next turn before Auguste could take steady aim at him. He had one slightly better chance and took it, firing off a round at a dead run, but he knew right away the shot was wide and the bullet had gone off into the forest. There was no way to stop the boy except to catch up, and Auguste made himself run harder than he had in many years, ever since he was a boy in the village and quite a lot lighter.

To the extent that Ben could be said to know anything now —anything that reached him through the enormous bleeding scream inside his head—he knew Auguste was close behind him, and when he heard the shot he expected to be dead—he almost wanted it—but somehow he wasn't and he kept on running.

And he expected to fall through one of the countless gaps in the boardwalk, but somehow he didn't, and he kept on running.

The boardwalk seemed to go on and on and on, as if he'd been running along a cliff in the forest forever and would forever go on doing so. Finally the boardwalk ended, and Ben reached the stairs leading up to the nightclub. He knew more of his enemies would be waiting for him at the top, and he had no plan now except to keep on running, more or less in a straight line, and to swing the machete at whatever lay in his path.

But climbing the irregular, undependable, moss-slimed steps long ago cut into or hammered onto the steep, almost sheer hillside was slower going than running on a level surface, and Ben had scrambled up only a few steps before Auguste came around the last bend in the boardwalk. Knowing he had no hope of getting away, Ben stopped to face his pursuer, heartily ready to give up and end the sound in his head.

Auguste was turning his torso as he ran, preparing to take another shot at the boy now that he was both closer and stationary. He realized he was enjoying himself, and wondered why, and then remembered he and Danton and Prosper had woken early and driven up here this morning to do some hunting in the old German's pristine hilltop forest, and—if you didn't count shooting the American soldier at the cigarette factory, which Auguste didn't, since that was more like target practice—this chase right now, and cornering the quarry on the stairs, was the closest he'd come all day to the real hunting he'd been looking forward to.

Before Auguste, still running, could finish aiming at Ben, waiting frozen on the stairs, most of the old boardwalk finally peeled away from the hillside, not instantly but without warning and fast enough that Auguste couldn't have reached a branch or root to grab hold of even if he'd tried, which he didn't. Instead, as the entire immense structure arced away from the slope, and even the long posts supporting it now tilted away groaning like trees falling a second time, Auguste fired one probably unintentional shot that sent a harmless bullet out into the night sky over the forest.

Then, shattering against countless trees and branches in their way, Auguste and a hundred tons of rotted lumber fell together into the ravine. Just a few steps below where Ben clung, trying not to look into the dark queasy depths as the crash of the collapse still went on far below him, the staircase ended in yawning space, its bottom steps ripped away with the boardwalk.

Up at the nightclub, Marcel had of course heard the terrible sound, like the entire back of the hill sloughing off into the forest, and he knew what had happened without going to look. Indeed he had no time to look, because the first embers of fire had risen through the floor and begun to attack the office itself. Giving up on the furniture for now, he focused on saving the nightclub's records and other documents, pulling stacks of papers out of desk drawers that had already begun to smoke. He could see, when he glanced through the doorway into the main room of the club, that the fire had traveled horizontally under the building even faster than it had climbed up, and if he stayed here in the office much longer he'd find the way out through the front of the club barred by flames.

He was working so single-mindedly, determined to do all a reliable watchman should do in an emergency like this, that he rolled aside first one and then the other of the bodies on the floor without the slightest hesitation when he needed to get into drawers they were blocking. The last thing he expected was for anyone to come back up through the door leading to the boardwalk that had just collapsed into the ravine. He was therefore unprepared when the little back door swung open and Ben staggered in with his bloody machete raised.

Marcel leaped back, and his eyes found his pistol, which he'd set on a high shelf to protect it from the fire while he worked. But the shelf was nearer to Ben than to him now, and Ben followed his glance and saw the gun. Swinging the machete once to ward off Marcel, Ben reached for the German's pistol. Empty-handed, Marcel retreated into the main room of the nightclub, where the gaps in the floorboards now resembled a glowing lattice.

Ben set down the machete so he could hold the pistol with both hands. Without pausing and with barely a flicker of recognition, his eyes passed over the bodies of Nabil and Prosper. He'd finally cornered the man who'd started everything when he came after the boys with a gun this morning at the house in the forest—a loaded gun, to point at a handful of scared seventh graders and threaten to shoot their dog!—and now, using the same pistol, Ben was going to finish what Marcel had started. That Marcel was unarmed just added to the symmetry: not one of the boys had been carrying so much as a pocketknife when Marcel showed up waving his pistol around like a big shot, and every other horror today had followed from that moment.

Ben stepped out into the main room with the pistol in both hands, just like Sean Connery. He was surprised by how much of the floor was already burning. In the flickering light and drifting smoke it would be much harder to find Marcel—and maybe Marcel wasn't even here anymore, maybe he'd run out through the front door onto the verandah overlooking the city and gotten away.

Pistol ready, Ben crouched down to check under all the café tables—an obvious place to hide—but Marcel wasn't there. He moved slowly toward the bar, the next logical hiding place. As he was straightening up after checking behind the bar—no one —he saw a movement to his left in the smoke and whirled toward it, and there stood Marcel. Ben pointed the pistol and took a deep breath, and Marcel lifted Théophile's homemade wooden spear and drove it straight through Ben's chest.

The spear extended a couple of feet both in front of him and behind him, and Ben dropped the pistol and took hold of the whittled shaft as if he meant to pull it back out. He stared down at it for a while, puzzled that it wouldn't move, then fell behind the bar. Looking down at the boy as he died, and making himself watch to the end, Marcel knew he'd regret this moment for the rest of his life. But if he hadn't done it, he knew he'd have spent the rest of his life regretting that too. So, either way, he had nothing to look forward to but regret.

It was too late now for Marcel to save the nightclub from fire, too late even to get back into the office to save the papers he'd set aside. And, with the door to the back stairs now cut off by smoke and flame, he could neither reach Danton and Auguste to help them—if somehow they were still alive after whatever had happened down there—nor even retrieve their bodies for burial. (Prosper he cared nothing for, and anyway his body too was inaccessible by now.)

But he could still reach Théophile's body, in the empty liquor storeroom behind the bar, where he'd watched the boys drag it at noon. And Théophile—whose hands were clean of any of the blood and ugliness and stupidity that over this long day had dragged down all the rest of them, men and boys—Théophile deserved better than to have his corpse left to roast like a pig in the nightclub.

There was no time to waste. He went into the storeroom and pulled aside the cloth that covered Théophile's body. And there, by the light of the flames from the main room, Marcel found Roddy's hiding place: he was lying on the floor, huddled right next to Théophile, sharing the cover of his Club Balafon tablecloth. Roddy stared up at him, wordless, and Marcel stared back. Finally Marcel said in French, "Get up, let's go."

4.

"COULD YOU LET Monsieur Leclerc know I'm here?"

"Of course, Monsieur Koeffler." The clerk at the front desk of the Sheraton Hotel began to turn over the pages of his registration book. "Leclerc?"

"Yes, Jean-Marc, Jean-Michel, something like that. A young fellow. I'll be up in the bar. He could meet me there."

Koeffler ordered his usual highball and had it brought to him out on the patio of the Sheraton's rooftop bar. The view of the city from here was spectacular, as always, and it eased Koeffler's slight annoyance at yet another social obligation tacked onto the end of his already long Saturday evening. If he'd known five years ago that this inheritance nonsense over the Club Balafon would still be hanging on, he wouldn't have been so agreeable about getting involved.

But maybe the visit of the grandson, this Leclerc boy, was a signal that the dispute over the will was coming to a close, and an extra half hour up on the roof of the Sheraton was a small price to pay if it helped settle the matter. Besides, the second social event of Koeffler's evening, the British Council reception just down the hill from here, had turned out to be less dull than he'd expected, so on the whole he didn't mind making one last stop.

It was only after he overheard the people at the next table remarking on it that Koeffler noticed the fire at the top of the German's hill. The span of the entire city separated him from the tiny flickering orange glow, high above but no brighter than the lights in those neighborhoods that had electricity, but Koeffler had been here long enough to know in a moment which hill it was.

The waiter at the bar leaned over him. "I beg your pardon, Monsieur Koeffler. The desk sent up to say that no Leclerc is registered here."

Koeffler finished his drink without hurrying. As he was getting up to leave he spotted the Minister of Telecommunications at another table, surrounded by the usual hangers-on from his people, the Hagaoua in the far north of the country—part of the never-ending geographic, religious, and tribal balancing act the President was so good at. The minister caught his eye and waved him over. Koeffler approached but didn't feel invited to sit.

The minister smiled. "Isn't that your nightclub burning over there?"

"Well, not exactly mine, but I was keeping an eye on it for the owners, yes. An inheritance dispute."

"You don't look very upset about it."

Koeffler laughed. "You know me too well, minister. If anything, it's a relief to have it off my plate."

"Still, it's a shame—the only place like it in the city, maybe in the whole country. You should have hired a night watchman to keep out arsonists."

"Oh, I don't think it was arson, at least not the way you mean."

The minister and his henchmen eyed Koeffler with interest. "You suspect someone?"

"Someone from the family is in town, and apparently went up there today to see it. I wouldn't be surprised if he took one look at what a wreck the place is and decided to burn it down so the relatives can stop arguing over it."

The minister glanced around the table at his friends and said

—in French, rather than in Hagaoua, because he meant for Koeffler to overhear—"There is no end to the cleverness of Europeans."

But Koeffler, as was expected of him, pretended to have heard nothing. "I'm actually here right now to meet the young man in question for a drink."

The minister laughed. "But he stood you up, because he's busy right now on the other side of town."

"Plus it turns out he's not even staying at the Sheraton. I assume my chauffeur just remembered it wrong—it wouldn't be the first time." Koeffler watched the distant fire for a moment. In Germany the hillside would have been teeming with the flashing lights of police cars and fire trucks by now, but in this country who was going to drive water to the top of a steep hill beyond city limits to put out a fire at an abandoned night-club?

The minister broke into his thoughts. "A telephone call would've saved you a trip up here tonight." Koeffler just nodded. The minister laughed. "If the telephone system worked, that is."

Koeffler smiled. "I may think such things, minister, but I prefer to let you be the one to say them out loud."

"Much appreciated." The minister swirled the pink ice in his glass. He was a Muslim, and drank grenadine in public. "It happens that we're meeting with the President Thursday to discuss a major upgrade of the telephone infrastructure. Is the West German government interested in playing a role? Public, private, or a combination. The contracts will be large."

Koeffler bowed slightly. "I'll pass the word on to my higher-ups, and I should have some kind of answer for you by Wednesday. I imagine it would be positive." He shook the minister's hand. "And, as always, thank you for the opportunity."

So his half hour at the Sheraton hadn't been a loss after all.

Turning for one last glance across the city at the distant glow on the hill, Koeffler left the rooftop patio and summoned the elevator, eager to go home and get out of evening dress.

When the reception was over, and the clean-up was over, and the jazz combo had finally packed up and left—they'd stayed and continued jamming through the clean-up in exchange for drinks—Mrs. Montgomery went to check on Roddy and found he wasn't home yet. She went back out to the large reception hall, where her husband was emptying ashtrays the clean-up staff had overlooked.

"Darling, what time did Rod say he'd be back?"

He stopped to think. "I don't believe he said."

"It seems awfully late."

"It is late. I wonder if those boys are planning to make another night of it at the house of one of the other fellows."

"Well, if so," she said, "I say no. I feel as if I haven't seen my own son for days."

"Days would be an exaggeration, I think," he said mildly, but on the whole he felt the same way. "Tell you what. We've been cooped up here all day getting ready for this bash and then living through it. I could use some fresh air, and I wager you could too. Let's get the motor, go find Rod, and if he's still awake we'll take the scenic way home and get a feel for the African forest at night."

"Brilliant. Just leave all the rest of that, it'll keep till morning."

Like everyone around them, Bijou and her grandmother had heard the gunshots coming from the direction of the cigarette factory after dusk. Unlike their neighbors, they knew what was going on and who was involved. No one had come back to the house afterward, but to Prosper's grandmother that was a good sign: if something had happened to Prosper, his Mtom friends Danton and Auguste would certainly have let her know.

So she spent the evening in her smoky little kitchen, staring into her fire and marveling at the brains and energy of her grandson—a man with almost no formal schooling, thriving by his own wits in the city, paying for his little cousin's education at the best girls' school in town, of course on top of the money he sent to the village for the rest of the family.

As for the little white boy, who would have predicted that puny weepy specimen would have enough smarts and guts to get away like that? You just never knew, even after a lifetime of sizing people up. But Prosper had said he had a way of making it all come out right. And, wondering if this was going to turn out to be another one of those mysterious deals of her grandson's that brought in a lot of money, the old woman dozed off by the cooking fire, smiling.

After finishing all of her homework, Bijou had gone to bed at her normal time, but for a long while she lay awake, staring up at the ceiling. She wasn't concerned about her cousin Prosper —she knew her grandmother was right when she said not to worry, Prosper wasn't going to let some little white boys get the better of him—and strangely she found she wasn't worried about Roddy either. She imagined him safe at home, curled up in bed, one pale uncovered arm stretched out over the bedspread as he slept, dreaming of her. Would a white boy even have a bedspread? Bijou remembered how little she knew about Roddy. She smiled, turned on her side, and fell asleep.

❖

As they drove, the Montgomerys pooled their recollections, but they had a hard time coming to any firm conclusion about where the boys might be. The note they'd left in the morning said they'd gone to Ben's house for breakfast, but by afternoon the two who came back had said they were at Jesse's Canadian mission dorm playing Monopoly, so Roddy's parents went there first.

Though it was now almost midnight, they could see a single light inside as they walked up onto the wide verandah of the old mission house. Mr. Montgomery knocked as lightly as he could, hoping to alert someone already awake without rousing the whole houseful of small children from their beds. As he and his wife waited by the door, he looked around the verandah, noting the distinctive features of equatorial African colonial architecture, making the case internally for this house as a landmark of that period, and wondering whether historic preservation was a cause the British Council could reasonably get involved in.

When Mr. Swenson answered the door he was still blinking as he awoke, though he was dressed, like a man who'd dozed off while waiting up. He'd expected to find Jesse at the door, and if not that then news of Jesse, so in his half-asleep state it took him a while to understand that Roddy's parents were looking for information rather than bringing it. He told them a rambling and confused story about one of the big girls reporting that Jesse had come by this afternoon on his way to a scavenger hunt, and a strange African man looking for Jesse later, but nothing at all about Roddy or any of the other boys. Shaking his head, Mr. Swenson finished by saying, "I've prayed on it. I guess I'll have to write to Jesse's parents again about his behavior."

As they got back into their car, Mrs. Montgomery said, "That man is too old to be doing what he's doing."

Mr. Montgomery laughed. "Too old is only part of it. Fine house, though."

The commander of the American Embassy's Marine platoon glanced at his watch and made a note that Corporal Cabrera had violated his report-for-duty time. He flipped to the previous page and saw Cabrera's name four times—and in the book was not a place you wanted your name to be. The officer had seen it before: a basically good man who couldn't keep his dick in his pants on weekends.

Though this assignment was considered an honor, he couldn't think of a single Marine—man or officer—who wouldn't rather be in Southeast Asia right now, instead of playing toy soldiers at the embassy in this African backwater. And maybe Cabrera's misbehavior—not just missing curfew, but all the crazy shit he got into—was just his way of saying he was bored and wanted back into the real fight. If so, he might get his wish, and sooner than he expected. The lieutenant closed the book and went to bed.

The Montgomerys agreed that Nabil's house seemed an unlikely place to find Roddy: they'd never heard of Nabil's father encouraging him to bring his friends there, whether for overnight or just to play. In any case, they weren't sure they even knew how to find it. So they drove to Ben's house.

The gate was open and there was a light on at the back of the house. A man whom they'd never met, but who looked like a bigger version of Ben, promptly answered the door. Mr. Welsh had just returned from a week at the ag research station up north

—a brutal drive, three flat tires in eleven hours—and he was making himself an egg for dinner while he thought about a paper he'd read recently on the comparative effects of soil temperature and humidity on germination periods in different varieties of rice.

He invited the Montgomerys in to join him, but they declined. He knew nothing about what the boys were up to—if they'd been here today there was no sign of it, and there usually was with boys—but he'd assumed when he got home to an empty house that both his wife and his son, and presumably the other boys too, were at the Saturday night movie at the American Club.

The Montgomerys both said, "Ah, of course, the club!" It was odd: they had a membership, naturally, and they knew Roddy spent a lot of time there with his friends, but they could never quite convincingly picture in their mind's eye their skinny little Scotsman lounging by a cabana-ringed pool eating a cheeseburger like some junior Hollywood tycoon.

Nabil's father, like Ben's, was alone in his house. He sat at one end of the long table in the dining room with a small glass of cognac in front of him. Just out of reach lay a stack of accounts and reports from the Chaloub businesses, and he could have stood up and leaned along the table and pulled them toward him to look over while he waited for Nabil to return, but he didn't.

He took it for granted that Nabil was at the American Club and would come home when the movie ended, presumably catching a ride with Ben, if Mrs. Welsh had sobered up enough by then. What preoccupied Monsieur Chaloub and kept him from giving his attention to his work was the conversation he needed to have with Nabil when he got home—the same one he'd meant to have at lunchtime, and that Nabil had so transparently dodged.

But maybe it was better this way, with the benefit of a few more hours to think it over, and a little cognac to soften his edges, and no servants in the house to interrupt or eavesdrop. In any case, it would happen tonight: Monsieur Chaloub could no longer put off telling Nabil he'd decided to liquidate the Chaloub businesses and leave the country. In recent years he'd grown resigned to the persistent corruption, the need to grease more and more palms to get anything done—something unheard of before independence—but now he was beginning to hear little whispers about nationalization, about "Africa for Africans," accompanied of course by a wink that with the right bribe and the right well-compensated local front man everything might be fine.

And beyond all that, he could no longer deny or explain away the toll the continental separation of the family had taken on both father and son in the past year. It was time to cash out the businesses while they still had any cash value, and time to reunite the family, if his wife would consider having him back, and time to start over again somewhere new.

But, though Monsieur Chaloub could muster all the logical and emotional reasons and they all pointed the same way, he knew it would be a difficult conversation. Nabil had been born in Africa, had been to France once, for a vacation on the Côte d'Azur—and had never been to Lebanon in his life. Monsieur Chaloub loved this country where he'd made his fortune, but it was with the attachment of an adult, and he tried to imagine what leaving here would feel like to Nabil, for whom this house, this city, this country, Africa itself, was everything.

It might be something like his own departure from Lebanon, as a young man many years ago—but he'd chosen that course himself, and he wondered how he would have reacted if his father had made the decision for him. Well, reflected Monsieur Chaloub as he looked at his cognac—though he was too sharp a businessman to believe it even at the moment he had the comforting thought—maybe it would turn out fine. After all, children were resilient.

As the last survivors of the S.S. Poseidon flew away in the rescue helicopter, a faint cheer rose from the couches and soft chairs and bar stools that had been drawn around to face the pull-down screen at one end of the main lounge of the American Club. Summer, the seventh and eighth grade teacher, was closest to the light switches, and each row of fluorescents she flipped on provoked a new groan from the sleepers now sitting forward and blinking as they returned from the excitement of a mid-Atlantic tsunami to the mundane reality of a Saturday night in Africa.

The two brightest girls in eighth grade, Heather Stone and Cheryl Larson, trapped Summer while she was fishing her shoulder bag out of the depths of the sofa. They were full of excitement about the movie and begged to be allowed to write their next book report on it.

"Um, girls, it's a movie. If you want to do a book report on the novel, you can do that. It's by Paul Gallico."

Heather groaned. "Come on, Summer! This is Africa! Where are we going to find some book?"

"Please, Summer?" Cheryl begged. "I'm sure the movie is exactly like the book, so what's the difference? Please?"

"You know we've already read everything worth reading in the school library. Please?"

Summer was inclined to give in, after suitable resistance—

she was against rules and boundaries and people who said no—
but before she could answer she saw a couple whom she
recognized as the parents of little Roddy Montgomery. She
couldn't remember ever having seen them at the club before,
and indeed they looked like they'd skipped the movie and just
walked in. After glancing around the room at all the people
stretching and getting up to leave, they approached her, almost
the only person they recognized here.

"Hi there!" said Summer. "Are you guys looking for Roddy?"

"Or any of those boys, actually," said Mrs. Montgomery.

Summer looked at the girls, and the girls looked at each
other. Heather said, "They said they'd be here, but we didn't
see them."

Mr. Montgomery said, "You saw them earlier?"

"Uh-huh, this afternoon. They were going swimming, and
they said they'd see us at the movie."

Cheryl didn't often contradict Heather, but she added,
"They only said they might be here."

"Roddy said that?" Mr. Montgomery heard Cheryl but went
on talking to Heather, because that was what everyone did.

"No, I didn't see Roddy," said Heather, "but you know those
guys—they're inseparable."

Summer smiled. "Good word, Heather!"

Cheryl said, "Ben's mom is around here somewhere, and
maybe she knows where they are." Then Cheryl and Heather
looked at each other, and thought about what Cheryl had just
said, and thought about Ben's mother, and at the same time they
both shook their heads and said, "No," and burst out laughing.

Mrs. Montgomery looked around the now almost empty
room. "I don't see her. Could she have gone already?"

"There's my mom," said Cheryl. "She'll know."

As the whole group reached her, Mrs. Larson finally
managed to pull Mrs. Welsh to her feet. "Come on, sleepy-

head. The boat sank. Time to go home."

But, just as the girls expected, Ben's mother knew nothing about where the boys were, and she didn't mention her own conversation with Ben here this afternoon because she'd forgotten it. She was startled to learn from the Montgomerys that her husband was back. "Holy shit, I'd better sober up and get home!"

She broke free of Mrs. Larson's steadying hand and began to walk toward the big French doors leading to the lawn and eventually to the parking lot. Then she stopped and turned to look at them all, squinting to focus. "Oh, wait, it's 1973 and I'm a free white woman—I don't have to sober up!" She walked on, almost in a straight line. At the doors she turned once more. "If you see Ben, tell him to be a little quiet when he comes in the house, okay?" Without waiting for an answer she stepped out onto the lawn, already wet with dew.

Marcel had repeatedly declined the offered beer, and he'd accepted the Fanta only to avoid appearing rude, but once Marie-Joseph put the cold bottle in front of him he realized how thirsty he was. As he drank, the women sitting around him at the plastic-covered table in Auguste's house watched him in complete silence. Danton's sister, who lived nearby, had joined Auguste's wife and his mother and his teenaged daughter, sweaty from the dancing that was still going on outside in the shanty town alley.

Marcel put the Fanta down on the table and waited for their questions, but they said nothing. He moved the bottle to cover a sunflower in the pattern on the plastic tablecloth, and waited, and still they said nothing. An unbearably cheerful song began outside, and Marcel cleared his throat and tried not to listen.

Maybe his prepared explanation had been too clear. They'd held a party up at the nightclub, there'd been a fire—the women all nodded: everyone in the shanty town had seen the glow high above them—and Danton and Auguste were dead. It was awful, but it was an accident—no one was to blame. He'd be telling Prosper's family the same thing right now, but he didn't know where Prosper lived. No doubt these women would pass on the news somehow.

Auguste's mother finally said, "What about those white boys?"

Marcel nodded. "Some of them died in the fire too."

"What was all that about, today? They came here looking for you, you came here looking for them... What was that?"

He nodded again. He'd had the long ride down the hill to prepare his story. "It was nothing—a game."

Auguste's daughter, whose eyes were wide with shock but who hadn't moved or cried since Marcel began his explanation, said, "They were talking about guns and shooting and setting a trap for you."

"I know." Marcel smoothed the already smooth plastic tablecloth and moved the Fanta bottle to cover a different sunflower. "It was just a stupid game. And then there was a fire. No one's to blame. It's just unfortunate."

He'd prepared himself for the beginning of this meeting—an unavoidable task, a duty—but now he realized he had no idea how to end it. They all sat and listened to the song outside. The last refrain finally faded away: *You make me so happy, so happy, so happy, so happy, so happy...*

In the silence that followed, Marie-Joseph folded her hands on the edge of the table and said, "It's God's will." She spoke for the first time in French, though all of them at the table were Mtom.

❖

Mr. Montgomery came back into his own house distracted and troubled and inattentive, and it was his wife who first noticed the trail of clothing leading down the hall. She took her husband by the hand, and together, without a word, they followed the shoes, the socks, the shirt, the shorts, and finally the underpants, which lay where they'd dropped, right outside Roddy's bedroom door. They quietly opened the door and crept in. Roddy was fast asleep, his body twisted, his fists clenched, his mouth wide open. Standing by his bed they listened to his breathing, slow and deep.

When they came back out and closed the door, Mrs. Montgomery began to pick up the clothes. She sniffed. "Ugh— everything smells like smoke."

"They must've made a campfire." Mr. Montgomery smiled. "Our little Scout! Where does he get that from, d'you think? We're neither of us especially outdoorsy, I'd say, wouldn't you?"

She nodded. "He's his own person, our Rod." She carried the bundle of clothes toward the laundry room. "He must've had quite a day, to be sleeping that hard."

"Well, I imagine they didn't sleep at all last night. Those boys never do when they're here. Can't think why they call them sleepovers."

She came back out of the laundry room and took his hand. "Let's let the poor thing sleep in tomorrow." He nodded, and together they headed toward their own bedroom. "And when he gets up, he can tell us all about it."

❖

When Marcel left Auguste's house and the weeping that had finally begun there, the party in the alleyway had ended, and he was alone as he walked out to the main road. He got into Prosper's Peugeot and took a deep breath: his duty was done. He was certainly not going to seek out Monsieur Koeffler and explain matters to him. He could barely recognize in himself the person who, at the beginning of this same day, had wanted to turn over all his problems to Koeffler and let the white man decide what to do. Now, only a few hours later, he was a free man, his own boss. After five years, his job at the nightclub had suddenly ended—there was nothing more to watch over.

Marcel had a car now: he knew Prosper had acquired the cream-colored Peugeot 404 with the deep red seats in some complicated and not quite legal way, and there was no reason to believe Prosper's survivors would come after Marcel for it, especially since they didn't even know who he was. And he had money, since he'd been paid today, as usual, for the week just ended. Plus he had an extra thousand francs: when he and the boy got into the car as they were escaping from the burning nightclub, he found the wad of ransom money on the front seat.

He said nothing about it as they drove down the hill and into the city, but when they reached Roddy's house—"Wait, this is where you live? Not the Lebanese boy?"—he pulled the two real CFA bills from the front and back of the stack of Monopoly money, and gave one to Roddy and kept one for himself. He didn't say, though it was clear to both of them, that the two matching bills were a private symbol of their agreement, the story they'd both tell to account for what had happened up at the nightclub today.

Marcel checked his new watch—the Matador's watch. Then he started the car and turned around to go back through the center of the city and get on the main road south. By dawn he'd be in Mtom country. When he reached his own village he'd go to the house of his father's junior wife and deliver Théophile's body for burial. And after that... Marcel decided he'd wait till tomorrow to figure that out—or maybe even Monday.

At the summit of the German's hill nothing remained of the Club Balafon but a few blackened and still-smoking timbers. And, after the earlier collapse of the boardwalk at the foot of the steep stairs down the back side of the hill, nothing now connected the old dead German's house in the forest to the ruins of the nightclub above it or to the world beyond—in fact there was nowhere convenient on the hillside from which to observe whether the house itself still stood. But a few feet of the boardwalk at the far end did survive, a short raft of fragile planks still anchored to the slope and leading nowhere. That fragment of boardwalk in turn held onto the little vandalized house, which remained there, surrounded by the African forest, floating over the ravine, forgotten.

STUART GELZER, the child of American missionaries, grew up in Cameroon and India. Over the years he's been a screenwriter, a film editor, a drama teacher, a film and photography teacher, and a singer specializing in folk music from the Republic of Georgia. Nowadays he does fine-art photography, writes fiction and travel memoir, and translates old French popular novels. He lives in Santa Fe, New Mexico.

BY THE SAME AUTHOR

Hoodoo Badlands

Six Reasons to Travel

Earthworm

translations from French

The Hunchback, by Paul Féval

Harry Dickson vs. Mysteras, by Jean Ray

Harry Dickson vs. Krik-Krok, by Jean Ray

Miss Musketeer, by Paul d'Ivoi

Queen of Illusions, by Paul d'Ivoi

CPSIA information can be obtained
at www.ICGtesting.com
Printed in the USA
BVHW011805160523
664275BV00016B/165

9 798987 808108